LAST
IMPRESSIONS

Jane Austen Investigations
Book Two

Laura Martin

SAPERE
BOOKS

LAST
IMPRESSIONS

Published by Sapere Books.

24 Trafalgar Road, Ilkley, LS29 8HH

saperebooks.com

ISBN: 978-0-85495-065-2

CHAPTER ONE

Outside the window of the carriage the snowflakes were falling in earnest, settling on the grass on either side of the long drive. When they had left home an hour and a half earlier the sky had been grey and heavy, and now Jane wouldn't be surprised if they were snowed in by nightfall.

Slowly the carriage rattled to a stop a few feet away from the imposing door of Melmont Hall, and two footmen hurried out.

"Miss Cassandra Austen, Miss Jane Austen, I was worried you wouldn't make it in the snow. Dreadful weather, threatening to spoil our plans," Mrs Paulson said as she ushered them inside and fussed around them, brushing the snow from their hair and helping them off with their coats.

"Our mother sends her apologies; she had a terrible head cold and could not face the journey," Cassandra said.

"Your poor mother. Never mind, we shall still have fun, shall we not? Our party will be small, but I wager we will have a wonderful evening."

It was warm in the hall and through an open door Jane caught sight of a blazing fire. She longed to slip away and stand in front of it, warming her frozen fingers and toes. The pretty satin shoes she wore had been no match for the cold temperatures in the carriage and silently she wished she had worn her sturdy boots instead.

"Let me show you to your room. Dinner is at seven, but I hope you will join us in the drawing room in half an hour. Miss Leveritt is here, and her skill on the pianoforte is unmatched in all of Hampshire."

"That sounds wonderful, Mrs Paulson."

Jane barely had chance to marvel at the portraits that lined the walls as they were hustled upstairs to their allocated bedroom. Melmont Hall was at least two hundred years old, but it was a house that had been built to last. Oak panelling lined the walls, and above their heads was a beautiful wooden coffered ceiling. On the walls, spaced at equal intervals, there were portraits of the Paulson family stretching back generations, all of them unsmiling and sitting upright, looking down at the people who walked beneath.

"Here is your room. The fire is blazing, and there is some water in the basin if you wish to freshen up."

"Thank you, Mrs Paulson," Cassandra said, stepping aside as a footman brought their bags into the room.

"I'm afraid we do not have a maid to dress you for the evening. Three servants left unexpectedly last week and it has been an awful inconvenience, especially with this house party arranged."

Jane turned, intrigued, but caught the look Cassandra gave her and resisted the urge to ask why the servants had left in such numbers. Melmont Hall was grand, but it wasn't huge like some country estates, and there was only Mr and Mrs Paulson in permanent residence. There would probably be eight indoor staff at most and perhaps a couple of gardeners and a groom. To have three leave, by the sounds of it quite suddenly, was more than a little inconvenient for Mrs Paulson and interesting for the gossips of their local society.

Knowing the best way to find out whether the three servants had been driven away by money woes, the butler's wandering hands, or a better offer from the next closest estate would be to make friends with one of the remaining maids later, Jane let the comment pass.

"Jane and I are used to helping one another dress," Cassandra said as the footman hurried out past her. "It will not be a problem."

At home they never had anyone but each other for help dressing, and they had been raised to care for their own clothes. The Austen household finances did not stretch to maids to do these things for them, and as such it felt strange if they did stay somewhere and a maid bustled in to help them dress.

Mrs Paulson left, closing the door behind her, and Jane edged closer to the fire, feeling the wonderful warmth spread through her.

"Do you think we were foolish to come tonight?" It had been threatening to snow all day, and now it seemed they may be trapped here at Melmont Hall if it kept settling as it was.

Cassandra shook her head before walking over to stand beside Jane and take her hand. "I think we all needed this."

Silently, Jane nodded. It had been a strange few months with her involvement in the tragic case of the murder of her friend, Emma Roscoe, over the festive period and then meeting and losing the man she had thought she was destined to marry. As always when she thought of Tom Lefroy, she got a lump in her throat and quickly turned away so Cassandra would not see the sadness in her eyes. For weeks her family had tiptoed around her, being overly solicitous with their sympathy. Only her brother Henry had treated her as if nothing had happened, declaring in his letters that he thought a little adversity was character-building.

Cassandra's latest mission since arriving back from Shropshire, was to see Jane out and about and enjoying herself. She hadn't openly declared this to Jane, but in the past week they had accepted five invitations to various events despite the weather being questionable, and Cassandra had even managed to persuade their mother to host a small gathering in a week's time.

"Tonight we will eat and drink, listen to some lovely music, and talk with friends. Perhaps after dinner there might be dancing or cards. If the snow keeps falling, it does not matter; we are warm and snug in this comfortable house with generous hosts."

"Of course you are right," Jane said, summoning a smile. Tonight she would not be morose.

They had both worn their best dresses, knowing they would arrive soon before dinner, so there was no need to change, but Jane took time to pin Cassandra's hair as she liked it and then see to her own in the little mirror on the wall.

Arm in arm they left the bedroom, following the melodic sound of the pianoforte as they descended the stairs. Mrs Paulson was a friend of their mother's and they had visited Melmont Hall on a few previous occasions, although never to stay before. The drawing room was at the back of the house, overlooking the formal garden with the dining room leading off on one side through double doors. It was a cosy room with heavy curtains and plush furnishings, the sort of room that encouraged you to relax.

"Come in, come in," Mrs Paulson said as they hovered by the door. There were a collection of other people in the room, the other dinner party guests. Some were acquaintances, but there were a few unfamiliar faces. "Let me introduce you to everyone," Mrs Paulson said, inserting herself between Jane and Cassandra and slipping her arms through theirs. "Over here playing beautifully on the pianoforte is the very talented Miss Leveritt."

Miss Leveritt looked up and gave a brief smile before her eyes focussed back on the sheet of music in front of her. Even with the distraction she did not miss a single note. Beaming proudly behind her was an older woman who bore a resemblance to Miss Leveritt.

"This is Mrs Leveritt, a close friend and neighbour, and over here we have Mr and Mrs Potter. They have just married and moved into the village."

"Lovely to meet you," Jane murmured before they moved on.

"Colonel Rushton I think you know, and he has brought a dear friend Dr Histon with him." Mrs Paulson looked around, beaming. "There, as I said, a small party, but I always think intimate is better, don't you?"

"I agree entirely, Mrs Paulson," Jane said, eyeing the guests. Only Mr Paulson was missing, although Jane wasn't surprised. He was older than his wife and eschewed company unless absolutely necessary. No doubt he would join them for dinner, but Jane could imagine him refusing to join in the pre- and post-dinner gatherings. It had been the same on the other occasions they had visited Melmont Hall.

Cassandra perched on the edge of an armchair, positioning herself so she was able to talk to the newlywed couple sitting next to her. Jane paused for a moment, listening to her sister properly introduce herself and regarding the young couple. They looked nervous, as if they didn't get to socialise much, but Jane knew Cassandra would soon put them at ease.

"What a beautiful room," Cassandra said with a warm smile, "and a much appreciated fire. Did you walk from the village, Mrs Potter?"

"We did, Miss Austen. I insisted, thinking it was terribly romantic in the snow. My dear Thomas was worried it may be too cold for me, but we made it without too many mishaps."

Dear Thomas. Closing her eyes momentarily, Jane gave herself a stern talking-to. She couldn't quiver and falter every time she heard the name Thomas, every time someone spoke in that lilting accent of his, every time she heard word of Lincoln's Inn Fields. Tom Lefroy was firmly consigned to her past, and she would not spend her weekend thinking of him.

Resolutely, Jane moved further down the room to talk to Colonel Rushton and his friend.

"It is a pleasure to meet you, Miss Austen," Dr Histon said, bowing over her hand. "Our hostess said you arrived in the snow this evening. Was the journey treacherous?"

"The roads were passable. When we left home it had only just started snowing, but a good layer had settled by the time we arrived. I am glad we are not due to return to Steventon this evening; I would not trust the carriage on the ice that no doubt will cover the roads."

"Indeed, it is a good thing that everyone is staying over," Colonel Rushton said, and they all glanced at the window.

It was dark outside and for a moment Jane could see nothing but the reflection of the candlelight in the room, but after a moment her eyes adjusted and she could make out a few details. The snow was still falling in large flakes, and now the ground was completely hidden under a thick white layer. It was hard to judge from inside the house, but she would guess it was at least a couple of inches deep.

"I do hope we aren't snowed in," she murmured, thinking of a few winters past when the snow had piled up against the doors and made leaving the house impossible. There was something magical about being snowed in when at home with adequate supplies and a good stack of firewood, but she didn't like the thought of being stuck at someone else's house, even if that house was as comfortable as Melmont Hall.

Shaking her head, Jane tried to dismiss the thought. There was nothing she could do about the weather, and they were here now. Hopefully tomorrow the sun would melt whatever snow had settled, clearing the roads for the journey home.

"How are you settling into civilian life, Colonel Rushton?" Jane asked as she moved away from the window.

"It is a very different pace, Miss Austen. I wake up every morning expecting the thrill of life in the army, and instead I am greeted by the prospect of tending my garden or caring for my chickens."

"In time do you think you will adjust?"

Colonel Rushton smiled indulgently. "I dare say I will. I spent twenty-five years in the army; I am being unrealistic to expect to leave behind everything I know and immediately fall into a life of contented fulfilment." He turned to his friend, clapping the other man on the back. "Dr Histon was kind enough to agree to come and stay with me for a few weeks to alleviate some of the boredom I find myself suffering from. I have pressed him for months to arrange a visit, and he has left his work for a few weeks to oblige an old friend."

"That is a kind thing to do. Have you known one another for a long time?"

Dr Histon returned his friend's smile. "We met in France a few years ago. We were in the middle of nowhere, camped in a muddy field in the middle of a horrendous march. It was dark and raining and I had come from the unenviable task of amputating a man's leg when I smelled the most wonderful cigar smoke. For a moment I could imagine I was at my club in London." The doctor grinned at Rushton. "Of course, it was this reprobate, wandering the camp having his nightly cigar. When he offered me one, I thought I had died and gone to heaven. I've been in his debt ever since."

"I did not realise you were in the army too, Dr Histon."

"I was. I left a few years ago to take over my father's practice when he died."

"Dr Histon extolls the change of pace from army life, but I argue he still has a job, a vocation that requires his attention. I am just an injured nag put out to pasture."

"I do not think anyone could compare you to an old nag, Colonel," Jane said, smiling at the image. Colonel Rushton was in his forties, but he was a man who clearly took the time to look after himself. Perhaps it was the years of army discipline, but on every occasion Jane had seen him he'd been perfectly groomed, and he kept himself in good physical condition, not succumbing to the expanding waistlines that plagued many men of his age.

As Jane spoke, she saw the butler enter the room and make his way to Mrs Paulson to whisper something in her ear. A moment later she stood, drawing the attention of all her guests.

"It is time for dinner," she announced as the butler opened the double doors leading to the dining room.

Dutifully, everyone stopped their conversations and filed into the dining room. Jane marvelled at the effort that must have gone into arranging the room, but it was to good effect. Candles flickered in a huge chandelier that hung suspended above the dining table, and decorative candlesticks were placed at intervals along the table and in the corner of the room. It gave the room a homely feel, even with the dark wood panelling and heavy furniture. The table itself was decorated with greenery, sprigs of holly and mistletoe. Nothing else was in bloom at this time of year and it made the room look festive, a reminder of the Christmas season just passed.

"Mrs Paulson, this looks wonderful," Cassandra said as she took her place at the table. Jane smiled across at her. They had been placed apart, as was expected in the complex rules of who sat where at a dinner party. Mrs Paulson had eschewed some of the guidelines, choosing to not balance the number of male and female guests, but she had kept to the rules of seniority within society. Jane and Cassandra were sat on opposite sides of the table, halfway down. To Jane's right sat Dr Histon and to her left Mr Potter.

Everyone sat and then looked expectantly at the head of the table.

"I do apologise," Mrs Paulson said, standing in a fluster. "Upton, will you let Mr Paulson know we are waiting for him?"

The butler bowed silently and disappeared from the room.

"Do you know our host?" Dr Histon asked as he leaned in closer to Jane, dropping his voice so she was the only one privy to his question.

"I have met him, yes, although it is Mrs Paulson I know better. She is a good friend of my mother's."

Dr Histon nodded, looking down the table.

"Unfortunately, my mother has a head cold and was unable to come today."

"That is a shame, although not unusual at this time of year."

"Do you know our host?"

Dr Histon began shaking his head, but before he could answer he was distracted by the butler re-entering the room, looking flustered. The elderly man leaned down and murmured something discreetly in Mrs Paulson's ear. She frowned and then stood, smoothing down her dress.

"Please excuse me for a moment," she said, then followed the butler from the room.

Jane watched her go and then stood herself.

"Jane," Cassandra said, trying to catch her eye from across the table.

Pretending she hadn't heard her sister, Jane slipped from the room, using the sound of hushed voices to guide her through the hall to where Mrs Paulson stood with the butler and a worried-looking maid.

"I took him a glass of whiskey at six o'clock, as I always do," the maid said, her hands trembling under Mrs Paulson's gaze. "That was the last time I went in."

"No one has seen him since?"

"No, ma'am," said the butler. "I have checked with the rest of the servants. No one has even tried the door, not until you asked me to knock for Mr Paulson."

"Is something the matter?" Jane said, moving closer. She might be shooed away, told it was none of her concern, but recently she was coming to learn that people accepted her presence in unexpected situations more than she thought they would.

"It's Mr Paulson," Mrs Paulson said, trying the door handle again, almost absent-mindedly. "He's locked the door and we can't rouse him." She let out a little sob of concern. "I'm worried something has happened to him."

Jane stepped closer, reaching out and placing a hand on the older woman's arm. "Try not to worry. Perhaps he has fallen asleep and hasn't heard the knocking. Is there another key?"

Mrs Paulson shook her head. "My husband likes his privacy. There is only the one key, and he keeps it with him at all times."

"I think it is in the lock," the butler said, motioning to the keyhole.

Jane crouched down in front of the door and put her eye to the keyhole. Sure enough, there was a dark shape obscuring her view of the room beyond.

"Is something amiss?" Colonel Rushton said as he came out into the hall. He was trailed by Dr Histon, who looked equally concerned.

"My husband isn't answering when we knock and the door is locked," Mrs Paulson said, and Jane could hear a subtle note of hysteria in her voice.

Colonel Rushton stepped forward and rapped sharply on the door. "Mr Paulson, is something amiss in there?" He waited for a moment and then knocked harder, hammering on the door with his fist.

They waited ten seconds, then twenty, but there was no hint of movement from inside.

"Stand back," Colonel Rushton said, taking a few steps back as if he was going to run at the door.

"Steady," Dr Histon said, placing a hand on his friend's shoulder. "Remember your injury. Let me."

Colonel Rushton looked as if he were going to protest, but a stern look from the doctor had him stepping back to make way.

Dr Histon eyed the door, pushing on it with a hand as if testing the weak points, and then he stepped back, lowered his shoulder, and ran at the solid wood.

Jane winced at the crunch of impact, feeling a reverberation of force as the moving man met the immovable wood. It didn't budge and Dr Histon let out a little groan as he rubbed his shoulder, but lined himself up again for another charge.

This time there was a splintering sound as the man collided with the door, but it wasn't quite enough to break the lock, and Dr Histon stepped back for a final rush.

The door gave way easily on impact this third time and Dr Histon went stumbling into the room. Immediately everyone began to crowd behind him, but he held up a hand, motioning for them to stay back.

Jane craned her neck, desperate to see the scene inside the study.

"No," Mrs Paulson whispered, shuffling backwards.

Jane caught sight of what lay beyond, and her hand flew to her mouth. The study was dark, lit by only two candles, but the flickering light was enough to reveal the lifeless body of Mr Paulson in his chair behind the huge desk. He was slumped backwards, half reclined, his body having slipped down a little.

Jane could tell he was dead immediately by the unblinking eyes staring straight ahead.

"He's dead," Dr Histon announced as he checked the old man's pulse.

Mrs Paulson let out a whimper and clutched at Jane's arm as Colonel Rushton brushed past her and strode into the room.

"Rushton, look at this," the doctor said, and Jane's attention was drawn back to the dead man in the study.

"He's been stabbed," Rushton said, leaning over the body.

CHAPTER TWO

For a long moment no one moved. Mrs Paulson was frozen in place, as if all the life had been sucked from her on hearing of her husband's death. Colonel Rushton and Dr Histon were staring at the dead man in the study, and the two servants stood in a daze, unable to comprehend the scene in front of them.

Thankfully Cassandra emerged from the dining room, the movement breaking the spell that held everyone in place.

"What's happened?" Her question was to the assembled group but her eyes were fixed on Jane.

"Mr Paulson is dead," Jane said quietly. "He's been stabbed."

Shaking her head, Cassandra peered towards the study and then turned away as if she didn't want to see. Jane wasn't squeamish, but she knew her sister sometimes felt faint when faced with the prospect of blood.

"Will you take Mrs Paulson to sit down? She's had a shock," Jane said, wanting to keep Cassandra busy.

"What will you do?"

Jane didn't answer. She had no authority here and as a young, unmarried woman it might be difficult for her to establish herself as someone to be listened to. Nevertheless, she had to try; that was what Lord Hinchbrooke, the local magistrate and her mentor, would prompt her to do.

Relieved when Cassandra took the pale Mrs Paulson and gently escorted her away, Jane took a breath to steady herself and then stepped fully into the study.

"Perhaps you had better join the ladies, Miss Austen," Colonel Rushton said, not unkindly. He and Dr Histon were still standing close to the dead man, regarding the scene in front of them.

"I may need your help, gentlemen," Jane said, deciding to play on both men's need to be of service. "You may not be aware, but I have recently been conscripted to help Lord Hinchbrooke, our local magistrate, in matters of the law. You may have heard of the sad case of Miss Roscoe, the young woman killed a few months ago at Lord and Lady Westworth's ball."

She waited for both men to incline their heads. It had been the talk of the local area for months, so they shouldn't have missed it, but it always surprised her what vital news passed some people by.

"In a moment I will ask one of the servants to ride out to fetch Lord Hinchbrooke and ask him to attend, but until he gets here I must insist on taking responsibility for preserving as much information as possible."

"What do you do for the magistrate?" Dr Histon asked. His tone was kind, as if he were trying to soften the implication that at most she must fetch him tea and organise his papers.

"I assist him with his enquiries. Take notes, discuss his observations," Jane said briskly.

Colonel Rushton was looking at her oddly, but he gave a sudden nod of acquiescence. "Whatever you say, Miss Austen. We need to seal the room and await the magistrate. I am eager nothing should be tampered with."

"Good."

Dr Histon was staring at the door and the broken lock that now protruded from it. Suddenly, he turned and walked over to one of the wide windows, testing the latch. Momentarily he opened the window, letting in a blast of icy air, then quickly closed it again. Systematically he moved to the other window and repeated the action.

"Both fully closed and latched," he said quietly. "From the inside."

Jane felt the weight of the implication sit heavily on her and for a moment tried to push it away. This early on she needed to work without assumption. Right now, before the scene had been properly examined and before the household had been questioned, there were a thousand possibilities as to what could have happened. She had to open her mind to all of them before she began eliminating the ridiculous and impossible until only one truth was left.

"Shall we step outside, gentlemen?"

She waited for Colonel Rushton and the doctor to step out and followed them, pulling the door almost closed behind her. The lock mechanism protruded from the edge of the door, stopping it from shutting completely.

"Upton!" Jane called, signalling to the butler to approach. "We need two servants to stand by this door and ensure no one goes in or out."

"Two?"

"Yes, please," Jane said, declining to explain her reasoning. Upton might have some loyalty to his employers, but he lived and worked with the servants, shared his meals and his lodgings with them. If a was servant responsible for this crime, the butler might feel it was his duty to protect them. The last thing Jane wanted was to leave the killer on guard and allow them to slip into the room and remove a vital piece of evidence.

"I shall organise it at once, Miss Austen."

"We will also need someone to ride out to alert the magistrate."

"Of course, Miss Austen, although…" Upton trailed off and glanced at the front door.

"Is it still snowing?"

In answer the butler moved towards the front door, pulling it open. Jane grimaced. If anything, the snow was falling thicker and faster now, settling on top of the already substantial layer of snow.

"It will be too dangerous. The roads will be impassable," Colonel Rushton said.

He was right, of course; it would be highly irresponsible to send anyone out in conditions like these, but Jane felt her pulse quicken as she began to realise the implications of being cut off from the world.

"Can I have my coat?"

"Do not be a fool, Miss Austen. You will not make it any distance in this weather. You risk too much," Colonel Rushton said, placing a hand on her arm.

"I am not going far," she said, lowering her voice. "I wish to circle the house."

For a long moment Colonel Rushton looked perplexed before understanding dawned in his eyes. "The snow," he said, nodding. "You're looking for footprints."

"Anything from the last hour may still be visible, but not for long with how quickly the snow is falling. We must make haste."

"Allow me to accompany you."

In truth she was hoping he might offer. It was dark outside and she didn't know the terrain. A candle was not going to stay alight for more than a second, and even an enclosed lamp would struggle in this weather. She feared venturing out alone and tripping on some concealed hazard, twisting her ankle and falling into the snow. At least with Colonel Rushton by her side she could lean on his arm as they battled the blizzard-like conditions outside.

"You cannot go out in those shoes," Colonel Rushton said, and Jane looked down at her feet, cursing her flimsy satin shoes for the second time that evening. "Bring Miss Austen a pair of boots," he instructed the footman, who hurried off to see to their demands.

"I will stay here," Dr Histon said as they made their preparations to go out. "I will ensure someone guards the door to the study, and then I will see to Mrs Paulson. She's had a shock. Unfortunately I did not bring my bag with me, so I have no potions, but reassurance is a wonderful medicine."

"Thank you, Dr Histon," Jane said. Both men were pale and drawn, and the doctor's hands were trembling as he ran them through his hair. She supposed that even for someone more familiar with death than the average person, seeing a man stabbed was far out of the ordinary.

The boots were slightly too big but Jane didn't complain, instead pulling the laces as tight as she could and knotting them securely. Once she was in her coat, she looked over at Colonel Rushton, who was turning up the collar of his.

"I am happy to go alone, Miss Austen, if you would prefer to stay in the warm."

"Thank you for the offer, but I will come. We will be back in the shelter of the house in a few minutes."

As they left, she saw Dr Histon instructing the footman and a maid to stand outside the study door and not let anyone in, and then he disappeared back into the dining room.

The wind whipped at their faces as soon as they stepped out of the door, and for a moment Jane couldn't see anything past a few feet in front of her. The snowflakes were the size of small butterflies and felt like tiny knife blades as they hit her face. Within a few seconds, she felt her fingers stiffen and begin to throb.

"It's a foul night," Colonel Rushton said as he offered her his arm. "Let us make haste, Miss Austen. I have a hankering for the roaring fire in the dining room."

With their heads bent against the wind, they began to trudge round the house, both silent in their concentration. Jane was hoping to spot a clear trail of footprints, perhaps some leading to the house and some leading away. Maybe even a forced window they had not noticed from inside the room. There was nothing at the front of the house, with even the carriage tracks and horse shoe prints from when everyone had arrived a few hours earlier already obscured. As they turned the corner, Jane's eyes flicked across the snow, but still there was nothing.

"No footprints yet," Colonel Rushton said, as he steadied her over a particularly rough patch of ground. "Although the study is at the back of the house."

At that moment, Jane felt her boot hit something slippery and she almost fell, her body stiffening instinctively to brace her for impact. Colonel Rushton gripped her arm a little tighter and Jane was able to steady herself, but she felt the muscles in her lower back protest.

Stepping even more carefully now, they rounded the corner and paused for a moment. Jane felt her heart sink. There was nothing, no incriminating trail of footprints, not even the hint of disturbed snow. It looked as though no one had traipsed through this part of the garden since the snow had begun falling hours ago.

"Nothing," Jane said quietly, pulling on the colonel's arm to prompt him to continue. They needed to walk round the entire house to ensure an intruder couldn't have got in any other way.

Once they were back at the front door they hurried inside, brushing the snow off their shoulders and hair. Jane felt the flakes on her face melting into little droplets of water and running over her skin.

"I saw nothing at all," Colonel Rushton confirmed, his voice subdued.

"I suppose it could have happened earlier," Jane mused, not convinced an intruder wouldn't have left at least some trace of himself leaving if he'd jumped from the study window and run off into the night.

"It could," Colonel Rushton said slowly, helping her with her coat. As Jane was about to walk away, the colonel reached out and grasped her arm, stopping her. "Can I beg a moment of your time, Miss Austen, before you charge back in there and start questioning people?"

"I looked like I was charging?"

"You have a certain expression of determination on your face."

Despite everything, Jane managed a weak smile. Her family often liked to describe her as determined, thinking it was less of an insult than some of the other words they could use.

"What is on your mind, Colonel?"

"I am concerned about how you plan to approach this. Surely you cannot mean to conduct questioning of the guests and servants as if you were the magistrate."

It was exactly what she planned to do. Jane bristled, only just managing to contain her exasperation.

"Of course not, Colonel Rushton. I know my place. I merely seek to preserve things until Lord Hinchbrooke is able to get here. Part of that preservation is asking a few simple questions to ascertain a sequence of events."

"Do you not think someone else would be better placed to do that?"

Silently she called him every foul name she could think of, upset that her vocabulary didn't stretch to much past scoundrel and cad.

"Someone like you?" she asked, trying to summon a sweet smile. She knew it ended up more of a grimace by the way Colonel Rushton recoiled from her slightly.

"I do have years of experience with the army."

"Forgive me, I did not realise your service included investigating violent crimes."

"It did not, Miss Austen…"

Knowing she was committed now, she pushed on, interrupting him. "Then your main objection must be that I am a woman." She paused and waited for him to look at her. It took a few seconds for him to meet her eye. "It is an objection, thankfully, Lord Hinchbrooke does not share." With a wave of her hand, she motioned they should return to the rest of the guests. "If it makes you feel better, we can make the enquiries together."

Colonel Rushton inclined his head, and Jane knew it was the best outcome she could have hoped for. The colonel was a decent man, well respected and with a certain authority from his decades of service in the army. She didn't doubt that when Lord Hinchbrooke arrived, he would include her in the investigation, but until then the other guests were not compelled to speak to her. Having Colonel Rushton by her side gave her more of an air of legitimacy.

The guests had returned to the drawing room, all thoughts of dinner abandoned. The room, which earlier had seemed so beautifully decorated, now felt garish and bright, and Jane had to close her eyes for a moment to allow them to adjust to the unforgiving light.

Everyone looked up expectantly as she and Colonel Rushton entered, their expressions a mix of curiosity and dread. Mrs Paulson sat in the corner of the room, half collapsed in an armchair. Dr Histon was on one side and Cassandra the other. The older woman looked pale and dazed and every few seconds would shake her head as if she could not believe what was happening.

The young newlywed couple, Mr and Mrs Potter, were sitting close together, Mr Potter's arm reassuringly draped around his wife's shoulders. Mrs Leveritt and her daughter sat across the room, looking shaken, the mother's hand resting on the daughter's leg.

Dr Histon stood as they entered, making his way over to them briskly.

"Mrs Paulson is in shock, unsurprisingly. I have made enquiries of the butler and they have some laudanum in the house, which can be used to settle nerves as well as for pain. Miss Cassandra Austen has been kind enough to offer to get Mrs Paulson settled upstairs, then I will administer it."

"Good idea," Colonel Rushton said, nodding at Cassandra, who started to rouse their hostess and help her to her feet.

No one spoke as Mrs Paulson left the room, and even once the door had closed behind her there was a sombre silence.

After a moment Jane cleared her throat, wishing Lord Hinchbrooke was here. His was a quiet, calming presence and he always seemed to know what to say to put people at ease.

"I am sure you are aware what has happened this evening," Jane said, looking from face to face.

"It can't be true. Dr Histon said Mr Paulson was murdered, that he was stabbed," Mrs Leveritt said. Her voice rose at the end with a hint of hysteria.

"I'm afraid it is true," Jane said calmly. "Before dinner, the butler could not get a response from Mr Paulson's study when he knocked on the door. Dr Histon broke the door down and he found Mr Paulson inside, dead." Jane closed her eyes at the image of the old man sprawled in his chair, no colour left in his face, no life left in his eyes.

"No," Mrs Leveritt said, shaking her head. "Surely it can't be."

"It is true," Jane repeated softly. "Mr Paulson was dead when we entered the room, stabbed with a knife."

"Are we safe? Is the intruder still here? We could all be stabbed in our beds," Mrs Leveritt said, her voice growing more shrill with each thought.

"Mother, we cannot think like that," Miss Leveritt said, taking her mother's hand and squeezing it. "I am sure whoever it is has fled. Why would they stay here?"

Jane exchanged a glance with Colonel Rushton, and wordlessly they agreed not to tell the rest of the guests what they feared to be true. There was no sign that whoever had killed Mr Paulson had left through one of the study windows, and no disturbance in the snow outside the study window to indicate someone had climbed out that way. She needed to have another look at the study, to work out exactly how the murderer had escaped and left the door locked on the inside, but right now she didn't need to add to the worries of the other guests.

"Normally in these circumstances someone would ride for the magistrate. We are lucky that Lord Hinchbrooke is a noble and conscientious man, interested in investigating the crimes committed in his area."

"Has he been sent for?" Mr Potter asked. It was the first time she had heard the man speak, and she detected a slight lilt to his words that indicated he wasn't originally from Hampshire.

"The snow is too thick and the roads dangerous," Colonel Rushton said with a shake of his head. "Hopefully tomorrow morning the snow will have melted enough to allow a rider through."

"What do we do until then?" Mr Potter said.

Jane took a deep breath, steeling herself for the next part. She had never struggled with defying people's expectations of her, had never wanted to fit into the stereotypical idea of what a rector's daughter should be, but she did still feel nervous at times at pushing herself forward. It was the same with her writing. She *knew* it was good, but every now and again she would sit down to write and be overcome by a wave of self-doubt that would prevent her from putting pen to paper. During that time she would be unable to look at her work rationally, unable to see the beauty in it, and then suddenly the doubt would clear like an easterly wind pushing away a cloud and she would be able to write again.

"I assist the magistrate in his work," Jane said, looking from person to person, making sure she held everyone's eye before moving on. "I know his procedures and how he normally approaches a tragedy like this. I will ensure any evidence is preserved until Lord Hinchbrooke arrives and will ask a few preliminary questions to gather some background for him. That way, when he is able to attend he will be able to move quickly and hopefully ensure that whoever has committed this terrible crime is brought to justice without any delay." Her declaration was a little exaggerated, but Jane did not think anyone would challenge her. She did work with Lord Hinchbrooke, although most of his work did not involve crimes such as this. Nevertheless, she had learned a lot when they had investigated the murder of Miss Roscoe together a few months earlier.

Mr and Mrs Potter nodded without protest, as did the young Miss Leveritt. Only Mrs Leveritt did not look convinced.

"We cannot wait for the roads to clear," she said, standing up. "The culprit will be getting away. We must reach the magistrate."

Colonel Rushton stepped forward, smiling in a gently reassuring manner. He commanded attention and just his presence seemed to soothe Mrs Leveritt.

"Miss Austen is right; unfortunately the roads are impassable. Tonight a terrible tragedy has occurred, and we are all caught up in the aftermath in less than ideal circumstances. We must pull together and help one another through. I will work alongside Miss Austen to ensure everything is in order when the magistrate arrives, and I assure you that as soon as there is a chance of getting through, I will ride for Lord Hinchbrooke myself."

Mrs Leveritt sat down, a frown still on her face but seeming to accept the situation more with Colonel Rushton involved.

"Thank you," Jane said, wondering what to do with the guests now. It was still relatively early, but she would rather they were out of the way whilst she and Colonel Rushton planned how they were going to approach the next few hours. "I know the hour is not late, but I expect you will want to retire to your rooms. I can see if the cook can arrange trays of food to be sent up."

Mr and Mrs Potter stood almost immediately, looking as though they wanted to distance themselves from events as quickly as possible. Jane felt sorry for them, caught up in this; it was hardly the evening any of them thought it would be.

Mrs Leveritt and her daughter also stood, conferring quietly before following the Potters out of the room.

Jane let out a loud exhalation and sank down onto one of the seats. The whole situation felt overwhelming, and she needed a moment to get the next steps straight in her mind. There were dozens of things that needed to be done, and they all vied for prime position in her mind.

"I think we should speak to the servants next," Jane said finally.

"First we need to discuss what we found outside."

"We didn't find anything outside."

"Exactly."

Jane closed her eyes and pictured the snow, unadulterated and fresh, not a single footprint or sign of disturbance.

"Whoever did it…" Colonel Rushton said, trailing off.

"They're still here."

At that moment, the door to the drawing room opened and Dr Histon entered, followed by Cassandra. Jane stood and went to her sister, aware that although Cassandra was a good person to have in a crisis, her sister was sensitive too.

"How are you?" she asked, dropping her voice so only Cassandra could hear.

Cassandra pressed her lips together and shook her head, tears glinting in her eyes.

"Mrs Paulson is asleep," she said, trying to be brisk. Later, when they were lying side by side in bed, she knew Cassandra would open up. They always shared secrets then, in the darkness. Somehow, not being able to see the other person made it easier to talk of their greatest hopes and fears. "What has happened here?"

"The Potters and Mrs Leveritt and her daughter have retired to their rooms," Jane said, glancing over at Colonel Rushton. "The colonel and I are going to speak to the servants next to find out if anyone knows anything helpful and to tell them what will be happening next."

Cassandra nodded thoughtfully, and Jane realised how exhausted she looked.

"Why don't you go upstairs and rest? I will not be long. There is a limited amount that can be done tonight." It was a lie, and they both knew it. Between talking to the servants, inspecting the room where Mr Paulson had been killed and formulating a plan for the next day, Jane knew she was likely going to be up until the early hours of the morning, but she couldn't tell Cassandra that. Her sister was loyal and generous and would offer to stay with Jane if she thought it would be helpful, even if all she wanted to do was to curl up under the bedcovers and pretend she was back home at the rectory.

"I think I will do that. Come with me, Jane. It doesn't need to be you who looks into this."

Jane smiled softly at her sister and shook her head. "I will try not to be too late, but perhaps you might lock the door until I come up. I will knock to rouse you."

Cassandra's eyes widened, and Jane could see she understood the implication.

"I will. Be careful, Jane."

Bidding the two gentlemen goodnight, Cassandra slipped out of the room and disappeared upstairs.

"Colonel Rushton tells me you suspect the killer is still in the house," Dr Histon said once Cassandra was out of sight.

Jane nodded, regarding the doctor. He could be helpful in checking over Mr Paulson's body. She knew it was something Lord Hinchbrooke normally tried to do as soon as possible, but she had no expertise in the matter. Dr Histon would be able to give his professional opinion on the death and no doubt his years as a doctor had given him a keen eye for those little details that might elude someone else.

"Yes, there are no footprints in the snow outside, and I doubt anyone would get very far in this weather. That's even before you get to the locked door in the study." She shook her head, aware already that it was going to be devilishly difficult to work out not only who had committed the crime but how they had done so. "Doctor, I wonder if I could ask for your assistance in a few minutes. First I need to talk to the servants, to reassure them everything is in hand, but then I thought you might be so kind as to take another look in the study with me. There might be something your medical eye spots that someone with no training would miss."

"Of course, anything I can do to be of help. My patients are normally living, but I have been around death enough to know the patterns things normally present with, and I can see if there is any disruption to what one would expect."

"Thank you."

"I will wait here until then. The fire is warm, and I spy a decanter of something to steady the nerves on the side table over there. Unless you have need of me before then?"

"No, no need before then. We will come back for you in a few minutes."

"Upton, gather the servants downstairs in the kitchen," Colonel Rushton instructed the butler as they stepped out of the drawing room.

"What about the two guarding the study? Shall I ask them to come?"

"Yes," Colonel Rushton said at the same time as Jane said a hurried, "No."

She saw a flicker of irritation cross the colonel's face, there only for an instant and quickly covered.

"Perhaps it is best if they stay at their posts and we talk to them separately afterwards," she said, trying to sound as reasonable as possible.

"You think someone is going to be foolish enough to try and sneak into the study with the house this full of people?"

"Mr Paulson was killed in a house this full of people."

Colonel Rushton blinked a couple of times and then inclined his head. "Let them stay by the study. We will talk to everyone else in the kitchen."

CHAPTER THREE

Together Jane and Colonel Rushton followed the butler to the kitchen. Most of the servants were gathered there already, talking in hushed voices. There was tension in the room, an underlying panic that felt as though it were bubbling to the surface and anything could make it explode.

"Perhaps let me take the lead here," Colonel Rushton murmured into Jane's ear. "These people are scared, and they will respect a voice of authority."

Jane pressed her lips together and motioned for him to go ahead, praying the snow would stop soon so the colonel could fulfil his promise and ride to fetch Lord Hinchbrooke himself. Anything to get him out of the house.

"Thank you for waiting so patiently," Colonel Rushton said, pacing in front of the large kitchen table as if he were addressing some of his troops. Standing facing him were four people. The cook and kitchen maid were easy to identify, and there was a pretty young woman whom Jane thought was probably a housemaid. Upstairs there was a footman outside the study, and of course Upton the butler, but it still didn't feel like many servants for a house of this grandeur. Before she started to speak, two young men came along the corridor and entered the kitchen, nodding politely at Jane and the assembled servants. By the looks of it they were grooms or gardeners, their coats buttoned high against the chill temperatures outside. Mrs Paulson had mentioned three servants leaving unexpectedly, and Jane wondered if they had made up the full complement or if there had been others who had left recently. She glanced at the faces, wondering who would be best to ask.

Upton was officially head of the staff, but he had a disapproving air about him, and no doubt he wouldn't give up the house's secrets that easily. Perhaps the housemaid was a better person to press. She would be privy to some of the private conversations Mr and Mrs Paulson had when no one else was around. People of a certain level of wealth always seemed to forget their servants had ears. The young kitchen maid looked petrified and was sitting with the cook's hand clutched in hers as if it were her only lifeline in a storm.

"As I am sure you're aware, Mr Paulson was found dead earlier this evening. He has been stabbed." The colonel paused for effect, looking from face to face. Jane regarded them too, trying to ascertain if there was a flicker of emotion or remorse on anyone's faces. It was too difficult to say. She didn't know any of these staff so couldn't tell if the stony expression on the housemaid's face was usual for her, or if the butler's stance, hopping from foot to foot, was how he normally reacted in a crisis.

The cook murmured something under her breath and shook her head, looking down at the table.

"At the moment the snow is too thick to get outside help. Hopefully in the morning it will melt a little and we will be able to send for the magistrate, but for now we have to make the best of things."

"What about the guests, sir?" the butler asked, looking to the doorway as if they might appear at any moment.

"The guests have mainly retired to their rooms."

"They'll be wanting dinner, I'm sure," the cook said.

"If you could see to sending up some trays with a little sustenance on them, I am sure it will be appreciated."

"Of course," Upton said, seeming to regain his composure a little and with it some of his authority. "We will see to it at once."

"We are asking that no one goes into the study where Mr Paulson's body is, not until the magistrate has been," Jane said, stepping forward. "In addition, we may need to ask a few questions to try and ascertain what happened earlier in the evening." She observed the panic in their faces before pushing on quickly. "It is merely to build a timeline of events; the questions will not be taxing."

"We acknowledge the shock of this evening's events and understand you will want to mourn Mr Paulson, but I ask for your help in this difficult time," Colonel Rushton said.

"I assure you everyone will cooperate fully," Upton said, nodding with complete confidence in his ability to compel the staff here to follow orders.

"Thank you."

They left before the servants could ask too many questions, and Jane was glad of it. Right now they were in shock, too dazed by the death of their employer to think of the consequences of some of the things Colonel Rushton had said. Soon they would realise they were all under suspicion, all liable to have their private lives poked and prodded to uncover any secrets, any motive for killing Mr Paulson.

"They're a quiet lot," Colonel Rushton said. Jane nodded. He was right; in a room full of people, no one had piped up and asked any difficult questions. No one had accused them of keeping everyone prisoner here or interfering with their rights. Perhaps it was down to shock, or perhaps there was another reason for the servants to be so quiet.

They found Dr Histon in the drawing room, nursing a glass of whiskey. He looked morose and dishevelled, and Jane had to remind herself this was a difficult situation for everyone involved. It would put a strain on even the strongest person, so she should think more charitably of the men who had volunteered to help her.

"Are you ready?" Colonel Rushton said to his friend.

"Yes. Shall we view the body?"

Jane went to fall in step beside them, trying to steady her nerves for what was to come.

"I think it might be best if you did not accompany us, Miss Austen," Colonel Rushton said, stopping and laying a fatherly hand on her arm.

"Nonsense," Jane said, shrugging him off.

"There is no need, and it will doubtless be a distressing experience. The doctor and I have, in our own ways, had the unfortunate experience of seeing death many, many times, but it is not something I would wish upon you."

Jane paused, with an effort managing to silence the tirade that was bubbling inside, straining to get out. He wasn't wrong; he and Dr Histon were likely hardened to death, having seen it many times before. It was disturbing to see someone lying there with no blood pumping around their body and no breath in their lungs. Jane thought back to the lifeless body of Miss Roscoe at the Westworth's ball. The images still haunted her dreams, even two months on, and she knew Mr Paulson's glassy, staring eyes would be added to that bank of disturbing pictures that sprung up in her mind unbidden.

"I thank you for your concern, Colonel Rushton," she said, trying to keep the irritated edge from her voice. "Please believe me when I say I am aware of the devastating effect examining a dead body can have on a person; however, Lord Hinchbrooke is insistent it be done. We have spent hours discussing the peculiar and enlightening findings one might make, little clues that might otherwise be missed."

"Dr Histon can look for you."

"And I am grateful for that, but Dr Histon comes at this from a medical point of view. The magistrate has shown me how to look at it from a criminal one."

Colonel Rushton removed his hand from her arm and stepped aside, not saying anything in answer as they quietly walked past the footman and maid guarding the study door and entered.

The room was still dark, with the two candles burned low and flickering in the darkness. Colonel Rushton paused in the doorway and sent the footman to fetch more. As they waited, Jane tried to use the pause to settle her nerves. Despite her speech to Colonel Rushton and the air of capability she was trying to exude, she felt petrified. There was a dead man sitting a few feet away, most likely stabbed by someone who was still in this house. The longer they had to wait for the magistrate, the more vital it was that she note down her observations so he could have a contemporaneous resource to work with.

Once the extra candles were in place and the footman had retreated out of the room, no one moved for a moment. Jane knew that if she wanted to be seen to be in charge of this situation, now was the time to step up, to show she could follow the meticulous procedures Lord Hinchbrooke advocated for.

"Dr Histon, I am going to approach Mr Paulson's body. Perhaps you would be so good as to accompany me and let me know your observations." The words sounded stiff, as if she were acting in a badly produced play, and Jane felt her stomach drop as both men's eyes focussed on her.

"Of course." The doctor strode forward, only hesitating when he got to the other side of the desk, and then he gripped the arms of the chair and moved it round so he could access the body.

Jane stood next to him, trying to take in every last detail of how Mr Paulson was sitting, knowing this was the last time he would be completely undisturbed. With solemnity and respect, Dr Histon took the dead man's hand and moved it to one side, so he could get a better look at the knife sticking out of his abdomen.

"Decorative handle — it looks like a letter opener, perhaps. Not a kitchen knife or anything that is used for heavy work."

Jane leaned in closer, trying to ascertain what the murder weapon could be from just the handle. It was about three inches long and was studded with coloured glass, the end curved into the shape of a dragon.

"Are letter openers sharp enough to stab someone?" Jane asked, glancing at the doctor.

"Anything is sharp enough, given the required amount of force. Even a relatively blunt object, if driven in with enough power, can pierce the skin and the layers of fascia." The doctor paused and then indicated the man's shirt. "I'm going to lift up the shirt and see what I can make out underneath."

Carefully Dr Histon untucked the shirt from the waistband of the dead man's trousers, pulling the edge up little by little in an attempt not to dislodge the knife. Jane could see some mild discoloration around the wound and some dried blood which stuck the shirt to the body at first.

"He has bled a little, but not extensively," the doctor said, seeing her frown. "At least, not externally. But see this discoloration here, around the wound?" He looked up at her and waited for her to nod. "It indicates internal bleeding. By the position of the knife, I would suspect the blade punctured the superior mesenteric artery. It would have caused catastrophic internal bleeding almost immediately."

"This superior mesenteric artery, is it hard to identify?"

"You're wondering if the perpetrator had specialist knowledge of the human body?" Dr Histon said. "It runs along this path here, not the easiest thing to find if you were aiming specifically for it, but the abdomen is crisscrossed by multiple large blood vessels. Even a random stabbing has a good chance of puncturing something. That's without even taking into consideration the devastation that can be caused by a wound to the bowel or the bladder or the kidneys." The doctor pressed around the blade, nodding in satisfaction. "The knife has acted as an obstruction, keeping the blood inside, but it has the same effect. Your blood is of no use to you outside the arteries and veins; if it is sitting in the abdominal cavity, it is as useless as if it were lying on the floor."

Jane straightened, catching sight of Mr Paulson's staring eyes. As gently as possible, she leaned in and closed them, noting how the body felt cold and stiff already. There was a waxy sheen to his skin, and his fingers were beginning to curl.

"Lord Hinchbrooke always advises to look under the fingernails and in the hands, in case the dead person has managed to grasp anything from their assailant."

Dr Histon picked up one of the man's hands and checked with a medical efficiency, then repeated the routine with the other hand.

"Is there anything else we should look at, Miss Austen?" the doctor asked softly, and Jane could see he was eager to step away from the dead man.

"No, thank you for your observations, Dr Histon. They are very helpful."

Dr Histon rearranged Mr Paulson's clothes, frowning as he tried to adjust the body in the chair. "We may have to move him before the magistrate arrives. I am sure there is a store room that could be used to keep him for now. Preferably somewhere dark and cold to slow down the process of decomposition."

Jane shuddered at the thought of the man rotting as the household continued their daily tasks around him. She knew the doctor was right; they couldn't leave this macabre scene in the study for days on end, and who knew how long it would be before Lord Hinchbrooke, or indeed an undertaker, could get through the snow?

"You're right, of course. When we are done in here, I will ask the butler to arrange it."

Turning her attention to the desk in front of Mr Paulson, Jane remained silent. At first glance, nothing looked out of place. If Mr Paulson had been stabbed in his chair, he had allowed the culprit to get close enough to wield the knife without allowing him to struggle. There were no strewn papers or items pushed onto the floor. The whole desk looked neat and orderly. In one corner was a pile of papers, the top piece covered in small, curly writing. He obviously shared her own resolve to not waste precious paper with empty spaces. She picked up the pile of papers, flicking through, noting an envelope discarded to one side, but when she pulled the papers from within, she was surprised to see the sheets empty, devoid of any writing.

"I'm not sure you should be touching those," Colonel Rushton said, leaning over her shoulder. "A man's private correspondence should remain private."

"Even if there is a letter in here declaring *I am going to kill you*, signed by the perpetrator?"

"Is there?"

"I won't know until I look."

Taking her time, Jane skimmed the words on each sheet of paper, discarding any that were clearly correspondence from the man's solicitor or land steward. The Paulsons owned an estate in neighbouring Dorset, and with that it would seem they rented out properties to a number of tenants and also had a few farms leased to tenant farmers. From what she could gather, Mr Paulson had delegated the day to day running of this estate to a land steward, but still liked to be kept informed of any developments.

Towards the bottom of the pile was a different sort of paper, and something about it made Jane pause. The writing was well formed and neat, but it had something about it that made it look a little too careful:

Dear Mr Paulson,

Please forgive me for writing like this. I know when I left I promised I would not contact you, but I find myself struggling and hoped you might help. Perhaps we can meet. You can reach me at the address on the envelope.

K

Jane turned the note over and then searched through the pile of papers for the envelope, but it was nowhere to be found.

"What is that?" Colonel Rushton asked, peering over her shoulder.

Jane resisted the urge to pull the letter away and instead handed it over, knowing there wasn't much more to glean from the short note. She wondered if it had been kept deliberately vague in case someone else spotted it. It had been shoved to the bottom of the pile of papers, either discarded as unimportant, or rapidly hidden when someone had entered the room.

Systematically Jane rifled through the remainder of the papers but did not find anything else, so she turned her attention to the rest of the desk. There were dregs of tea left in a cup to Mr Paulson's left and an ink pot and set of pens to his right.

With one last look at the desk, Jane stepped away, letting her eyes flit over the rest of the room. It was unremarkable really, like a hundred other studies of wealthy men around the country, or so she imagined. There were two comfortable, high-backed chairs off to one side, a wall lined with bookcases, a large fireplace, and of course the desk and chair behind it. The desk was directly opposite the door and formed the centrepiece of the room, drawing your attention to the shiny mahogany. There were two windows, and Jane went over to inspect these now.

"I do not have an answer," Colonel Rushton said, coming to stand beside her.

"They're both locked?"

"Not locked, but secured from the inside. It would be impossible for someone to escape this way and then close and secure the windows."

Jane looked around the room. There were no other doors, no other way in or out of the room. It was an old house and conceivably there could be a priest's hole or something similar, but surely Mrs Paulson or one of the staff would have mentioned it when Mr Paulson was first found dead.

"The door was locked from the inside, and the windows were secured from the inside. There is no other way in or out of the room," Colonel Rushton said.

"Dr Histon," Jane called, waiting for the medical man to finish his inspection of the body and straighten. "Could Mr Paulson have moved around after he was stabbed, before he died?"

Dr Histon glanced at the large man slumped in the chair and considered for a moment.

"It is not inconceivable he could have staggered a few steps. Death would have been quick, but not instantaneous."

"Could he have walked to the door, locked it and made his way back to the desk?"

"Don't be ridiculous," Colonel Rushton said, shaking his head. "What man gets stabbed, lets the perpetrator escape, and then locks himself in his study to die after?"

"Perhaps he did not realise quite how serious his injury was," Jane murmured. It didn't sit right with her either, but until she could work out how the murderer had attacked Mr Paulson and escaped a locked room, it would be hard to find who had stabbed the man in the abdomen.

"It is possible, I suppose," Dr Histon said quietly, looking from the chair to the door and nodding his head slowly. "Sometimes in the moments before death, our actions are not the most logical. It would not be inconceivable to imagine Mr Paulson's mind was clouded by the rapidly approaching darkness and he acted irrationally."

It was a theory, although an unsatisfactory one.

CHAPTER FOUR

On her way upstairs Jane paused outside the door to the master bedroom, wondering if Mrs Paulson was inside or if she slept in her own bedroom, as was the custom for many women of her social standing. Jane's parents had always shared a bedroom and she liked to think it was out of more than necessity. The rectory was a decent size, although not large like Melmont Hall, and there probably was enough room for a separate bedroom had her parents wanted a different arrangement. If all the family were home it could feel overcrowded, but that hardly ever happened, with her brothers mostly leading their own lives away from home, stopping in for the occasional visit but hardly ever more than one at a time. She and Cassandra shared a room, falling asleep beside one another every night, and Jane missed her sister if she wasn't there.

She dreaded the time when Cassandra's fiancé would return. Of course, she was happy for her sister, for the prospect of her marrying a decent man and having a family of her own, a household of her own, but in the quiet moments, when Jane allowed her innermost thoughts to come to the fore, she sometimes wished things weren't going to change.

Perhaps that was why the short liaison with Tom Lefroy had hit her so hard. They'd barely known one another, yet...

Jane shook her head. She'd promised both herself and Cassandra she would not wallow. Outwardly she would be happy for Cassandra and her happy ending, and she would work on being inwardly happy too.

Softly she knocked on the door, waiting for a moment before twisting the handle. The bed was undisturbed, freshly made that morning for a man who would never sleep in it again. Mrs Paulson must be elsewhere.

Jane carried on to her room, wondering if Cassandra was asleep and hoping she had taken her advice and locked the door. She knocked, three sharp raps on the door, and heard immediate movement inside.

Cassandra opened the door, her face pale and drawn, concern in her eyes.

"It's late, Jane. You must be exhausted."

Slipping inside the room, she felt some of her tension ebbing away as Cassandra locked the door behind her.

"Let's get you undressed, then you can tell me everything when we are in bed."

Silently Jane nodded, taking a few moments to allow the events of the day to rush through her mind without examining them. Lord Hinchbrooke advocated this approach. Often they would sit and play chess together, and he would tell her of interesting cases he had been involved in or criminals he had sentenced in his court. As they focussed on the chess pieces, he would impart little pieces of wisdom, speaking in his slow, melodious voice, a natural teacher who could make even the dullest subject seem fascinating. He had told that sometimes your brain needed time to work through everything it had seen and heard, time to put the pieces of the puzzle together into a coherent order and to spot the anomaly. That was what she was hoping for. It had only been a few hours since they had found Mr Paulson's body, but already Jane's head felt like it was going to burst with all the facts and observations she'd gathered. At the moment none of it really made sense and she was desperately hoping a little time would allow the information to settle and slot together.

Cassandra helped her with her dress, lifting it over her head and ensuring it was neatly packed away whilst Jane unlaced her stays and stepped out of her petticoat. Once she was in her nightclothes she slipped into bed, feeling a weariness descend over her. Normally she was a poor sleeper, restless in bed and never able to rid her mind of the thousands of thoughts that flooded through it, but perhaps tonight she might get some respite in sleep.

"The door is locked?" She watched Cassandra go over and try the handle.

"It's locked."

"Good."

Cassandra fussed around for another few minutes and then slipped into bed beside her, blowing out the lone candle as she did so. The room was dark, the only light the faint glow of the embers in the hearth from the fire that had been laid earlier that evening. Jane lay there without moving for a few minutes, her eyes adjusting to the dark.

"Does it have to be you?" Cassandra asked eventually.

"No one else has experience in investigating a murder."

"Surely Colonel Rushton has some skills that would help."

"He certainly thinks he does," she muttered, knowing she was being uncharitable. "Lord Hinchbrooke will be here as soon as the snow has cleared, and I hope he will allow me to assist him again, like he did with Miss Roscoe."

Cassandra was silent for a long time, and Jane could almost hear the words of protest running through her head. Words she knew would do no good spoken out loud.

"You think the killer is still here, don't you?"

"Yes," Jane said. There was no use denying it. Anyone could see a locked door, and no tracks in the snow pointed to an assailant from inside the house.

"And you think that person could pose a threat to anyone who might uncover something. That's why you were so keen for me to double-check the door was locked."

"Whoever it is has killed once. I do not know for sure, but I can imagine it is easier a second time."

Cassandra shuddered and Jane reached out and put a hand on her arm. They were of very different temperaments, despite having such a close relationship. Cassandra was softer, more forgiving, gentler in nature. Jane knew some people found her sharp-tongued and abrasive, and often were taken by surprise by her desire to smash through the expectations people had of her as an unmarried daughter of a rector. Whereas Jane looked at a matter like the murder of Mr Paulson as a challenge, a puzzle to be worked out, her sister instead saw the dangers.

"Then you have to step away, Jane. You cannot make yourself into a target."

"The safest thing to do would be to unmask the killer. That way, they could be detained until the magistrate arrived."

"Surely if someone feels you are getting close to uncovering the truth they will strike out, panic even."

Jane didn't answer. Her sister wasn't wrong, and she didn't have the words to reassure her.

For a long while they lay there in silence. Cassandra's breathing became heavier and more even as she relaxed, but Jane could tell her sister wasn't yet asleep.

"Go on," Cassandra said eventually. "Tell me, although I can't promise to be awake when you're done."

"Are you sure?"

"Just nothing gruesome. I don't want nightmares."

"The last person to see Mr Paulson alive was the maid at six o'clock, when she took a glass of whiskey into the study. At that time, Mr Paulson was alive and well. An hour later at seven, whilst we awaited his presence in the dining room, the butler Upton could not get an answer from the study. After knocking and knocking, Dr Histon broke down the door and confirmed Mr Paulson was dead and had been stabbed. On further inspection of the room, it was apparent that the door had been locked, the windows fastened from the inside and there appears to be no other way into or out of the room." Jane paused, closing her eyes for a moment, wondering if there was a simple explanation she was missing. "What's more, when Colonel Rushton and I took a walk around the house, there appeared to be no tracks in the snow, although it is conceivable that they were covered by fresh snowfall."

"It is a mystery," Cassandra murmured, her voice heavy with sleep.

"It is." Jane could see her sister's eyes closing in the darkness and held back any further speculation, instead allowing Cassandra to drift off to sleep. She wished she could do the same but knew she was likely in for a night of tossing and turning in a strange bed, perhaps with a few hours of snatched sleep in the early hours of the morning.

Trying to clear her mind, she thought first of Tom Lefroy, but quickly recoiled from the idea of spending her night pining for him. Instead, she tried to focus on the book she was writing. The familiar world she was building soothed her nerves and finally allowed her to relax, and she picked over the story already written and her ideas as to what should come next.

CHAPTER FIVE

Jane was awake early, trying to lie as still as possible so as not to disturb Cassandra. The light hadn't begun to filter through the curtains yet and outside it was deadly silent, with the snow muffling the sounds of any wildlife that ventured out. Somewhere upstairs she heard the stirrings of the earliest risers amongst the servants. There were the quiet creaks of doors and groans of floorboards as they felt their way in the darkness, getting ready for another day and a house full of guests.

Sometimes she wondered how they knew it was time to rise, time to start clearing the fireplaces of the vestiges of the fires laid before and setting new ones. Time to heat up the stove and put that first pan of water on to boil, or gather the eggs for breakfast. It wasn't as though all the servants had timepieces, yet they still managed to start their days well before the rest of the household awoke.

Carefully Jane slipped out from underneath the sheets, feeling with her feet for the slippers she had brought with her. The floor was cold, and she inhaled sharply until she managed to find her slippers, only then relaxing. Wishing there was a little more light to guide her in this unfamiliar room, Jane bumped into the edge of a chair, sending it clattering a few inches across the floor as she made her way over to the window. For a moment she paused, looking back over her shoulder at the bed, but although Cassandra shifted and turned over she did not wake.

Pulling back the curtain far enough to reveal the view, Jane positioned herself on the wide sill behind the heavy fabric, sitting with her legs bent in front of her, side on to the window.

Outside, everything was peaceful and still. It looked like a scene from a beautifully illustrated book, the snow thick and undisturbed, obscuring the shapes of the trees and bushes, smoothing the edges and making the landscape look soft and surreal.

Leading from one bush out into the open was a small set of footprints, perhaps a fox or a badger, some animal that had ventured out a little way into the snow and then having realised there was no food to be had in this weather had retreated back the way it had come.

The snow had stopped falling now, although the clouds still looked heavy and thick in the dark sky. It was difficult to tell quite how much lay on the ground, as there was no obvious point of reference. The bushes and trees in the garden all looked much shorter than usual, and the statue that stood at the entrance to the formal garden was certainly at least a quarter under the snow, but it was difficult to see whether it was that deep everywhere or if the snow lay in drifts, piled where the wind had blown it.

"No one is going anywhere today," Jane murmured to herself, leaning her forehead against the window. If they were lucky, the sun might appear later in the morning and warm everything up enough for the snow to start melting, but in reality she doubted it. Even if there was a significant lift in temperature the roads would be icy, far too treacherous for anyone to make the journey to Lord Hinchbrooke's ancestral home fifteen miles away.

She was on her own. Of course, Colonel Rushton would volunteer to help, but whether that was a blessing or a hindrance was yet to be seen.

As she sat there in the darkness she tried to recall everything she knew about Mr Paulson and realised it was little. Mrs Paulson was a friend of her mother's, a woman of about the same age as Mrs Austen, although she had never thought to enquire where they had met. Mrs Paulson and her mother were of a similar age, so it was most likely they had grown up together, but Mr Paulson was a different matter. He was older than his wife by about fifteen years, not so much as to provoke comment, but noteworthy all the same. Jane wondered if he had been married before his union to Mrs Paulson, or if he had remained a bachelor. Mr and Mrs Paulson had remained childless, but she realised she didn't know if he had children from a previous marriage.

What she needed was a talkative maid. Mrs Paulson would be too distressed to answer anything but the most basic of questions, and Jane knew she couldn't treat the poor woman heartlessly and insist she give a full history of her husband's life whilst she was still in shock from his death. A maid would know the family gossip; Jane just needed to find one who didn't believe in discretion.

Quietly she rose and pulled on her dressing gown, creeping over to the door and opening it. She glanced back at Cassandra's sleeping form in the bed before slipping out into the hallway. Soon the house would slowly creak to life, but before it did Jane might find the perfect opportunity to discuss things with the housemaid she suspected was working her way around the downstairs rooms, seeing to the fires.

A whimper made her pause in the long, upstairs hallway, the sound causing her pulse to quicken. She wished she had a weapon with her, anything to give her a little bit of courage as she made her way through the darkness.

The sound had come from a room across the hall, and Jane padded over to it, conscious that she didn't want to go bursting in if she had merely heard the Potters bidding each other good morning or Mrs Leveritt soothing her daughter's fears.

There was another whimper and Jane looked over her shoulder, torn between leaving whoever was in the room to their privacy and going in.

After a few seconds' hesitation, she knocked quietly on the door.

"Hello, is anything amiss in there?"

When she didn't get an answer she tried the door, and when the handle gave way she stepped inside.

It was darker in here than in the hall, with the curtains pulled completely shut, and it took a moment for Jane to work out the layout of the room. Her heart was hammering, as if trying to escape through her breastbone, but even taking slow, deep breaths was not enough to quell the apprehension she felt mounting inside her.

"Miss Austen, is that you?"

Mrs Paulson's familiar voice was querulous and sounded confused, and Jane quickly rushed further into the room, wanting to reassure the older woman that it was not anyone wanting to do her harm.

"Yes, Mrs Paulson, I heard a noise and wanted to check on you."

"That is so kind, Miss Austen. You are so terribly kind. Everyone is."

"Can I get you anything, Mrs Paulson?"

Mrs Paulson gave a sob in the darkness, and Jane heard a rustle of sheets as she adjusted her position in the bed.

"Come sit with me, dear, just for a minute."

"Of course."

Jane perched on the edge of the bed, able to make out the outlines of the furniture in the room now as well as the pure white of Mrs Paulson's nightclothes. She had to muffle a cry when Mrs Paulson reached out and took her hand, grasping it tightly in her own.

"I have such a heavy head."

"Dr Histon gave you something to help you sleep."

"Tell me, Miss Austen, it all really happened, didn't it? It wasn't just an awful dream?"

"It all happened, Mrs Paulson." There was no point in being anything but direct, even though the sob that came from Mrs Paulson was difficult to hear. Jane wondered if she had truly loved her husband, or if it was the life that was irrevocably changed that the older woman was ultimately mourning. Mr Paulson had always come across as cantankerous and rude, but Jane was well aware people were different in private. She had no idea if the marriage between the Paulsons had been a contented one, whether each morning they took breakfast together or if they did their best to avoid one another's company all day.

Jane opened her mouth to ask a question and quickly closed it again. She might be direct and sometimes a little insensitive, but she was not cruel. There were other ways to find out what she needed without pressing the grieving widow.

"Will you stay with me, Miss Austen?"

"Of course."

Jane shifted her position a little as Mrs Paulson rested back on the pillows. She wasn't sure what Dr Histon had given her the night before, but it seemed to be quite long-acting, for the older woman's breathing soon deepened as she drifted back into unconsciousness.

Jane waited until she was sure Mrs Paulson wasn't going to wake up again imminently and then crept from the room. Downstairs there was more movement now and she hurried along the upstairs hallway, eager to speak to the housemaid before she finished her early morning duties away from the rest of the staff. People always seemed more likely to talk if other ears weren't listening, and she couldn't imagine Upton's unwavering gaze making even the most talkative person want to gossip about the night's events or their employer.

"Good morning," Jane said softly as she entered the dining room. Despite her quiet approach the maid jumped, placing a hand over her chest and quickly getting to her feet. After a moment she seemed to remember herself and dipped into a curtsey.

"Good morning, Miss. Is there something I can help you with?"

Jane regarded the maid. She was older than Jane had first thought, perhaps in her early twenties, although she had a round, youthful face that made her look a decade younger at first glance. She was pretty in an innocent way and had big, trusting eyes that at the moment were filled with fear.

"I'm sorry to disturb your morning work. I'm sure you have a lot to do before everyone is up and about," Jane said, glancing over her shoulder to check they were not being observed. "I will try to be as quick as possible, but I wondered if you might have a few minutes to answer some questions."

"I'm not sure I should," the young woman said quietly. "Mr Upton said we should wait for him to be present, that it wouldn't be right for us to talk to anyone without his supervision."

The Austen family had never employed a butler; their household was too modest to need it, and her father's income didn't stretch past Mrs White and Lizzie, who helped cook and clean. Still, she had come across enough butlers to know that they occupied a unique position within the house. As a servant, they had the responsibility of overseeing all the household staff below them and often didn't develop the friendships or share in the camaraderie that made the long hours and constant demands bearable. Upton seemed organised and officious, and Jane could imagine him not being the most popular member of staff amongst the maids and footmen.

"Of course you must listen to Mr Upton's advice," Jane said with a smile, "when it comes to answering questions about the murder of Mr Paulson, but I hoped to learn a little more of the set-up in the house, that is all. Normally I would ask Mrs Paulson, but I thought it might be better to spare her what I can."

"You don't want to ask me about the murder?"

"Not yet, not unless there is anything you want to tell me." Jane waited, her eyes searching the maid's and seeing the struggle as she tried to decide whether to obey Upton or help her mistress.

"I suppose it couldn't hurt to talk about Melmont Hall, although I do have a lot of fires to clean and set for the day."

"Let me help you. We can talk while we work."

"Oh, I couldn't allow that, Miss. You're a guest, and you'll get all dirty."

"I don't mind a little work in the mornings. Pass me that spare apron."

There was another thick apron hanging over the basket the maid had set beside the fireplace with everything she needed to sweep out the remnants of the fire the day before and lay a new one.

The maid still hesitated so Jane moved to take it, tying the straps around her waist. Kneeling down, she set about with a brush, getting into the corners of the fireplace as her mother had taught her. Jane was expected to help around the house at home, with no job too menial. Her mother advocated for a family life where they all did their share of domestic labour whilst giving thanks that they could afford some help in the form of their maid Lizzie.

"What's your name?"

"Charlotte, Miss. Charlotte Harper."

"Have you worked here long, Charlotte?"

"Three years now, Miss. Before that I was a maid for Mrs Keeting in the village."

"Do you like working here, Charlotte?" It was a question meant to set the young woman at ease, but Jane could see it had the opposite effect. She remembered the recently departed staff and knew it was vital she found out what had caused such an upheaval here at Melmont Hall.

"It is a good job, Miss," Charlotte said carefully, starting to polish the grate. She attacked it with vigour, focussing on the task and not looking up to meet Jane's eye.

"Not an easy job, though, I can imagine."

"No, it is a large house, and there is much work to get through each day."

"I understand a few of the servants have left recently. That must make your job harder."

"It's been double the work since Kitty left. Normally in the mornings she would do the upstairs fires whilst I did the downstairs. Then we'd clean the downstairs together and tackle the bedrooms after that. It's so much harder to make a bed when there's not someone on the other side, pulling the sheets straight."

"It's a lot more work for you. Have the other people who've left impacted on you as well?"

Charlotte shrugged and paused for a moment, regarding the grate as if contemplating whether it was shiny enough. "Benjamin Grout was a lazy scoundrel anyway. Although Mr Upton moans that a house this size should have more than one footman, I don't think he's been too missed. Then there was Fran Adams; she was a general maid, helped a bit upstairs and in the kitchen. She was quiet, liked to keep herself to herself, but she did everything that was asked of her without a complaint."

"Did they all leave at the same time?"

Charlotte sat back on her haunches and glanced at the door.

"All within a couple of days of each other. Don't ask me why. Mr Upton might be able to tell you, but he discourages gossip, and if he heard any of us discussing it we would be harshly reprimanded."

Jane nodded thoughtfully, knowing she would come back to the subject but deciding to dig into something else first and build up her rapport with the young woman.

As the maid finished polishing the grate, Jane began setting the fire ready for its next use, building it up in layers as her mother had showed her. They worked in silence for a short amount of time before Charlotte stood and indicated they should move on to the next room.

"Who is left here? With regards to servants?"

"There's Mr Upton, of course; he's overall in charge. Then Mrs Brown, the cook; she's in charge downstairs. She's got Moll under her; that's the kitchen maid. Upstairs there's me, Fred Giles the remaining footman, and Mary Wright, who is the mistress's lady's maid. Then there are two grooms, Gabriel and Peter Jones, and a young lad who helps in the stables, but his mum has taken ill so he's gone back home for the week to see her."

"Does everyone else live in?"

"Yes. Mrs Brown has a room downstairs next to the kitchen, and everyone else lives at the top of the house. The grooms have their own cottage by the stables."

The next room on the maid's list was the drawing room. It felt cold and hollow, not like the glittering room they had entered the night before to the sound of Miss Leveritt playing the pianoforte.

"Is Mrs Paulson a good mistress?" Jane asked, lowering her voice as they set the basket and brush down next to the fireplace.

"Oh yes, Miss, the very best. She's so kind and caring. She was the one who insisted Johnny went home to see his mother, even when Mr Upton said it would set a dangerous precedent and every servant would be begging time off to visit ailing relatives."

Jane could imagine Mrs Paulson gently overruling the butler on a matter such as this. She *was* kind, the sort of woman who wouldn't think twice about helping out a friend in need, even if it meant disadvantaging herself.

"What about Mr Paulson? Was he a good master?"

Charlotte hesitated, pretending to focus on sweeping out the ash from the fire the night before. "I didn't have much to do with him, Miss," she said eventually.

There was something important here, something the young maid would tell her if Jane trod carefully and asked the right questions. Something that might reveal a motive for the murder of Mr Paulson.

Jane stood, wiping her hands on her apron, before crossing the room and looking out into the hall. When she was satisfied there was no one else there, she closed the door, trying to mute the click of it closing by pressing her hands against it.

"There's only you and I here, Charlotte. Anything you tell me does not have to go any further, and perhaps it would be better if you told me now rather than the magistrate thinking you've held something back from him."

"It's nothing really, Miss Austen, nothing definite. And my mother always told me not to say anything unless you were completely sure of your facts, otherwise it was no better than malicious gossip."

Silently cursing Charlotte's mother, Jane nodded as if considering the maid's position.

"I do understand. The thing is, I have heard rumours, terrible rumours. I know when Lord Hinchbrooke, the magistrate, arrives, he will go straight to Mrs Paulson and ask her about them, and I worry it will cause her undue distress. I only ask for your help to spare Mrs Paulson the pain some of these questions may cause."

"It's only rumour," Charlotte repeated resolutely, then sat back on her heels and sighed. "Although if enough people add to that rumour, I suppose it is harder to dismiss."

Jane remained silent, hoping the young maid would push on without any further prompting.

"People said Mr Paulson could be a little … overly familiar," Charlotte said, her voice barely more than a whisper.

"Have you ever seen it?"

Charlotte shook her head and bit her lip. "He's never taken much notice of me — only to ask me to fetch some hot water or hurry up tidying his study. That's why I hesitate to repeat it."

"Where have you heard this from, Charlotte?"

"Lots of people. The maids all warned me when I started, said I was young and pretty, and as I was the new one around the house he was bound to take an interest. Even Mrs Brown took me aside and told me to make sure I was never in a room alone with him if I could help it."

"But he never tried anything?"

"Not once." Charlotte shrugged. "I thought perhaps it was a rumour that had got out of control — you know how these things do."

Jane remained quiet, sensing that there was more.

Charlotte took a shaky breath. "But then things happened with Kitty. She moaned about it, but sometimes I saw her secretly smiling, as if she was pleased as punch to get attention from the master."

"What happened with Kitty?"

"I don't know *exactly*; she was coy about it, even though you could tell she wanted us to ask, to force it out of her. At first she started showing off little trinkets, gifts he'd given her, and then she began talking about the future when she wouldn't have to put up with the drudgery of maids' work any longer."

"She expected something to change," Jane murmured, knowing she needed to speak to Kitty but having to acknowledge it was impossible with the snow as it was.

"Then suddenly she was gone, her and Benjamin and Fran all in one foul swoop. There was no explanation, and we were told we were to have no contact with them."

"They were all dismissed without warning?"

"Kitty and Benjamin were. Mr Upton marched them right off the estate with their little bundle of belongings. Fran they were kinder to, and I think she's gone to work for another household in the next village."

Jane thought back to how Mrs Paulson had described the departure of her staff and wondered if the mistress of the house was aware of the true circumstances around it. She had made it sound like the two maids and the footman had left of their own accord, but this story Charlotte was telling was vastly different.

"Where has Kitty gone, Charlotte?"

The maid shrugged. "She has family in the village, so I expect she's back with them, but we were forbidden from contacting Kitty or Benjamin. This job might not be perfect, but I'm not naïve; I know it is better than so many positions out there. I wouldn't go against Mr Upton, not openly."

"So you haven't contacted her?"

"No."

Jane sat back, wondering what to make of all of this, wondering if Mr Paulson's wandering hands were the reason for his murder or if it was merely a distraction from the true motive, a mere added layer of complexity in the household rather than a justification for someone to kill him.

Before she could ask any more, the door from the hall opened and Upton strode into the room. Charlotte's eyes widened and quickly Jane bent over, slipping the apron off before the butler could see and somehow blame the poor maid for Jane's insistence she help.

"What is happening here? Harper, you should be finished with all the downstairs fires by now and starting upstairs. What is the meaning of this delay?"

Jane stood, brushing down the skirt of her nightdress and pulling her dressing gown a little tighter around her body.

"Please do not blame Miss Harper, Mr Upton," Jane said, wondering whether the butler was as officious and pompous as he appeared or if it was a façade he put on for his role. "I struggled to sleep and came down here early. Miss Harper was kind enough to let me chatter to her as she worked, but I do not doubt her kindness has delayed her. I am sorry for that."

Mr Upton looked as though he would have reprimanded Jane, but her status as a guest stopped him from doing anything but giving a stiff bow and then glaring at Charlotte until the young maid hurried out of the room.

"I understand you have positioned yourself to hold some authority here in lieu of the magistrate," the butler said, barely suppressing a sneer, "but I would thank you not to talk to the servants without me present."

"Why?"

"Excuse me?"

"They are all adults, all perfectly capable of holding a conversation without your supervising eye. Why would you want to censor what they say?"

"It is not a matter of censorship…"

"Tell me what possible reason you could have for needing to be present when I speak to them, then?"

The butler drew himself up, as if trying to use his superior height to gain an advantage. Jane barely noticed. She was petite and had been all her life; men towering over her and trying to intimidate her with their physical size was nothing new. She was secure in the knowledge that she could best most of them mentally, and perhaps they knew that too; perhaps that was why they felt the need to demonstrate their physical strength. Jane responded by taking a step closer to Mr Upton, then another, closing the gap until he was forced to take a step back to maintain a polite distance.

"Mr Paulson trusted me with the running of this house, and until I receive instructions to the contrary, I will continue safeguarding this household as I see fit, as my late master would have expected of me."

"He expected you to intimidate and censor the servants?"

"You are being wilfully antagonistic, Miss Austen," the butler said, raising his voice a little. She stood still, not saying anything, wondering if he would realise how inappropriate this conversation was. "I can assure you Mr Paulson's murder has nothing to do with any of the staff at Melmont Hall."

"How can you know that?"

There was a long pause, and the butler regarded her with an inscrutable expression before giving the smallest bow she had ever seen and turning away.

Jane watched him go, knowing there was no point in hurrying after him. In all likelihood he had said it merely to rile her, but if the butler did know more about Mr Paulson's murder, she doubted he would reveal it to her alone. Perhaps later, with the authority of Colonel Rushton by her side, or even better Lord Hinchbrooke, if by some miracle he made it through the snow.

As she made her way back upstairs, determined to dress, eat a quick breakfast and then make a plan as to how to best tackle the rest of the day, she saw Mr Upton pause outside the study door. It was no longer being guarded, but the door was pulled closed. As she watched, the butler placed his hand on the wood and opened it just a little, peering inside. Then he seemed to change his mind, shaking his head and moving away.

Jane watched him until he disappeared down the stairs to the kitchen, wondering what the butler had been looking at.

CHAPTER SIX

"I woke up this morning, and for a moment I wondered if this had all been a bad dream," Mrs Leveritt said as she cracked open the top of her boiled egg. Miss Leveritt sat with a straight back next to her mother, her eyes downcast. "Truly I cannot believe this is happening to us."

"To Mr Paulson," Miss Leveritt corrected.

"What was that, dear?"

"It was Mr Paulson who was murdered, Mama, not us."

"Well, I know that, of course, but we are the ones suffering now. To be caught up in such a scandal — it is unimaginable."

Miss Leveritt stood, pushing her chair back abruptly so it scraped along the floor with force.

"Please excuse me," she said to the table in general, turning and walking from the room.

Jane looked at her breakfast. It was beautifully presented but she had no appetite, and for the last five minutes she'd done little more than nibble on some toast and push the rest round her plate. Briefly she gripped Cassandra's hand and then stood, following Miss Leveritt from the room. The young woman had disappeared by the time Jane had made it into the hall, but she guessed she'd headed upstairs and hurried after her.

"Miss Leveritt!" Jane called as the woman paused at the door to one of the guest rooms.

Miss Leveritt hesitated, not moving for a moment before finally turning around. Jane could see there were tears in her eyes.

"Has something upset you?" It was a ridiculous question to ask in a house where a man had been murdered less than twenty-four hours previously, but Jane had to ask it anyway. She thought of Lord Hinchbrooke's gentle, reassuring manner when he spoke to those closely involved in a crime and tried to emulate his air of calm.

Miss Leveritt bit her lip and shook her head but wasn't overly convincing. Jane bustled over to her, knowing the overbearing mother was probably not far behind.

"You were visibly upset at breakfast, Miss Leveritt. What distressed you so?"

"I cannot say. You will think me terribly selfish. I *am* terribly selfish. Please, it has nothing to do with the death of Mr Paulson, I give you my word."

"Is it to do with your mother?"

Miss Leveritt grimaced, and Jane knew she was at least partially right.

"Why is it we spend our youth trying not to emulate our mothers, ridiculing everything about them, but then find ourselves mimicking the very flaws we hate in our own behaviour?"

Jane smiled softly, thinking of her own mother. Mrs Austen was a formidable woman in her own way, gentle, supportive, but with the heart of a lion. To the outside world she seemed the perfect rector's wife, deferring to her husband, keeping the home running smoothly, giving birth to and raising a brood of children, but behind closed doors there was so much more. Jane had seen her mother cajole her father down the right path many a time — once over the decision to take students when money was a little tight, and another time to let go of an old animosity for the good of the family. Still, her mother was not perfect, and she knew exactly what Miss Leveritt meant. There were times when Mrs Austen became over-enthused about Jane's prospects for marriage, inviting potential suitors to take tea with them or go for a stroll after church on Sundays. Jane always rolled her eyes and huffed, never caring for her mother's choices, but Mrs Austen would smile and tell Jane she would do the same for her daughter one day.

"Listening to my mother, I felt sick; she's so consumed by her own concerns, how this tragedy will affect us, rather than thinking of poor Mrs Paulson and her loss. Then I realised I was fretting over the same thing. I had barely spared a thought for Mrs Paulson; instead, I had tossed and turned all night worrying about what this would do for my prospects. I'm just as bad as her."

"It is a natural response," Jane said kindly, wondering how Mr Paulson's death could affect Miss Leveritt's future. She was a neighbour, a friend, but any further connection had not been apparent. "I think everyone first thinks of themselves; it is how we are made, a mode of self-preservation, I suppose. Those that tell you their every thought is charitable are lying. It is more important what you do next, how you consider others after that initial selfish thought."

Miss Leveritt considered this for a moment, her shoulders slumping.

"Does Mr Paulson's death affect you, Miss Leveritt? I mean, of course, apart from being so close to the tragedy of it now?"

For a moment Miss Leveritt didn't answer, her hand still resting on the doorhandle to her room, and then she nodded.

"It's my whole future," she whispered, tears forming in her eyes.

Jane reached out and took Miss Leveritt's hand from the doorhandle then turned it herself, waiting for the young woman to enter the room before following her in. It was similar to her and Cassandra 's room but had a view out over the front of the property rather than the gardens at the back.

Out of the window Jane could see the snow was just as thick as the night before, and the sun, although unobscured by clouds, looked weak in the sky.

Miss Leveritt flopped down on the edge of the bed, brushing away a tear.

"Mrs Paulson offered to sponsor me for the season."

"In London?"

The young woman nodded and Jane inhaled slowly. That was a reason to be shaken by events.

"She is so kind and generous," Miss Leveritt said, breaking off to suppress a sob, "but of course it will not happen now. Mrs Paulson will be in mourning and I…" She trailed off, a desolate look in her eyes.

"Was there a reason Mrs Paulson made this kind offer?" It was a big commitment for someone who was not close family. There would be the cost of moving a household to London for a few months, buying new dresses, and hosting dinner parties and soirées.

"She has always been kind to us. My papa died a few years ago. It has not always been easy, but my mother sacrificed a great deal to ensure I had a good education and all the opportunities she felt should be afforded to me. Mrs Paulson saw our struggles and offered to help." Miss Leveritt lowered her voice, as if aware it was a subject she shouldn't be talking about. "The hope was in London I would find a gentleman wealthy enough to take care of me and my dear mama, who would see my accomplishments and not be put off by the lack of a dowry."

Jane nodded, understanding the sentiment behind this but wondering if it were true. Most marriages were dealt with as business transactions, even many of those claimed to be love matches. There was still a dowry to be paid, terms to be agreed.

It was kind of Mrs Paulson to offer to take Miss Leveritt to experience all the delights of the London season, but without any dowry Miss Leveritt would likely still struggle to secure a suitable match.

"Now I will be stuck here in Hampshire with no prospects and forced to accept any offer to save my mother and I from complete ruin."

"Surely you still have a little time?"

Miss Leveritt sniffed and then gave a sad smile. "Look at me, talking about myself. This is what I meant. Poor Mr Paulson lies cold downstairs and all I can think about is my predicament."

"Did you know Mr Paulson well?"

"No, not really. We would sometimes see him when we visited Melmont Hall, but only long enough to bid him good morning."

"But you must know Mrs Paulson well."

Miss Leveritt smiled. "Yes, she is a dear friend of my mama's and often visits us at home. She was a frequent visitor when I was growing up, always bringing freshly baked cakes or some treat we would otherwise not be able to afford."

"She is a generous woman." Jane stood, thinking to leave Miss Leveritt in peace. Mr Paulson's death would have far-reaching consequences. They hadn't even touched on what would happen to his wealth and property now he was dead. The land wasn't entailed and Mr Paulson had no title to pass on, so he might have left his wife a generous settlement, but equally he could have followed a more traditional path and left the entirety of his fortune to his closest male heir.

It was something else to ask Mrs Paulson about when the widow was up to some gentle questioning.

CHAPTER SEVEN

Jane returned downstairs to find the servants in uproar, gathered in the hall and mumbling rebelliously. She groaned when she saw Colonel Rushton had gathered them and wondered what he had said that was so controversial that a group of normally well-controlled people were protesting so loudly.

"I am not saying that at all," Colonel Rushton said, holding his hands out to try and make the gathered group listen. The Potters were peering out of the dining room, looking to see if there was an escape route past this melee, and after a moment they retreated back inside. "I merely meant that if there was a hiding place, someone who lives here, who works here, is more likely to know about it."

Jane hung back for a moment, wondering what would happen next and not wanting to align herself with the colonel if he was going to turn the servants against him.

"You're saying one of us did it, one of us killed Mr Paulson."

"That's not true," Colonel Rushton said slowly, shaking his head.

"Blame the servants. That's what always happens. Accuse those with less chance of fighting back."

"No one is being accused of anything."

Jane stepped forward, trying to look suitably grave and perplexed at the turn of events, and remembering the magistrate's calm, authoritative manner, a manner he used to his advantage at moments like this.

"We are all scared," Jane said quietly, not raising her voice so everyone would have to remain quiet to listen to her. "For every single one of us this is unprecedented, to be in a house where such a tragedy has occurred. I know I lay in bed unable to sleep last night, and I am sure many of you did too." She paused, looking from face to face. "*No one* here is accused of anything. We do not know how this happened, let alone who did it, and I promise you there will be no false accusations here, no efforts to scapegoat someone who is innocent. When the magistrate arrives you will see he is a fair and honest man who has fought his whole life to stop the disadvantage the poor and working classes face in court." The servants remained quiet and Jane pushed on, knowing she had to turn this into something productive or the divide between the guests and the servants would widen. "For now, Colonel Rushton and I hoped for your help with trying to solve the mystery of how Mr Paulson was found in a room locked from the inside. This is an old house, one which holds many secrets, and some of you have lived here for years. You may know of nooks and crannies that would be otherwise difficult to find. We merely ask for your assistance with identifying anywhere that might help."

At first no one answered, and Jane could see they were picking over her speech, working out if she could be trusted.

After a long pause, the kitchen maid tentatively raised her hand.

"Yes, Moll, is there something you think might help?"

"It's only a rumour, but when I started, someone told me there was a priest's hole somewhere in the house."

"Nonsense," Mr Upton said quickly, glaring at the young girl. "They were mocking you. If there was such a thing, I would know."

"Thank you, Moll," Jane said, taking a moment to flash the maid a reassuring smile. "Can you remember any other details?"

With a glance at Mr Upton, she shook her head then looked down at the ground, her cheeks flushing at the attention.

"Has anyone else heard of a priest's hole here at Melmont Hall?"

There was shuffling of feet and Mrs Brown declared, "I need to get back to the kitchen. Come on, Moll, we have guests to cook for."

"I heard the same rumour," Charlotte, the housemaid, said quickly, glancing after Moll and giving her a small smile, "but I think maybe it was only a rumour, told to whoever the new maid was, like you might say the house was haunted."

"No one said where it might be located?" Colonel Rushton asked, his demeanour calmer now.

"No."

"Thank you," Jane said as the staff began to drift away.

"You have a way with words, Miss Austen," Colonel Rushton said in a tone she couldn't quite place. Either he was impressed with her handling of the situation or annoyed that she had needed to rescue him from the irate servants.

"Thank you," she murmured.

"A rousing speech," Cassandra said as she came out of the dining room. "My sister should have been in the army, should she not, Colonel, motivating the troops for the battle lines?"

Jane suppressed a smile, clasping Cassandra's hand.

"Will you help us?"

"Of course, what do you need help with?"

"I think the Colonel and I are of the same mind; we need to work out how the assailant managed to escape, with the door locked from the inside."

"You want to search the study again? I thought you did so last night."

"We did, but not thoroughly. That was more to look at the papers and to see Mr Paulson's body where it lay."

Cassandra shuddered.

"Do not fear," said Jane. "Mr Paulson was carried downstairs to a cool storeroom last night. He is no longer in the room."

"If Miss Austen is not comfortable assisting with the search, I am sure Dr Histon and I can manage," Colonel Rushton said.

Jane looked over to where the doctor had joined his friend and smiled weakly, hoping Cassandra would agree to stay. Otherwise, she would be outnumbered again.

"I am happy to help," Cassandra said quietly.

Jane was the first one to the door, pushing it open and feeling the chill of the room as she stepped inside. No fire had been lit in here today and much of the residual heat had escaped from the room now, giving it a cold, unwelcoming feel.

It wasn't a large area to search, especially if they were looking for a hiding place.

"If we are looking for a priest's hole or something similar, does it solve the problem?" Cassandra asked as she followed Jane over to the bookshelves. "Surely it still doesn't explain how the door was locked from the inside, unless we're suggesting the assailant was still there when Mr Paulson was found."

Jane paused, shuddering at the thought of unearthing some miniscule hiding place, then looking in only to see eyes staring back.

"I don't know," she said, beginning to pull the books from the shelves in sections, and checking the wooden panelling at the back of the bookcase before replacing the books and moving on. "I think it is highly unlikely there is a secret hiding place, but until we have searched thoroughly, until we have ruled it out, I think the *possibility* of one will overshadow the case."

Cassandra nodded thoughtfully and moved to the other end of the bookshelves, working her way into the middle from the opposite direction. Behind them, Colonel Rushton and Dr Histon were rolling up the heavy rug that almost reached the corners of the room to inspect the floorboards underneath.

"Perhaps while we're here it would be a good use of time to discuss how we all knew Mr Paulson," Jane said, trying to keep her tone casual. Colonel Rushton was an acquaintance but nothing more than that, and before yesterday she had never met Dr Histon. They both might have respectable professions, but that didn't rule them out as suspects. As a medical man Dr Histon was no stranger to death, and Colonel Rushton had presumably killed his fair share of people in combat. Their involvement in the murder was unlikely, but not impossible, and she would have to tread carefully in the process of ruling them out.

"Cassandra and I barely knew Mr Paulson, although we have visited Melmont Hall on a few occasions. Our mother is friends with Mrs Paulson," Jane began, hoping the men would follow her example.

Colonel Rushton paused in what he was doing but then nodded curtly. "I suppose you are right, Miss Austen; we have no cause to trust one another any more than the other people in this house. I did know Mr Paulson, but we were not close. I have had a home in the area for the past twenty years, and we have met on a number of social occasions. I always got the impression Mr Paulson was a man who liked to keep to himself and we never struck up a friendship, but that is not to say there was any bad blood between us. My friendship was with Mrs Paulson, as is the case with most of the guests here, I believe."

It fitted with what they knew of the victim, a man who preferred to stay in his study than join his wife's dinner guests for drinks and conversation in the drawing room.

"How about you, Histon? Did you know our victim?" Colonel Rushton asked.

"No. As you know, I am not from the area. I do not think I had ever met either Mr or Mrs Paulson before we arrived at Melmont Hall yesterday afternoon."

Jane turned back to the bookcase. She and Cassandra worked systematically, getting through the books quickly despite the high volume. It was soothing to do something so repetitive and gave Jane a little time to gather her thoughts. There was still so much she didn't know, still so many questions to ask. In the midst of all the chaos she had almost forgotten about the note from *K* found on the desk, perhaps the most vital piece of evidence. She glanced at the window, knowing the snow would still be too thick for anyone to venture out but hoping it might have melted a little. It was impossible to tell, of course, from in here. It might be six inches deep or two feet; only by stepping out would she really know how stranded they were.

Colonel Rushton and Dr Histon had the rug pushed back over half the floor now and were examining the floorboards, tapping on them and pressing to see if anything moved. In any other circumstances the scene would have been comical, two such distinguished men crawling round trying to find a hiding place that probably didn't exist, but now it just served to highlight how in the dark they were as to how this murder had been committed.

Out of the corner of her eye, Jane saw movement by the door to the study and caught a glimpse of Upton standing there watching them.

"Do you need something, Mr Upton?" she called, making him start at being caught.

"You won't find anything," Mr Upton said, stepping onto the threshold but not entering the room. "I have worked here for fourteen years. If there was a priest's hole or a secret passage, I would know about it."

"Most likely," Jane said, not wanting to antagonise the butler. He still could be their greatest ally in finding out exactly what went on in this house. "In truth, I do not expect to find anything, but this locked door confounds me, and until we can work out *how* this crime was committed I think we owe it to Mr Paulson to be as thorough as possible."

"You're wasting your time. The locked door has no relevance. *That* is clear as day…"

He shook his head and then spun abruptly, walking away.

For a long moment Jane watched the doorway, wondering if the butler was simply miffed at having his expertise ignored or if he had some deeper knowledge of how the crime had been committed.

"What a strange thing to say," Dr Histon said, sitting back on his haunches. Colonel Rushton nodded in agreement, and Cassandra glanced at Jane. It was strange, something else to be probed and prodded when the time came to interview the butler.

It took the better part of an hour to finish searching the study, and when they had Jane flopped down into one of the armchairs with a loud sigh. She hadn't truly expected to find anything, but it was still disappointing to come up with nothing during their search.

"Let us think about this logically," Dr Histon said as he took the chair at an angle to her own. Cassandra perched on the arm of Jane's chair and Colonel Rushton leaned against the wide windowsill. "The door was locked, we all saw that, the key on the inside. The windows too were secured from the inside. There is no hiding place in this room, nowhere a killer could be concealed." He paused and closed his eyes, considering the matter for a moment. "Could it be as simple as there was another key and the lock was turned from the outside, with the key on the inside still resting in there?"

"Can that happen?"

Dr Histon shrugged. "It seems farfetched, does it not?"

"Miss Austen?" The voice of Mary Wright, Mrs Paulson's lady's maid, startled Jane from her thoughts. "Mrs Paulson is asking for you. She says she has a confession to make."

With wide eyes Jane glanced at Cassandra and swallowed, her tongue sticking to the roof of her mouth. Suddenly she wished she was back home, curled up in an armchair and reading her favourite novel by the fire. She had never treated an investigation as an amusement, a distracting way to spend a few days, but now it felt real and devastating and she wished she had no part in it. Surely kindly Mrs Paulson couldn't have murdered her husband. If such a generous woman had, there would be no hope for the rest of society.

CHAPTER EIGHT

The walk upstairs seemed impossibly long, and with each step it seemed to Jane that her heart grew heavier. By the time she had reached the door to Mrs Paulson's bedchamber, she felt as though she had trekked ten miles through the thickest snow.

"Come, my mistress is still resting in bed. She is eager to see you," Mary Wright said. The lady's maid was approaching middle age, with the first grey hairs streaking her otherwise dark hair. She was dressed in a high-collared black dress with her hair pulled back into a severe bun, but despite all of this her face was soft and her lips full, and if she let her hair tumble about her shoulders she might even be called attractive.

Despite the maid's pleas Jane hesitated outside the bedroom door, taking a moment to steel herself before she walked in. Mrs Paulson's bedroom had a rustic, traditional charm. That wasn't to say the furniture differed greatly from the opulence of the rest of the house; the four-poster bed looked solid and well made, but instead of being topped with the most expensive fabrics there was a homemade quilt covering the sheets. It was the same for the pictures on the wall; instead of masterpieces by well-known artists, there were children's drawings and paintings, all lovingly displayed for Mrs Paulson to see. It was as if the downstairs rooms told one story — the story of the wife of a wealthy and successful man who diligently made their home a place people coveted an invitation to — and this room told another. Up here, she could retreat amongst the familiar and comforting, the little things that made this house feel like a home.

"Miss Austen, thank you for coming," Mrs Paulson said, pushing herself up in bed. She looked a decade older than she had the night before, her cheeks sunken and hollow and her eyes red-rimmed and desolate. Dressed only in a nightdress and thick dressing gown, she had the bedcovers pulled to her waist, as if she hoped to collapse back onto the pillows once this interlude was over.

"How are you feeling, Mrs Paulson?"

"Groggy. I cannot abide sleeping potions; my head feels as though it is not my own." She paused and then patted the space next to her. "Come sit with me, Miss Austen."

Jane did, feeling her heart thumping and wondering if the other woman could hear it.

"I am so sorry for your loss."

For a moment Mrs Paulson did not respond, instead staring out into the distance. She only seemed to recover when Mary Wright, her lady's maid, came and sat in the chair close to the bed.

"Would you like privacy, ma'am?"

"No, Mary, stay. Unless you object, Miss Austen?"

"Whatever you would prefer," Jane murmured.

"Mary is such a comfort to me, and she long ago discovered the worst of my secrets."

Jane couldn't imagine the charitable older woman harbouring secrets. It was like thinking her own mother might have confidences she concealed from her husband or family.

"Your mother told me of your involvement in that sad case at the Westworths' estate, where poor Miss Roscoe was killed. I understand you helped the magistrate."

"I did."

"And even after the culprit was found, he continued to take an interest in you?"

Jane inclined her head.

"That is why I wanted to talk to you, Miss Austen. When Lord Hinchbrooke arrives, I know you will have his ear; no doubt he will look to you to inform him of what has happened here at Melmont Hall."

"I think you are right, Mrs Paulson." Jane kept her replies simple, knowing that if Mrs Paulson was going to confess to some involvement in her husband's murder, then it would not take much to spook her and make her reconsider her confession.

"Then you must tell Lord Hinchbrooke I am responsible." She said it clearly, so there could be no mistake as to what she was declaring.

For a long moment Jane did not say anything, trying to choose from the dozens of questions that were fighting for prominence in her head.

"To be clear, Mrs Paulson, you are saying you killed your husband?"

Mrs Paulson glanced at the maid sitting at her side, who reached out and took hold of her mistress's hand.

"I am responsible for his death, Miss Austen, and I will face any and all consequences with my head held high." The choice of words seemed unusual, and Jane knew she needed to poke at this some more.

"Please excuse my bluntness, but did you take a knife and stab him?"

Again there was that glance at Mary Wright as if seeking guidance. It wasn't unheard of for a mistress of the house to grow close to her lady's maid. They spent a huge amount of time in one another's company, and if their temperaments were well suited often they became one another's confidantes, but Jane wondered if Mary might have some sort of hold over the older woman, even though she was doing nothing more than sitting serenely in the chair by the bed.

"Did you stab Mr Paulson?" Jane repeated, her voice not unkind but her tone a little more insistent.

"Does it matter? I have confessed, that should be enough."

"I am not entirely sure what exactly you have confessed to."

"*I* am responsible for the death of my husband. That should be all you need to know."

Jane sat quietly for a moment and then shook her head. "I do not believe you."

"You must believe me. I am a friend of your mother's, an upstanding member of the community, an honest woman."

"Who for some reason is lying right now," Jane said as gently as she could.

"Perhaps it is best you tell her the truth, ma'am," Mary said softly, her eyes pleading with her mistress. "You can make Miss Austen understand."

Almost a minute passed in silence as Mrs Paulson considered her maid's words and the situation that faced her. Abruptly she nodded, flopping back onto the pillows as if exhausted by the decision. She closed her eyes, massaging the gap between her brows before she started talking.

"I did not stab my husband, but I wish to take responsibility for his death."

"You wish to confess to a murder you did not commit?"

"It was my actions that led to his death, Miss Austen. I am guilty. I understand that a crime like this needs to have an answering punishment, and I wish to be the one who takes that punishment."

"Lord Hinchbrooke is a reasonable man," Jane said slowly, "but there is no scenario where he will let an innocent person take the blame for murder, not even when there are extenuating circumstances as there must be for you to even suggest such a thing."

"Please, ma'am," Mary said, squeezing her hand reassuringly.

"Is it you? Did you kill him?" Jane asked, turning on the maid. She knew she needed to keep calm, to not lose her patience, but it was difficult. She exhaled sharply and shook her head. "I am sorry, please forgive my outburst."

"But the question still stands," Mary said softly, holding Jane's gaze.

Nodding her head, she wondered if the maid would answer as cryptically as Mrs Paulson.

"No, I did not kill Mr Paulson."

Lord Hinchbrooke had told her some magistrates thought they could tell a person's guilt or innocence by looking them in the eye when the witness or accused answered a question. He had chuckled in a self-deprecating manner and told her he did not share their talent. Some people were skilled at spinning webs of deception; they practised it every day, even when there was no real need to. Other people looked guilty as hell even when the worst thing they had ever done was forgo putting any money in the church collection pot.

Still, there were no outward signs of deception on Mary Wright's face. She held Jane's gaze and didn't rush to give reason after reason as to why she couldn't possibly be guilty.

"Please," Jane said, turning back to the older woman, "tell me what is going on here. You say you are guilty but did not wield the knife. Did you press someone else to stab your husband? Is that it?"

"No," Mrs Paulson said sharply and then let out a groan, covering her face with her hands. "This is such a mess."

"My mistress is not a murderer," Mary said quietly, and then looking at Mrs Paulson, said, "I can tell it, if it is easier."

Mrs Paulson shook her head and took a long, shuddering breath.

"I say I am guilty, Miss Austen, for I believe I am. I knew something terrible had occurred and I did not do enough to rectify the situation. My inaction led to the death of my husband, and if I do not step in, it will lead to the ruination of a young life."

Pressing her lips together, Jane remained silent, sensing the older woman was on the cusp of explaining her confession and not wanting to say anything to make her change her mind.

"My husband..." she began and then trailed off, shaking her head and covering her mouth with her hand. "My husband was a wealthy man, well respected in our social circle. His family have owned Melmont Hall for generations, and he has held positions on various boards and charitable trusts over the years. All that said, he was not a *good* man."

Jane felt her eyes widen at such a direct attack on Mr Paulson's character by his wife.

"He was never outwardly cruel to me, never beat me or even chastised me in front of friends," Mrs Paulson said, shaking her head as if this was little to be thankful for, and Jane supposed she was right. It was a risk for a woman to marry, one that most women had to take, for the alternative was even less attractive. Still, giving up any modicum of independence, accepting that your husband owned everything that had once been yours and by law even had the right to beat you, was hardly something to be celebrated. Unbidden, thoughts of Tom Lefroy popped into her head and instinctively she knew he would be a good husband, a kind husband. She may have only known him for a short while, but she could see he had a good heart, and that didn't easily change in a person.

Mrs Paulson took a shaky breath and continued, "But he did ruin people's lives."

"Whose lives, Mrs Paulson?"

"Over the years there have been almost a dozen that I know of, but likely there are more. Young women, mainly, all pretty, all at least a few rungs below him on the social ladder. Most recently it has been maids, but in the past there were others. The daughter of the local vicar was the most scandalous, but thankfully after that debacle he seemed to keep things within the household."

"He had a relationship with all these women?"

Mrs Paulson nodded, not able to meet Jane's eye. "He would pay them special attention, flatter them, buy them gifts and take them to places they otherwise wouldn't get to go. I do not think he ever forced himself on anyone, but that does not excuse his behaviour, nor what came next."

"What came next?"

"Inevitably the young woman would become pregnant and my husband would then lose all interest in her and his bastard child growing inside her." Mrs Paulson shook her head. "In the beginning I think he paid for them to visit someone who could get rid of the baby, but that is unreliable, of course, so he then arranged for the children to be delivered to the orphanage after birth."

Jane wondered how many children there had been over the years. If Mrs Paulson knew of almost a dozen, no doubt there was at least double that number, maybe triple.

"After one particularly disastrous case, I stepped in. I knew I could not prevent his liaisons, but I wanted a different fate for these poor young women whose lives were ruined for the sake of his pleasure. I set up a charitable foundation for young, unwed mothers. They get a room and their food, get to keep their children with them, and in exchange they do needlework or something similar. It isn't ideal, but it is something at least."

"Is this close by?"

"No, I thought it best to put it somewhere far, far away." Mrs Paulson looked down at her hands where they rested on the bedcovers, every so often scrunching the sheets and then smoothing them out. "Otherwise, the temptation…" She trailed off and Jane leaned forward, eager to hear more.

"The temptation to visit the women, you mean?"

For a long moment Mrs Paulson was silent, and Jane wondered if she had lost her nerve. After what felt like an eternity she began speaking again, quietly this time.

"I do not know if you are aware, Miss Austen, but Mr Paulson and I had a son. He was the light of my life, the sweetest, most adorable boy you could ever have met."

Jane shifted in her seat. This was a surprise. Her mother had known Mrs Paulson for some years, yet she had never mentioned a child. Perhaps it had been too painful a subject and over the years the older women had silently agreed not to speak of it to spare Mrs Paulson some of that pain.

"My Charles. He was four when he died."

"I'm so sorry," Jane said quietly, knowing that losing a child must be the hardest thing to bear.

Mrs Paulson sniffed and Mary reached out to squeeze her hand again.

"It was a long time ago, but it still hurts. People expect you to get over your grief as the time passes, but it never goes away. Things around you change, but the grief doesn't."

"You cope admirably well, ma'am," Mary said softly.

"It hurts all the more knowing my husband sired children with these women he had illicit affairs with. You would not believe how hard it is to keep away, to stop myself from visiting them, from looking at the children and wondering why they all get to grow up when my Charles did not." She let out a little sob. "You see, Miss Austen, I am a terrible person, devoid of all humanity. These are innocent children, yet sometimes I find myself wishing to bargain one of their lives for that of my son."

"They are only thoughts," Mary said, as if she'd had this discussion a thousand times before. "You would never act on them. Who amongst us hasn't wished for something we shouldn't? Our every thought cannot be charitable. It is your actions that show the person you truly are."

In that moment Jane saw the respect Mary Wright had for her mistress and wondered what bonded these two women together so closely. There might be a gulf between them in social status, but there was an understanding that flowed from one to the other that hinted at a close friendship.

"I am struggling to see why you think yourself guilty of contributing to your husband's death," Jane said slowly, trying to take in everything Mrs Paulson had revealed so far. It made everything more difficult. There were now scores of potential suspects, people whom Mr Paulson had wronged. As well as the women themselves, there were fathers and brothers and beaus of the women in question, perhaps even some of the children who had grown up, if he truly had been at it for as long as Mrs Paulson implied. And if it was someone from the past, the question of *why now* would have to be answered.

Mrs Paulson glanced at her maid again and then gave a little sigh that Jane thought signified she was ready to tell everything now.

"I do not know how much you have discovered already, Miss Austen, but I mentioned when you arrived that last week two maids and a footman left abruptly."

"So I understand."

"One of the maids, Kitty, was having an affair with my husband. He had wooed her, promised her the world, and they had been finding opportunities to be intimate for the past four months. Unfortunately for Kitty, she found out she was pregnant a few weeks ago."

"Mr Paulson decided to end things then?"

"Yes. It was all horribly predictable. I am not privy to what my husband promised these girls, but she seemed to think he was going to provide for her and the child."

"Had he done that before?"

"No, never. He paid them much less than would be fair." She scoffed. "As if anything could be fair in these circumstances. I mean to say he paid them less than it costs to feed and clothe a child for sixteen years. Normally they are ushered out of the house quietly, and I assume he only released the meagre funds he bestowed upon them in exchange for some sort of agreement that they would not sully his doorstep again."

Jane thought back to the note she had found hidden amongst Mr Paulson's papers. If it was from Kitty, which seemed likely, she hadn't been begging or pleading or even threatening to expose his philandering ways. The young woman must still have wanted to believe the older man's lies, to cling to some hope that she wasn't about to be abandoned.

"Do you know what happened when your husband told Kitty things were ending?"

Mrs Paulson shook her head and glanced at her maid.

"I overheard a little," Mary said quietly. "Not what Mr Paulson said initially, but I saw Kitty run from his study in distress. She barrelled into Benjamin, the footman who has been dismissed as well."

Jane nodded slowly, trying to fit the pieces together.

"Benjamin always had a soft spot for Kitty, and he took her downstairs to the kitchens. She must have told him everything, for within a few minutes he was charging through the hall, and he flung open the door to Mr Paulson's study without even knocking. There was a great argument, and Mr Upton had to go in and intervene. Mr Paulson could be horrible when his blood was up, and I doubt he took too kindly to a servant speaking to him with a complete lack of respect."

"What happened then?"

"Mr Upton hauled Benjamin out of there and told him and Kitty to pack their bags immediately. They were escorted off the grounds."

"There was another maid, Fran, I think, who left as well? What was her part in this?"

Mrs Paulson grimaced and shifted in bed.

"From what we can glean, Fran was simply in the wrong place at the wrong time. She was cleaning the copper pans in a room off the kitchen, minding her own business, but Kitty and Benjamin had their talk where she could overhear them. Later that day Fran went to Mr Upton, and he took the matter to my husband. I can only assume my husband thought he could keep the matter quiet by dismissing her."

"Mr Paulson didn't know that you knew about his —" Jane hesitated, searching for the least offensive word — "affairs."

"No. Typical man, he thought I didn't take notice of anything outside my rose garden or embroidery."

"He didn't know what you did for the women pregnant with his children? About the charitable organisation?"

It seemed unlikely he had no knowledge of his wife's interests.

"I am no fool, Miss Austen. Over the years I have taken care to support many charities, so this is just one among dozens. It is hidden in plain sight, and as such I do not think Mr Paulson knew what I was doing."

Jane sat back and exhaled, wondering if this was the answer. It gave many people a motive, but most acutely it meant they would have to consider Kitty and Benjamin as viable suspects. She knew Lord Hinchbrooke's next actions would have been to track them down, question them, and try to ascertain if someone could vouch for their whereabouts at the time of the murder. But being trapped here meant that Jane was unable to do that.

"So you see, Miss Austen, I am responsible. If Kitty has anything to do with this murder, I am as culpable as she. For years I have sat in the shadows, observing my husband's despicable behaviour and done nothing about it. I was not brave enough to confront him, to threaten to expose him to those he enjoys the approval of in our social circle."

"Hush, ma'am," Mary said, standing up decisively. "I think Mrs Paulson has exerted herself enough for now, Miss Austen. I am sure if you have any more questions, she would be happy to answer them once she has rested."

Mrs Paulson settled back on her pillows with her eyes closed, a look of resignation on her face. Jane wondered if she felt lighter, unburdened, having confessed her knowledge of her husband's actions.

"I have one last question, a practical one," Jane said as she stood.

Mrs Paulson didn't open her eyes.

"Who inherits?"

"I can answer that," Mary said, ushering Jane to the door. "It was no secret. There is a nephew who will inherit the house and some of the money. Mrs Paulson gets the manor house in the village and a generous allowance. She will be well provided for."

"And the nephew?"

"I've never met him, Miss. I don't think he has ever visited England. Mr Paulson's sister moved to America many years ago and the boy was brought up there."

"Thank you," Jane said, stepping out of the room. She turned back to ask one final question, but already the door was shutting.

For a moment she didn't move, wondering if it was normal for a lady's maid to have such a say over whom her mistress saw and spoke to. She thought of Mrs White and Lizzie at home. They were part of the family, certainly encouraged to speak their minds and involved in all the drama that came with family life. Jane supposed it wasn't much different for Mary Wright. Mrs Paulson was isolated, living alone with a husband who didn't care for her and no children, no other relatives in her day-to-day life to be a close confidante. It wasn't that surprising that she had found someone she could trust, someone who was there every day, helping her with all manner of personal things. Mary was sharp and intelligent, and Jane did not doubt that was the reason she had risen to become lady's maid, perhaps the most important position in the household after the butler, housekeeper and cook.

"Everyone needs a friend," Jane murmured to herself.

Jane contemplated the closed door and decided to leave her questions for now. No doubt it was a difficult time for Mrs Paulson, and there were plenty of other people to talk to. Their hostess could rest, and later Jane would visit again to ask the rest of her questions.

CHAPTER NINE

"The atmosphere in here is awful," Cassandra murmured as Jane came to join her, Dr Histon, the Potters and the Leveritts in the drawing room. Mr and Mrs Potter were sitting on a sofa, heads bowed together and talking quietly. Mrs Leveritt was pacing backwards and forwards in front of the long windows, glaring at the snow as if the force of her stare might encourage it to melt quicker. Miss Leveritt sat morosely on the piano stool, flicking through sheets of music without much enthusiasm. The doctor was sitting on his own, a book in his hand, but Jane could see by the lack of eye movement he was not reading it.

"I suggested we come in here a few minutes ago, as people were just milling around the house, but now I wish I hadn't," Cassandra said, shaking her head. "It is as if I have collected misery in one room, and now we must be subjected to it."

"Fortitude, my darling," Jane said, taking her sister's hand. "We shall get through this."

"How was Mrs Paulson?"

"Overwhelmed and exhausted." Jane glanced at the other people in the room and leaned towards Cassandra. "I will tell you all about it later. Where is Colonel Rushton?"

"I do not know."

Jane sat back in her chair, drumming her fingers on the arms, trying to decide what needed to be done next. There were still the rest of the guests to question, and all of the servants, but she didn't know where was best to start.

Her thoughts were interrupted by a piercing scream that sent chills through her and immediately made her jump to her feet.

The door to the room burst open and Charlotte, the housemaid Jane had spoken to earlier, burst in, her eyes wide. For a moment she stood there, trembling and unable to speak.

It was Cassandra who went to her and took her hand. She brought her into the room fully, settling her on a free chair and kneeling down beside her. Jane was ever grateful for the softness of her sister, the generosity, the instinctive kindness. Jane herself was a great observer, seeing the little nuances of people's personalities, but Cassandra was better at dealing with them directly.

"It is Charlotte, is it not?" Cassandra said softly.

The maid nodded, looking around her in a daze.

"What has happened, Charlotte?"

"It's Mr Upton," Charlotte managed to say after taking a shaky breath. "He's out there, in the snow."

Jane immediately went to the window and peered out, looking in both directions but unable to see anything untoward.

"He's out the front," Charlotte said and then buried her face in her hands. "There is a lot of blood."

Jane felt a cold dread settle over her, and she spun and raced from the room. Only when she was almost at the front door did she realise there was someone behind her.

"There may be something I can do," Dr Histon said.

Together they paused on the threshold and then stepped out into the snow. Immediately Jane's feet were soaked, her satin shoes ruined and the cold seeping through her stockings. At first she could not see anything untoward, and only when she stepped out a little further did she notice the still form in the snow to the left of the door. There was blood, startlingly red against the pure white, splattered out about a foot and hinting at a violent death.

Cautiously Jane moved towards the butler, peering down. Dr Histon was less hesitant and quickly crouched down beside the body, feeling for a pulse. After a moment he looked up at Jane and shook his head.

"Dead. His body is still warm, though, despite the cold. He hasn't been out here long."

"Can you see…" she said, trailing off as her eyes rested on the top of the butler's head. There was a bloody mass matted into his hair.

"A blow to the head," Dr Histon confirmed. "Would have killed him instantly, by the look of it."

"What was he hit with?"

They both looked around, eyes searching the snow for any hint of a weapon, but there was nothing visible.

Jane shivered and Dr Histon stood up, his trousers and shoes soaked from the snow.

"If we bring his body inside, I can have a look to see if there is anything else we are missing," Dr Histon said, running a hand over his brow. He looked older, more haggard, than he had the night before, and Jane had to acknowledge the toll this string of tragedies was taking on all the people at Melmont Hall.

"Yes. Good," Jane said, trying to stop her hands from shaking. A second murder confirmed what she had feared all along. Whether it was a servant or a guest, the person who had killed Mr Paulson and now Mr Upton was still with them.

As they reached the front door Colonel Rushton stepped out into the snow, his face pale.

"They said it was the butler," he said, peering over Jane's shoulder.

"Yes."

"Good Lord," Colonel Rushton murmured and placed his hand over his face momentarily. "What have I done?"

"You, Colonel?" Jane asked sharply.

"Do not look at me like that, Miss Austen. I did not kill Mr Upton," the colonel snapped and then seemed to deflate. "He came to me and asked for a private word about an hour ago. I shrugged the man off, told him I would see him later. I wanted to use the opportunity to check the upstairs rooms, the ones on the second floor that are barely used. I had the notion someone might be hiding in there, waiting for the snow to clear."

"He knew something," Jane said, frowning. "He knew something and he had decided to tell you. Colonel, it is important, where were you when the butler approached you? Who else was there?"

Colonel Rushton nodded thoughtfully and didn't answer for a moment.

"It was at the end of breakfast. The Potters were there, and the Leveritts. Your sister was there, Miss Austen, talking to Dr Histon. Although I doubt anyone could have overheard the butler — he whispered his request in my ear. He could be very discreet."

"What about servants?"

"Just the footman and the housemaid, no one else."

For a moment Jane felt paralysed and wouldn't have been able to move a single limb even if there had been a fire raging around her. There was another man dead, and she couldn't help but feel some sense of responsibility.

"I will organise someone to help me get the body inside," Dr Histon said, and Jane nodded gratefully.

"We need to tell everyone."

"There will be panic," Colonel Rushton warned.

"It is unavoidable. Do you wish to inform the guests while I tell the servants?"

Jane took a moment before she headed for the stairs that led down to the kitchen. She wasn't surprised to see the servants all gathered there, faces full of concern and talking in low voices amongst themselves.

"It is true?" Mrs Brown, the cook, asked as Jane stepped into the kitchen.

Jane nodded, feeling suddenly a little light-headed. She pulled out a stool and sat down on it heavily, smiling weakly as Moll brought her a cup of water.

"A few minutes ago Charlotte found the body of Mr Upton outside. It looks like he has been hit over the head."

"Is he dead?" Moll asked, her eyes wide.

"Yes. I am sorry."

Before Jane could say anything else, Charlotte came stumbling into the kitchen and Mrs Brown quickly got up and drew the younger woman into her arms.

"Hush, now, you've had a shock. You're safe, my dear."

Jane watched silently, wondering how many of the servants would stay once the snow cleared and how many would decide a regular wage was not worth the upset they had witnessed here and leave to look for employment elsewhere.

"If anyone has any information about what happened to Mr Upton, I would be very grateful for your confidence."

"It was terrible," Charlotte said, looking around the room, wide-eyed. "I was tidying Mr and Mrs Potter's room when I glanced out of the window and I saw his body in the snow."

"Did you see anyone with him?"

"No. He was already on the ground. Poor Mr Upton."

"When was the last time anyone saw Mr Upton?"

"He came down to the kitchen after breakfast was cleared," Mrs Brown volunteered, glancing at the clock above the door. "Must have been about half past nine."

That was whilst she had been upstairs with Mrs Paulson.

"Anyone else?"

There were vague shakes and murmurs that Jane took to mean no, no one had seen him after half past nine.

It was quarter to eleven now, which meant Mr Upton had been killed in the last hour and a quarter.

"Fine," Jane said, standing. Suddenly she had the urge to get out of the dark basement rooms, to be somewhere with sunlight. She gave the servants what she hoped was a reassuring smile, made some vague promise that they would get to the bottom of it, and dashed up the stairs. At the top she almost barrelled into Dr Histon and Mr Potter, who between them were carrying Mr Upton like a sack of potatoes.

"Mr Potter volunteered to help," Dr Histon supplied, sweating with exertion. Mr Potter looked pale and as if he might be regretting his act of charity, but as Jane watched they descended the stairs, no doubt to place Mr Upton's body in the same storeroom where his master lay, cold and dead.

Cassandra hurried out to join Jane and linked her arm through her sister's, bending her head close.

"You'd better come in," Cassandra said. "Mrs Leveritt is hysterical and no one knows what to say to calm her."

Reluctantly Jane entered the drawing room. Colonel Rushton was standing to attention next to the door, looking at the scene with undisguised bewilderment. Mrs Potter looked bereft without her husband and Jane realised she had never seen the young woman on her own, so devoted to one another were the newlyweds. Mrs Leveritt was pacing by the window, her daughter hovering nearby and looking completely overwhelmed.

"There is a *killer* loose in this house and we are trapped here. It is torture and I cannot bear it any longer. Every moment we stay here, we're at risk. Does nobody else see it?"

"Mama, please sit down. We are all worried…"

"Not worried enough," Mrs Leveritt declared and gripped her daughter's hand. "Come, dearest, it is time for us to leave."

"You cannot leave," Colonel Rushton said, moving ever so slightly so he was more in front of the door. "It would be suicide."

"As is staying here. I would prefer we took our chances with the snow."

"You do not know the terrain, Mrs Leveritt," Jane said, trying to keep calm. "The snow is piled in drifts, obscuring the landscape. You could fall in a ditch very easily and may not be able to get out."

"If we stay here, we will be murdered in our beds."

"Mama, no one has been murdered in their bed," Miss Leveritt said quietly. "Please just sit down and think about it."

"I am your mother and you will do what I say. We are leaving. Someone kindly fetch our coats."

Jane watched as Miss Leveritt fought every instinct to agree with her mother. She could see the young woman had been brought up to be obedient. It was apparent in everything she did, from how she took her place at the piano at her mother's request, to her agreement to the plan that she would travel to London with Mrs Paulson for the season to find a wealthy husband and save the family from ruin. Miss Leveritt was a good and loyal daughter, and now she was faced with choosing between doing what her mother told her and doing what she knew was right.

After a few seconds of silence, Miss Leveritt lowered her head and Jane knew common sense had lost.

"Yes, Mother," Miss Leveritt murmured.

Mrs Leveritt followed her daughter out into the hall and everyone else crowded behind them. Colonel Rushton was at the front of the group, and now he stalked over to the front door.

"I cannot allow you to leave," he said as Miss Leveritt reappeared with their coats. "It would be irresponsible of me."

"You will not stop us."

"Please," Jane said. "The snow is melting; we have not had any more. I think tomorrow someone may be able to make it to the village and get a message to the magistrate. Wait one more day."

Mrs Leveritt spun and fixed her eyes on Jane. "Your mother ought to be ashamed," she said. Her voice was low now, but somehow this was worse than when she had been almost screaming. "Raising a daughter who takes pleasure in meddling in affairs such as these. I will not have my daughter tainted by it."

Jane recoiled as if she had been slapped and was thankful for Cassandra's supporting arm. Without another word, Mrs Leveritt pushed past Colonel Rushton and walked out into the cold, Miss Leveritt trailing silently behind her.

For a long while no one spoke; they just huddled around the door, watching the two women struggle onwards in the snow. Whilst everyone else was preoccupied, Jane tugged on Cassandra's hand and quietly pulled her away.

"Do not listen to her," Cassandra said firmly before Jane could get any words out. They had slipped into the Paulsons' private sitting room and Jane had sunk into a chair. She felt physically weary, and the temptation to walk out into the snow as the Leveritts had done was great. "Everyone knows you get no pleasure from this."

"Do they? They think it unnatural for a woman to be involved in a magistrate's work."

"They know nothing about it. Lord Hinchbrooke knows you; he has seen what you are capable of. *He* is the only one with an opinion I would take any notice of."

"What if he arrives and is aghast at how involved I have been, at how I have been acting as magistrate when in reality I am nobody?"

"You are not nobody."

"I am a woman. I am from a family with nothing to distinguish it from thousands of others across the south of England. I am no peer of the realm or decorated soldier. I have no official role with Lord Hinchbrooke."

"You may not be a man, a peer, or a magistrate, but what you have, and what Lord Hinchbrooke can see, is a spark inside you. One day, you will set this world on fire."

Jane closed her eyes, playing Mrs Leveritt's words over and over again in her mind. She took no pleasure in investigating these crimes, but she could not deny there was a spark of exhilaration there, a feeling of anticipation for the challenge of gathering people's stories and piecing together the information.

"No wallowing," Cassandra said, pulling Jane to her feet. "There is too much to do, and if you bow out now you will leave Colonel Rushton to take charge."

Jane allowed herself a small smile at her sister's master manipulation. Cassandra was quiet, kind and always underestimated; she could read people well and always knew which sensitivity to press on if she needed to get her way.

"Someone should update Mrs Paulson," Jane said, thinking of their hostess closeted in her bedroom and Mary Wright standing guard.

"I am happy to do that, if it will help you."

"Thank you. Now I have to go and admit Colonel Rushton has had a good idea, even if he did allow Mr Upton's murder to happen by not listening to him sooner."

Jane paused outside the drawing room, aware that the number of people in this house was quickly dwindling. Inside, there were only Dr Histon and Colonel Rushton, the two men conferring with their heads bent together, and the Potters, looking even more shocked than they had before.

"They have not returned?" Jane asked hopefully, glancing out the window.

"No. They have disappeared," Colonel Rushton said, his voice heavy with regret. "Their chances of making it to the village are slim. Did you see the thickness of Miss Leveritt's coat? It was barely more than a dressing gown."

"Colonel Rushton, you said you had a thought to search some of the abandoned rooms."

"Yes, I had a thought that if someone had come from the village or further afield and committed the murder of Mr Paulson, then we know they couldn't have left the house in the snow, not without leaving a trail — but this is a big old house; there are plenty of places to hide."

Jane nodded, feeling like a fool for not suggesting it herself. It wasn't impossible that someone had sequestered themselves somewhere in the house before the guests arrived the day before, waited until he coast was clear to kill Mr Paulson, and were now hiding until they had an opportunity to flee.

"We should search the house from top to bottom," Jane said decisively. "Check every room, every possible hiding place. That way, if we don't find anyone…" She trailed off.

"We know it is one of us. Servant or guest," Colonel Rushton finished for her. "I shall arrange it, Miss Austen. Dr Histon and I will conduct the search, and perhaps Mr Potter will agree to accompany us. If there is anyone hiding here, then we will ferret them out."

He was already halfway to his feet when Jane rested a hand on his arm. "I admire your enthusiasm, Colonel, but I wonder if it might be more appropriate to have a servant assist us. We are proposing to invade their one small area of freedom, the room they call their own in a world where they own little else."

Colonel Rushton looked like he was about to refuse, but Dr Histon leaned in. "Not a bad idea, Arthur. Let everyone feel they have a representative. You and I, Miss Austen, for the ladies, and a servant — they can choose amongst themselves who they want."

"Fine," Colonel Rushton said abruptly. "I shall see to it. I will meet you upstairs in five minutes."

Jane watched him leave and then sank down into a chair with a sigh, closing her eyes and rubbing her head.

"A headache, Miss Austen?" Dr Histon said. "I may have something to help with that."

"No, I am fine, Dr Histon. It is worry, that is all."

"You can let Colonel Rushton and myself conduct the search if you are struggling, Miss Austen. It will not be a defeat."

Jane smiled at this and opened her eyes to look at the doctor. "Is it that obvious?"

"Colonel Rushton is a dear friend, but he is a typical soldier," the doctor said. "He likes everything to be in its place and it gives him no end of consternation when it is not."

"I am out of place?"

"I think you do not fit neatly into the confines of the roles society sets for us, but do not misunderstand me — that is not a bad thing. It does mean certain people can be threatened by you, as they have no reference, no prior knowledge of anyone like you."

"Right now, I do not feel like a threat," Jane said, taking a moment to smooth down her hair and her creased skirt.

"Come, let us make our way upstairs. We wouldn't want Colonel Rushton to start without us."

He offered her his arm as if they were about to take a stroll through Hyde Park together and led her upstairs. The house was laid out over four floors in total, with the basement containing the kitchen and the storerooms as well as a small set of rooms each for Mr Upton and Mrs Brown. The ground floor had the usual mix of private family spaces and rooms for entertaining. The first floor was exclusively filled with bedrooms, including the master suite and Mrs Paulson's bedroom. The second floor was crammed with rooms, with a nursery and room for a nanny or governess at one end of the hallway and at the other multiple small bedrooms for the servants.

It was darker up on the second floor, with smaller windows set higher in the walls than elsewhere in the house. Jane shivered, feeling a sudden surge of nerves. Rationally she knew it was unlikely there was anyone hiding here undetected, but if there was, and they disturbed them, this person had already killed twice. They wouldn't hesitate to kill again.

"Shall we start in the nursery?" Dr Histon suggested.

Part of Jane wanted to wait until Colonel Rushton and whichever servant volunteered arrived, but she knew time was of the essence and there was plenty to do, so she nodded and pushed open the door to the room.

It was a beautiful room, decorated with light blue wallpaper and with a small bed over to one side. There was a rocking horse in the middle of the room and a basket of toys at the edge. It looked as though the child that lived there had just gone out to play and soon would be crashing back into their bedroom, ready to gather up their treasured possessions.

Jane paused for a moment, wondering how often Mrs Paulson came up here. She could picture her sitting on the edge of the bed, hugging the beloved teddy bear to her chest, weeping for the son who would never get to grow up.

Dr Histon must have picked up on the reverie, for he had fallen still as well, his expression morose.

"Such a tragedy," he murmured, shaking his head.

After a minute Jane roused herself and Dr Histon followed suit, gently opening the door to the adjoining bedroom for a nanny or governess and checking there was no one hiding in there.

"Do we check under beds and in cupboards?"

"I think we have to," Dr Histon said, dropping to his knees and peering under the narrow bed. "Otherwise we might miss something."

They had finished with the nursery by the time Colonel Rushton made it upstairs, accompanied by the young, scared-looking footman.

He was barely an adult, his body tall and lanky as if he had only just stopped growing upwards, and he had yet to gain any muscle on his thin frame. His skin had an oily sheen to it, and there were a few spots on his chin and forehead.

"It's Fred Giles, isn't it?" Jane said, trawling through her brain to remember the footman's name."

"Yes, ma'am."

"Thank you for coming to help us."

"He didn't have much choice," Colonel Rushton murmured. "Mrs Brown refused to be part of anything and forbade the girl she keeps by her side from leaving the kitchen. The housemaid was still in shock from finding the body of the butler, and Mrs Paulson's lady's maid is still closeted with her mistress."

"We are very thankful you have come to join us, Fred," Jane said gently. "We need to search the house, room by room, to check no one is here that shouldn't be."

Fred swallowed a few times, his over-large Adam's apple bobbing up and down before he nodded.

"Can you tell us which room belongs to which person?"

They were further along the corridor now, away from the nursery and in the part of the house that looked stripped bare. Gone were the plush carpets and richly decorated walls; instead, there were bare floorboards and whitewashed walls.

"This first room is mine," he said, looking around nervously. "I used to share it with Benjamin, but they haven't found a replacement for him yet, so I've got it to myself for a while."

"Good, and the rest?"

Fred pointed to the rooms one by one. "Charlotte has the next room, and Kitty used to have the one next door to her. Moll has the little room on the end." He turned to face the other side of the corridor. "Mary Wright has this first room to herself, and then the next two are used for storage."

They moved together down the narrow corridor, hesitating outside the servants' doors. It felt like an invasion of their privacy, but Jane knew it was necessary. In a few minutes they would be downstairs, checking all the guests' rooms in the same way.

"Right," Jane said, reaching out for the handle of the first door. Out of the corner of her eye, she saw Fred Giles flinch as she pushed it open, revealing the room beyond. He seemed to visibly relax once the door was open, and she wondered if he had been worried about anything private he might have left on display or something more.

Dr Histon moved along to the next room and Colonel Rushton started on the other side of the corridor, directing the footman to search the storerooms with him.

There wasn't really much to search. A bed was pushed up against each wall, and next to each bed was a little wooden table. At the end of one bed was a trunk, no doubt where Fred Giles kept his personal possessions. The walls were bare and the room looked desolate. Jane couldn't imagine living anywhere without any comforts. There wasn't even a picture on the table or any personal items to make the room feel more homely.

She crouched down, looking under the two beds. Finding nothing, she backed out of the room.

Mary Wright's room was completely different. It was the largest of the servant's rooms up here and housed a comfortable bed as well as a little writing desk and a chair. On the walls there were three paintings, and a little miniature sat on the bedside table. You couldn't completely disguise the fact that this was a servant's room, but Mary had done a good job of trying.

"Nothing," Jane said as she backed out of the room. Fred and Colonel Rushton had finished with the storerooms and Dr Histon had been into the maids' rooms.

"Let us continue downstairs," Colonel Rushton said.

Jane hung back, allowing the colonel and Dr Histon to lead the way and falling into step with the young footman.

"Tell me, how are you, Fred?" Jane asked, seeing the startled expression on the young man's face at being addressed so directly.

"Fine, ma'am."

"Good, this all must be a lot to cope with."

"Yes, ma'am."

"You're only young, Fred. Tell me, have you been with the household long?"

"Six months, ma'am."

"How old are you?"

"Seventeen, ma'am."

"And how do you find it working here at Melmont Hall?"

"Very good, ma'am."

"You like everyone you work with?"

He hesitated for a fraction of a second, only noticeable because his other answers had been so quick.

"Yes, ma'am."

"But there are tensions, are there not? It would be unusual if there weren't. There are tensions in every household."

"I suppose, ma'am."

Jane paused, feeling that she wasn't getting anywhere and conscious that they would soon catch up to Colonel Rushton and Dr Histon. She decided to try a different line of questioning.

"It must have been hard having to share a room with Benjamin."

Fred glanced at her and then nodded.

"Constantly together in your duties in the daytime and then sharing a room in any free time. It must have been difficult."

"Only the senior staff have their own rooms — that's what Mr Upton said."

"Yet you and Benjamin were the only ones sharing. Why was that?"

"Moll's room is tiny, so you couldn't get anyone else in there. Charlotte is head housemaid, so she had her own room."

"What about Kitty?"

Fred shrugged, not meeting her eye.

Jane nodded silently. So the staff were all aware of Mr Paulson's affair with Kitty and had seen how he had favoured her.

They were down the stairs now, outside the first of the guest bedrooms. Colonel Rushton and Dr Histon were already inside, checking under beds and in trunks.

Jane lowered her voice so only the young footman could hear. "Upstairs, before we went into your room, you were nervous."

Fred's eyes flicked to hers for an instant, and he looked like a rabbit caught in a snare.

"No, ma'am."

She considered how to handle this. Fred was scared. At seventeen he lived away from his family, away from the people who had previously guided and protected him. Now there had been two murders, and she doubted anyone had taken this young man aside and helped him through the shock and confusion he was feeling. Still, she wasn't here to mollycoddle him. She was here for answers.

"You were nervous, Fred. Right now, I am jumping to all kinds of awful conclusions about what you worried we would find in your room. Perhaps a bloodied fire poker that was used to kill Mr Upton, or perhaps a secret key that allowed you to lock the study door from the outside?"

Fred shook his head vehemently, going pale.

"I didn't do anything," he said, his voice rising in panic.

"Then tell me the truth. That's the only way I can be sure of your innocence."

There was a long pause, and Jane could almost see the cogs turning in his head. Then he gave an almost imperceptible nod.

"I thought Benjamin might be there."

"Benjamin? The footman who was dismissed last week?"

Fred nodded.

"Why would Benjamin be there?"

Looking around furtively, Fred lowered his voice. "He made me promise not to tell anyone. Said I would just get in trouble if I did."

"You will not be in trouble if you tell me the truth now, Fred."

There was another long pause as Colonel Rushton and Dr Histon came out of the first bedroom and closed the door, making their way into the next room. When it was only Jane and the footman in the hallway, he spoke again.

"He came back here yesterday morning. I saw him slip into the house whilst Mrs Brown and Moll were in the cold store."

"What did he want?"

"He said he'd come back to collect something and it would be best if I pretended I never saw him. He told me he would be out of the house in two minutes and wouldn't return."

"What did you do?"

"What could I do?" he said miserably, and Jane got the impression he was scared of the other footman.

"Did you see where he went, what he wanted to collect?"

"He was sneaking around, trying to make sure no one saw him. I know he went into Mr Paulson's study because I followed him. Mr and Mrs Paulson were in the drawing room having tea and discussing the dinner party."

Jane felt her pulse quicken and her muscles tense in anticipation.

"What did he do in the study, Fred?"

Fred shrugged. "I don't know. Mrs Paulson rang the bell in the drawing room and I had to go. When I came back, the study was empty."

"You didn't see Benjamin leave?"

"No."

For a long moment Jane closed her eyes, trying to piece together the new information. "That was why you were worried Benjamin might be in your room? You think he is still here in the house?"

"He *hated* Mr Paulson — he wouldn't stop talking about him every night when I wanted to be asleep. He went on and on about what a scoundrel he was, how he was taking advantage of Kitty."

"Benjamin admired Kitty?"

"He thought he had a chance with her, but even *I* could see she wouldn't settle for a nobody like him."

"This is what led to Benjamin confronting Mr Paulson when Kitty was upset?"

"He would have done anything for Kitty. Anything at all."

Anything like murder? Jane wondered.

"I don't know if he's still here," Fred said, running a hand through his oily hair. "But I didn't see him leave. And if he's here, it means he could be the one…" He trailed off, his eyes wide. There was fear in them, but also a hint of excitement.

"Thank you for telling me all this, Fred. If Benjamin is here in the house, we will find him."

Together they joined Colonel Rushton and Dr Histon as they went into the next room, a bright and sunny bedroom the Potters had been allocated for the weekend. It was a comfortable but simple room, with a large double bed, a chair and a little table as well as a wide window seat. It only took a few seconds to search, and as they left the room Jane caught hold of Colonel Rushton's arm.

"Fred is concerned the other footman, Benjamin, might be hiding in the house somewhere. Apparently he slipped into the house yesterday before the snow and Fred did not see him leave. He may have gone, but there is a real chance he could be here."

"And could be our murderer," Colonel Rushton said, nodding thoughtfully.

"Let us leave no corner unsearched."

CHAPTER TEN

Jane flopped down on the sofa and closed her eyes, thankful for a few minutes alone. The rest of the search had taken two hours, and they had not turned up anything. No secret hiding places and no disgruntled footmen concealed in the shadows, ready to confess to murder.

Her head was pounding, the weight of responsibility pushing down on her shoulders, and she longed for a few moments to clear her mind.

"Here you are, Miss," Charlotte said as she entered the drawing room, brandishing a pair of heavy boots.

Jane opened her eyes and smiled weakly at the housemaid, taking the boots from her.

"Let me help you, Miss," Charlotte said kindly, kneeling down in front of Jane and helping her slip off her still wet satin shoes. The boots were a little on the large side, but they would do for a short trip outside.

"There has been no sign of Mrs Leveritt and Miss Leveritt returning?"

"No, Miss," Charlotte said, biting her lip and looking out the window. "Do you think they'll make it to the village?"

Jane tried to picture the terrain between Melmont Hall and the village and grimaced. She had only travelled the route a couple of times, and always in a carriage. Even then it had seemed a fair distance, although perhaps it would be closer if you eschewed the roads and travelled over the fields. There would be hidden perils that way, though, ditches and uneven ground under your feet.

"I hope so," she said, not wanting to think of the alternative. If only they had waited a little longer. There hadn't been any more snow today, and Jane thought what was there had perhaps melted a little. If it was a few degrees warmer tomorrow, she thought there was a chance someone would be able to make it.

"If they get to the village, they'll contact the magistrate, won't they?"

Jane hoped so, but Lord Hinchbrooke lived some fifteen miles away and it was unlikely a message would get through to him any time soon, even if the Leveritts did make it to the village.

"I'm sure they will, Charlotte. What will you do once the snow has cleared?"

"I want to go and see my mama," Charlotte said quietly. "I'm a grown woman, but all I can think is that an embrace from my mother will make things better."

"Isn't it peculiar how the ones we love can make us feel safe and secure just with their presence?" Jane thought of Cassandra, of the confidence her sister gave her, the knowledge that whatever she did, Cassandra would be there, supporting her.

Outside Colonel Rushton was waiting, blowing on his hands to warm them.

"Ready?"

"I am, Colonel."

"Good. Let us search."

He offered her his arm and Jane took it. The ground was far too slippery, the terrain too treacherous, to refuse to hold onto the man's arm out of principle.

They were heading to the collection of outbuildings associated with Melmont Hall. There were grand stables with a little cottage attached where the two grooms lived. Next to that was a small barn and a half tumbled down outbuilding at the end of the row. So far, they hadn't had much contact with the grooms. The young men had been informed of the deaths but had opted to keep away from the house, and away from suspicion.

First they searched the stables, the barn and the outbuilding that currently housed a couple of carriages. Only once they were satisfied did they knock on the door to the cottage.

"Afternoon," a young man said as he opened the door. "Wondered when you would come."

"Let them in, Peter," a voice called from inside.

The man called Peter stood still for a few more seconds, then reluctantly stepped to the side.

"Excuse my brother," the man inside the house said. They stepped directly into the kitchen, and Jane was struck by how homely the room was. She had expected the grooms' quarters to be cold and bare, but this was by far the most welcoming servant's room they had been in. "Tea?"

"Yes, please," Jane said, surprising herself. The smell coming from the pot bubbling on the stove was good, and she suddenly felt ravenous. A cup of tea would go some way to settling her stomach.

"Please sit. I'm Gabriel Jones, and this is my brother Peter."

"Jane Austen," Jane said, holding her hand out and shaking Gabriel's. Peter took up a position in the corner of the room and scowled.

"Colonel Rushton," the colonel said, declining the offer of tea.

"We're searching every room, every building, to see if we can find anyone hidden that shouldn't be here," Jane said, wondering if the grooms would allow them to search their home.

"There's no one here," Peter said. "You can take my word for it rather than rummaging around my house."

Jane looked at the young man and nodded pleasantly. There was no way she could force him to open up his house for their search.

"My brother is right. There is no one here but us," Gabriel said, pouring the tea.

"We will have to check," Colonel Rushton said, standing.

Jane placed a hand on his arm in warning, but he shrugged it off.

"Are you saying you don't believe us?" Peter's voice lowered a fraction, and Jane felt a sliver of dread.

"I don't know you," Colonel Rushton said, looking with disdain at the younger man. "Why would I trust you?"

"You are in our house, Colonel. I advise you to be careful."

"Correct me if I am wrong, but the house belongs to Mr and Mrs Paulson, does it not?"

There was a long silence as Peter took a step forward and drew himself up to his full height.

"It is our home, Colonel," Gabriel said eventually, "even if the bricks and mortar belong to someone else."

Unable to bear the mounting tension, Jane stepped forward and placed herself between the men.

"We have got off to a poor start," she said, keeping her expression serious. This had gone past what a little joviality and forced smiles could solve. "I understand completely that this is your home and what an intrusion it is for us to want to poke around in it. Perhaps you will allow me to explain a little?" No one uttered a word, so Jane pushed on as if they had all agreed. "Mr Paulson is dead, murdered. We know someone came up to the house from the village yesterday morning; they were seen close to where Mr Paulson was murdered. What we do not know is whether they left soon after, returning whence they came, or if they hid themselves somewhere in the area, either in the house or outbuildings."

Peter grunted but backed off a little. Gabriel was looking at her with interest.

"You're talking about Benjamin Grout?"

"You've seen him?"

"Yesterday morning, about eleven. He came through the woods at the edge of the estate rather than up the main drive. I didn't think much of it — there is a shortcut that way from the village, an overgrown path, but it does take fifteen minutes off the walk."

"Did you see where he went?"

"Slipped into the basement via the servant's door."

"And did you see him come out?"

Gabriel shook his head. "I was moving hay from the barn into the stable for the extra horses we knew we would have to house for the duration of Mrs Paulson's house party. I was in and out of the buildings."

"So he could have left and you wouldn't have seen him?"

"Easily."

"Did you see him at all, Mr Jones?" Jane asked, turning to the other brother.

"No."

"Peter was mucking out the horses and cleaning the stables so that all the routine jobs were done before we got the extra horses in to look after," Gabriel explained.

"Thank you. What you tell us ties in with what other people have said, but it is good to build a picture of Benjamin's movements."

"You think it was him?"

Jane sighed. "Benjamin shouldn't have been here; he didn't want anyone to know he was here. It doesn't seem as though he was visiting for a valid reason, but at the moment it would be nothing more than speculation to say he was involved."

"But he is who you are searching for?"

Jane nodded, seeing the brothers exchange a glance she was unable to interpret.

"We wouldn't shelter him," Peter said vehemently.

"You don't like the man?"

"No."

There was no elucidation, just a continued dark scowl from the young man.

"Show the colonel the cottage, Peter," Gabriel said quietly. "We have nothing to hide."

For a long moment Peter didn't move, and then without another word he turned and walked out of the kitchen door and into the house beyond. Colonel Rushton hesitated for only a second before following him.

"Sit," Gabriel said once he and Jane were alone. "I'll make you that tea."

The water was already boiled, so it only took a minute for him to finish preparing the cup of tea. He set it down in front of her.

"Is there a reason your brother doesn't like Benjamin Grout?" Jane asked as Gabriel sat down with her, his own cup of tea warming his hands.

"Apart from his personality?"

"He wasn't the most popular member of staff in the house, I gather."

"Far from it. I suppose you have heard all the gossip?"

"About Benjamin?"

"About Kitty." Gabriel said her name quietly, glancing at the door through which his brother had disappeared. "And the trouble she's caused."

"I've heard a little."

Jane leaned forward, wondering if there was something she was missing.

"Benjamin Grout was obsessed with her. Used to fawn over her like a lovesick boy. Wouldn't leave her alone a lot of the time. Kitty would run over here and flutter her eyelashes and ask for sanctuary for a few minutes from him."

Jane nodded, hoping Gabriel would go on.

"Peter was susceptible to her charms. She's a pretty young woman and knows how to get her own way. Had all the men in the Hall wrapped around her little finger."

"Your brother would let her in?"

"Yes. Nothing untoward happened, but she used to sit here and giggle at his jokes and ask him about horses. Sometimes she would tell him what a pain Benjamin was being."

"I can imagine that didn't sit well with your brother?"

"No. He warned Benjamin to back off, to stay away."

"Did Peter think he and Kitty might have a future?"

Gabriel swallowed and looked down at his tea for a moment. "I don't want you getting the wrong idea. Peter comes across all fierce, but he's a kind lad, naïve in many ways. He wouldn't hurt anyone." He paused as if considering whether to go on. "He hoped one day he and Kitty might be married. Of course, from the start I thought it unlikely. I'd seen her with other men around the house, probing until she found their weaknesses and then exploiting them. I never thought she really cared for my brother."

Jane cleared her throat, wondering how to ask about the relationship between Kitty and Mr Paulson.

"Did your brother know about Kitty's entanglement with Mr Paulson?"

"Yes. It broke his heart. When she became involved with the master, she stopped coming by, stopped talking to Peter completely. She had found a better prospect and dropped Peter so fast it was obvious she had never really cared for him."

"Your brother must have been upset."

Gabriel looked at her quickly, assessing the question.

"Not with the master. He wouldn't do anything to harm him."

Jane was about to try and gently probe a little further when Peter came crashing back into the room, Colonel Rushton a few steps behind.

"You think I killed that disgusting lecherous pig?" Peter asked, his voice raised.

"Did you?"

"No, but I am thankful he is dead. A man like that…" He trailed off and shook his head.

"A man like that what?" Jane said, standing up so he wasn't looming over her quite so much.

"A man like that doesn't deserve to be alive. Gabriel told you what Paulson did to Kitty?"

Jane nodded.

"She wasn't the first, either; there have been others. Used and then quietly disposed of, sent away when he gets fed up of them or they're with child."

"That must have made you angry, Peter?"

"Not as angry as some."

Jane thought this was likely to be true, but the groom did seem to have an explosive temper. If Mr Paulson had been found struck over the head or beaten to a pulp, a crime committed in a fit of rage, she might believe Peter Jones had something to do with it, but the murderer in this case had been cold, calculating and meticulous. It didn't fit.

"Did you see Kitty after she was dismissed?"

"No. Mr Upton marched her off the grounds and told her she was not welcome back."

"You haven't been into the village to see her?"

Peter looked away for a fraction of a second, and Jane could see he was considering whether to lie.

"No," he said after a moment.

"What about the murder of Mr Upton?" Colonel Rushton said from his position in the kitchen doorway. "Do either of you have anything to say about that?"

Gabriel shot his brother a warning look and then spoke quickly.

"We didn't know him well. I can't say I particularly liked the man — he liked to think of himself as better than the other staff — but I barely knew him. We had little to do with most of the servants in the house. We cook for ourselves, take care of our home ourselves — we barely come into contact with most of them."

"How about you, Mr Jones?" the colonel said, turning to Peter.

"As Gabriel said, I hardly knew the man. I would greet him if I saw him, but no more than that."

"Neither of you saw anything around ten o'clock this morning, around the time of his murder?"

They both shook their heads. "We were in with the horses, giving them some fresh food for the day."

"Thank you," Jane said quietly, smiling at the two men. "You have been very helpful. If you do think of anything else, will you let myself or the colonel know?"

Gabriel inclined his head and moved to the door, opening it for them.

The air was biting outside, but it was a relief to step out of the tiny kitchen. Once they were a little way from the cottage, Jane let out a loud breath and gave herself a shake.

"There was nowhere for anyone to hide, or to be concealed," Colonel Rushton said. "The cottage is tiny, just another room downstairs and then two basic bedrooms upstairs."

"From the sound of it, the Jones brothers would have no reason to shelter Benjamin Grout anyway." Jane told him what Gabriel had revealed about the footman and his obsession with Kitty.

"We keep coming back to this damn maid, don't we?" Colonel Rushton said. "Please excuse my language. The stresses of the last two days are catching up with me."

Jane waved a dismissive hand and thought about what Colonel Rushton had said. He was right: whichever angle they looked at it from, the motive for Mr Paulson's murder was in some way related to Kitty. The killer could be Benjamin Grout, who had been obsessed with Kitty and dismissed after his altercation with Mr Paulson. Or it could be Kitty herself, come to avenge the cruel way she had been brushed off. Even Mrs Paulson had a motive, fed up with her husband's philandering ways.

None of it was building into a cohesive picture, though. She sighed and told herself to slow down. On the last case she had assisted Lord Hinchbrooke with, he had told her to forget about trying to piece everything together at first. If she worked on gathering the information and asked as many questions as she could, with everyone's answers and the evidence mounting up, something would reveal itself.

As they rounded the corner they almost crashed into Dr Histon, who looked up at them in surprise.

"Are you going for a stroll, Doctor?"

"You laugh, Miss Austen, but I felt compelled to stretch my legs. I hate being cooped up inside, so I decided to risk the perils of the ice to get some fresh air, even for a few minutes. Even so, it is a little too cold even for me. I think I will return to the house with you," Dr Histon said with a shiver.

They had just reached the front of the house when a movement in the distance caught Jane's eye. At the very limit of her vision, she could see a small black dot moving towards them. It wasn't going fast, but there was an air of urgency about it.

For a few moments all three stood watching it, and then Jane squinted and cried out.

"It's Miss Leveritt!" she said, immediately taking off down the drive, slipping and sliding as she went.

Colonel Rushton soon caught up with her and steamed past, and a second later Dr Histon followed, making good progress on the way to Miss Leveritt. As they drew closer, Jane could see how the young woman was struggling. Each step seemed a gargantuan effort, and before they could reach her she collapsed into the snow.

By the time Jane had reached Miss Leveritt, Colonel Rushton had already helped her to her feet and was supporting her around the waist, his shoulder propped under her arm.

"Can you walk?" he asked. "I would carry you, but this shoulder of mine will give out and we'll both end up in the snow."

"I can walk," Miss Leveritt said through chattering teeth.

Jane whipped off her coat and placed it over the young woman's shoulders, with Dr Histon coming to support her on the other side. As they made progress towards the house she kept glancing over her shoulder, wondering if Mrs Leveritt would appear out of the snow at any moment, but as the minutes ticked by it seemed more and more unlikely.

CHAPTER ELEVEN

"Please, Miss Leveritt, sit down," Cassandra said, gently pressing the young woman on the shoulders until she settled back onto the sofa.

"I need to find my mama."

"The men are out searching," Jane said, not moving from the window. "They will do whatever they can to find her. Perhaps you can tell us which direction you went in? It may make it easier for them."

Miss Leveritt let out a little sob. "I don't know. Everything looked so different in the snow — there wasn't anything familiar at all. It felt as though we were walking in circles, and then mama fell." Her voice was rising with a note of hysteria, and Cassandra shot Jane a warning look.

Jane grimaced, looking at the sky. There were some clouds gathering, but no snow as yet. The searchers had a chance of finding Mrs Leveritt as long as a fresh layer of snow didn't come down and obliterate the tracks Miss Leveritt had made getting back to the house.

"You just focus on getting warm," Cassandra said, tucking the pile of blankets more securely round the young woman.

"I thought a hot drink might be welcome," Charlotte, the maid said, hurrying into the room. She held a steaming cup in her hands and passed it over to Miss Leveritt, watching whilst the young woman took a sip. "Any sign yet, Miss?" Charlotte enquired as she moved over to join Jane by the window.

Dr Histon, Colonel Rushton and Mr Potter had all gone out to search, accompanied by the young footman Fred and the two grooms from the cottage next to the stable. It was a good sized search party that would be able to cover a wide area in good time, but Jane still wished she could be out there with them. She hated waiting, hated sitting around doing nothing, when there was action to be taken.

"Did you get anywhere near the village?"

Miss Leveritt shook her head. "I don't think so. There was no sign of it, but with this snow it could be just round the next bend and you wouldn't even know. When Mama fell, it took me fifteen minutes to get her out of the ditch and back on her feet." Miss Leveritt shuddered at the memory. "She couldn't put weight on her ankle so I said I would get help, but I didn't know whether to carry on or retrace my steps. Maybe it would have been better to have kept trying for the village. Maybe it would have given Mama a better chance."

"You did very well, Miss Leveritt," Cassandra said, patting her on the hand. "You must not fret too much. I am sure she will be found soon."

Jane peered out the window, wondering if Cassandra's words were true. It would be easy to follow the footprints; the difficulty was the speed at which they could progress through the snow. Mrs Leveritt had been wearing a coat, hat and gloves, but she was hardly dressed for the arctic conditions. If she was unable to move, Jane wasn't sure how long it would be until all the heat was sapped from her and her body shut down from exposure.

Resting her head on the windowpane, she jumped when Cassandra came up behind her and placed a hand on her shoulder.

"Miss Leveritt has drifted off to sleep. The rest will do her good," Cassandra murmured. "How are you, Jane? You look fraught."

"What a day," Jane said, leaning back into her sister.

"What a day," Cassandra echoed quietly. "Do you think you're any closer to finding out what happened?"

Jane thought about the question for a long time before answering. She had spoken to some of the guests and servants, gathered a lot of information, inspected two bodies, looked at two crime scenes and searched the whole of Melmont Hall from top to bottom, and right now she didn't feel like she had made much progress at all.

"I know a lot more than I did," she said slowly, "but it is hard to work out what is relevant and what is useless noise, complicating things."

"Is there someone you suspect?"

Jane shook her head slowly. "No, but I think I may have found the motive. Mr Paulson was a bit of a scoundrel; he liked to engage in physical relationships with young women, mainly maids. From the sound of it, he would choose one every year or two to have an affair with for a few months until he got bored of her or she became pregnant; then he would send her away with a small amount of money and a refusal to acknowledge the child."

"This has happened more than once?"

"Multiple times, by the sound of it. The maid who was dismissed last week, Kitty, she was the latest."

"He sent her away?"

"Yes, and Kitty was popular with the male servants too. It is easy to imagine someone convincing themselves they were defending Kitty's honour by killing Mr Paulson."

Cassandra sucked in a breath and closed her eyes.

"That is quite a motive."

"It is. It's the only real motive I have come up with from talking to people. He wasn't the most pleasant of men, but no one has talked about money woes or a tendency towards violence or really anything else that could be construed as a reason to kill the man."

"That is why you were so keen to search the house, to see if someone involved with Kitty could be hiding here."

"They weren't. We were very thorough — I don't think we missed anywhere."

"What about the locked door?"

Jane groaned, clapping a hand over her mouth as Miss Leveritt stirred behind them on the sofa.

"I cannot work it out, Cassandra. Nothing makes sense. There is no way someone could have locked that door from the outside, and there was no other way out of the room."

"Mr Paulson couldn't have done it himself?"

"Why would he stab himself?"

"Remorse, perhaps."

"He's been at it for decades, Cassandra, having his fun with vulnerable young women and then discarding them. Why would he grow a conscience now?"

Cassandra shrugged. "It was just a thought. It could explain why the door was locked."

"I may not have known him well, but I can't see Mr Paulson feeling remorse about *anything*, especially not enough to stab himself in the stomach."

"You're right. I am sure it is an excruciating way to die."

Jane stood, stretching out her back. "There's still much to do. I haven't spoken with the Potters yet, or Dr Histon really, although I don't think any of them had a long acquaintance with Mr Paulson, so it is difficult to see how they would have a motive. I have only talked to a few of the servants. Perhaps I will turn something up there."

"You do not have to solve this thing before Lord Hinchbrooke arrives, Jane."

"I know. My main concern is that no one else gets murdered before we can find the murderer."

"Do you think that is why Mr Upton was killed?"

"So far, I have assumed so. I suppose there could be someone with a grudge against both Mr Paulson and the butler, but who would hate them both enough to want to murder them? I think it more likely Mr Upton was killed because he knew something that could identify the killer." Pausing, Jane realised this was an angle she hadn't looked at closely before, trying to work out what it was Mr Upton had known or seen or heard. It must have been damning enough to make him think he knew what happened, and somehow the murderer had worked out that the butler was close to revealing his information and had struck before he could.

There were too many possibilities. Perhaps he had seen someone near the study when they shouldn't have been, or overheard an argument between Mr Paulson and the murderer. Perhaps he had worked out who could have killed Mr Paulson and left without leaving a trace, the study door locked from the inside.

"I do not know," Jane said, covering her eyes with her hand.

"I heard the news," Mrs Paulson said, bursting into the room, making Miss Leveritt stir and sit up on the sofa. "My dear Miss Leveritt, whatever could you have been thinking, going out in the snow like that?"

"My mama insisted, Mrs Paulson, and when she gets a notion in her head…"

"Have they found her? Is your mama back with us?"

Miss Leveritt shook her head and a tear slipped down her cheek. "Come, my dear," the older woman said, sitting down on the sofa beside her. "Don't cry. I assume the colonel is leading the search. He is a very capable man."

"The snow is so thick," Miss Leveritt sobbed. "It's impossible to make much progress."

Jane observed the older woman with Miss Leveritt and marvelled at how she had roused herself to comfort her young guest. Jane knew a little of the relationship between Mrs Paulson and Miss Leveritt, aside from the proposition that she would sponsor the young woman's season and hopefully turn the family's fortunes around by introducing her to a wealthy husband, but here her affection was evident. She looked at Miss Leveritt protectively, as if she wanted to gather her in her arms and shield her from all the evils of the world.

"Come, we will not give in to grief or melancholy. Your mother is a strong woman. Once Colonel Rushton finds her, she will need a little warming up, that is all."

Jane turned back to the window and frowned, wondering if she was imagining movement amongst the snow-covered trees. She watched and then called out.

"I see someone."

Sure enough, there was a shape moving towards the house. Miss Leveritt shed her layers of blankets and ran to the window, a flicker of hope in her eyes. As they watched, the shape slowly became bigger. There were others trailing behind.

"They're returning," Jane said, wondering if they had Mrs Leveritt with them or if the conditions had been too dangerous to continue the search.

"Can you see my mama?" Miss Leveritt said, her voice small.

No one replied. As they squinted out into the snow, Jane thought she could make out the form of one person supporting another, but she didn't want to get anyone's hopes up.

Their progress was painfully slow, but it soon became apparent that wasn't just because of the deep snow. Every fifty yards they would stop and pass a burden between them, before starting up again with a new person carrying the load.

"They're carrying something," Jane said. "I think it is your mother."

Miss Leveritt let out a strangled sob of relief and then realisation dawned on her. "Why isn't she walking?"

"Perhaps the ankle she hurt is paining her too much," Cassandra said softly.

"Perhaps."

Mrs Paulson sprang into action, pulling the bell cord. When Charlotte appeared, she instructed the maid to prepare Mrs Leveritt's bed with a bed warmer and extra blankets and to build the fire in the room so it was blazing.

It was Gabriel Jones who made it over the threshold with Mrs Leveritt in his arms. The other men were close behind but he shrugged them off, clearly concerned at the delay that might occur if he handed her over before taking her upstairs.

"This way," Mrs Paulson instructed, taking charge, shaking off her own grief to provide for her friend in a crisis.

Jane didn't follow upstairs, knowing there would be enough people in the bedroom with Mrs Paulson, Miss Leveritt, Dr Histon and a maid or two bustling around. Cassandra hesitated and then waited a few seconds before following, ensuring she wouldn't get in the way but ready to lend a hand if she was needed.

The men were all inside now, although Peter Jones was noticeably absent. The colonel must have seen Jane glancing out the window in concern, because he began to explain what had happened.

"Mrs Leveritt was only half a mile from the village. Mr Jones thought he could make it the rest of the way to the village and leave a message with the innkeeper. If the roads from there clear before ours do, they will be able to send for the magistrate without any further delay."

"Is he coming back here after?"

"That was the plan. He didn't struggle in the snow, not like the rest of us."

Jane saw how haggard and exhausted the colonel looked, and then glancing around, she saw the same tiredness reflected on the faces of the other men.

"Come and sit down," she said, ushering them all into the drawing room. "Sit down and I shall organise hot drinks."

Mr Potter and Colonel Rushton traipsed in gratefully, divesting themselves of coats and gloves as they went. Fred, the young footman, hesitated on the threshold.

"You can go in too, if you wish," Jane said gently. "Or, if you would prefer, I am sure Mrs Brown has a warm spot by the fire downstairs."

"Thank you, Miss. I think I'll go downstairs."

Jane followed him down, asking the cook to prepare some hot drinks for those who had been out in the snow.

"Of course," Mrs Brown said. "I'll send Moll up with a tray when they're ready."

Returning to the drawing room, Jane took a seat across from Colonel Rushton, eager to find out exactly what had happened. However, she was aware that he was likely to want a few minutes of rest before she started interrogating him.

"You look like a racehorse straining at the bit, ready for the race to begin, Miss Austen."

Jane smiled, sitting back in her chair.

"I am sorry, Colonel. I will give you a moment to recuperate."

"A moment? You are relentless, Miss Austen."

"Is that a compliment, or are you pointing out a flaw?"

"It depends on the circumstance." He sighed and flexed his fingers towards the fire for a moment and then turned to her. "We were able to follow the Leveritts' trail through the snow. There isn't much more to it than that."

"How far had they got?"

"They'd taken quite a circuitous route and the walk was strenuous, but they'd made it about two thirds of the way to the village. If Mrs Leveritt hadn't fallen, I think they would have had a good chance of making it."

Jane lowered her voice. "And Mr Jones has gone on to ask the villagers to send a messenger to Lord Hinchbrooke when the road is clear."

"Yes. He volunteered," the colonel said slowly. He looked over his shoulder before continuing in barely more than a whisper. "He was keen, a little too keen."

"You think he had an ulterior motive?"

"If he is guilty, it was a good opportunity to distance himself from the house before our suspicions could fall on him. When the roads clear, he will have a head start from the village."

"You don't think he's coming back?"

"I think there's a good chance he's met up with the maid Kitty and together they're planning on fleeing the area."

Jane considered his suggestion for a moment and knew it wasn't without merit, but she couldn't quite tie it together. If Peter was the killer, he would have had to get into the house unseen, somehow murder Mr Paulson in the locked study and slip away unnoticed. The house had been busy with guests and servants, and surely someone would have noticed the groom where he shouldn't have been. One of the guests or house servants slipping out of the study wouldn't have seemed strange to anyone observing, but Peter Jones would have looked completely out of place.

Mr Upton's murder didn't have the same problem, but she was working on the assumption that Mr Upton had seen something he shouldn't have or deduced who had committed the crime. As far as she knew, Peter Jones had not had any contact with anyone in the house. He wouldn't have known Mr Upton was eager to speak to Colonel Rushton or that he might reveal something.

"I suppose it could fit," Jane said, not completely convinced. "We shall see if he returns."

Colonel Rushton scoffed but looked quite pleased with himself, no doubt already quietly congratulating himself on solving the crime.

"If it was him, how did he do it, though?"

"Who knows? Perhaps he has some tool for pulling stones out of horses' hooves that can grip the key through the keyhole to turn it from the other side."

"Does such a thing exist?"

Shrugging, Colonel Rushton turned his attention to Moll, who was hovering nearby waiting to give him his hot drink.

"Don't just stand there, girl. Pass it over."

Moll did, her hand shaking and spilling some of the dark liquid as she did so. Terrified, her eyes darted up to meet Colonel Rushton's as she backed away.

"Clumsy fool," he muttered, wiping the droplets off his trousers.

"I am sorry, sir," she managed to stutter.

"Get back to the kitchen with you, before you can make any more mess."

Jane watched in surprise. She knew Colonel Rushton must be exhausted from the foray out into the snow and everyone's nerves were frayed today with two dead bodies rapidly cooling in the storeroom downstairs, but this was completely out of character.

She didn't say anything, wondering whether to excuse the snap as a reaction to a stressful couple of days or whether it was his true personality shining through. Colonel Rushton was an acquaintance, nothing more, a man she had met on a few social occasions when they had talked about the weather or the state of the harvest that year. She didn't know him, not really. She thought of how he had inserted himself into the investigation, trying to push her out, suggesting it was no place for a woman. That could be his opinion, but what if there was a more sinister reason for wanting her to have nothing to do with it?

Slowly she stood, brushing down her skirt. She smiled at Mr Potter as he caught her eye, then she left the room. Outside she paused, bracing herself against the banister on the wide stairs and taking a few deep breaths until the light-headedness dissipated.

What she wanted was some fresh air, to go for a brisk walk and allow all the warring thoughts in her mind to settle, but that was impossible in the snow. She was trapped here with no possibility of escape, unable to walk five feet without bumping into another of the guests or servants, any of whom could be a murderer.

Jane rushed up the stairs, almost at the top before she heard the creak of a door below. As quietly as possible, she peered over the banister, surprised to see the mousy Mrs Potter creeping out of Mr Paulson's study. For a long moment Jane could not move, wondering if there was an innocent reason for Mrs Potter to be in the room where their host had been murdered. Jane watched as Mrs Potter hesitated outside the drawing room before entering, a smile now plastered on her face.

She was ready to go marching downstairs, demanding an answer when she heard voices coming out of the Leveritts' bedroom. She was relieved to see Cassandra and Mrs Paulson slip out.

"How is she?"

"Dr Histon is hopeful she will recover. Her hands and her feet are taking a while to warm, but other than that she does seem to be rallying. She's sleeping now and he has given her something for the pain in her ankle," Cassandra said. "She needs to rest now. Miss Leveritt is insisting she stays with her mother."

"What an ordeal," Jane murmured.

"What fear does to us," Mrs Paulson said, shaking her head. "Mrs Leveritt has always been superstitious. I suppose it was too much worry to think she might be under the same roof as a murderer."

"How are you now, Mrs Paulson?" Jane asked their hostess.

"Feeling a little better, thank you, my dear. Isn't it marvellous how the body responds to a crisis? Half an hour of running round and organising things and I have barely thought of the events of the last couple of days at all." She did look brighter, with two spots of colour on her cheeks and a vitality in her eyes that had not been there earlier in the day. "I suppose I should check on the Potters; I do feel sorry for them, getting dragged into all this. I only wanted to make them feel welcome in the local area."

Jane thought of Mrs Potter creeping out of the study and wondered how well Mrs Paulson knew the young couple. Even though she was trying hard, she couldn't think of an innocent explanation for why Mrs Potter had been sneaking round as she had.

Sighing, she acknowledged that a few minutes earlier she had been adamant it was Colonel Rushton who had committed the murder, and she still couldn't shake the idea that perhaps he had been so keen to take over the investigation so that he could manipulate the facts. However, she had no proof of this, just a feeling of dislike towards the man.

"She's asleep," Dr Histon said as he came out and joined them in the corridor. "Let us pray death does not claim another this weekend."

CHAPTER TWELVE

They were sitting in Jane and Cassandra's bedroom, huddled around the bed like a circle of witches. Jane was leaning with her head back against the headboard, Cassandra perched on the end of the bed and Mrs Paulson on the other side, her feet dangling off the edge.

"I can't believe it of her," Mrs Paulson said, shaking her head vehemently.

"How well do you know her? How well do you know either of them?" Jane asked quietly, wishing Mrs Paulson's voice wasn't so loud.

She had hurried Cassandra and Mrs Paulson along to her bedroom to discuss the Potters before they went back downstairs, but so far Mrs Paulson was stuck on disbelief rather than giving her any useful information.

"Admittedly not that well. They only moved into the village a few weeks ago, but they are decent people, well-mannered. You can tell they're from good stock."

"But do you actually know anything about them?"

Mrs Paulson considered a moment. "I know what they've told me. They're newly married. Mrs Potter has some family connections in Petersfield so wanted to be close by, but not too close, and Mr Potter is not from the area."

"That's all?"

"I don't go prying, my dear. I met the Potters in the village and started conversing, and the invitation sprung from that."

"You met them once and then invited them to spend the weekend at your house?" Jane asked incredulously.

"In retrospect it seems a little rash, but how was I to know my husband was going to be murdered? Do you truly think it was the Potters? She seems so sweet, and he appears completely harmless."

Jane leaned her head back and closed her eyes. If she was truthful, she was hopping from theory to theory with no real proof. There could be an innocent explanation as to why Mrs Potter had been in the study. Perhaps she was secretly a fan of the macabre, or maybe she had dropped an expensive earring somewhere and wanted to check the floor.

"I will have to ask her what she was doing, but it will be difficult to know if she is lying."

"I'm sure you'll find out, Miss Austen. Mary has kept me up to date with your progress so far, and we think you're doing a wonderful job."

Jane was taken aback by this. She hadn't known Mrs Paulson was well enough to take such an interest and certainly hadn't realised the lady's maid had been checking on her progress.

"Whilst I have you here, Mrs Paulson, I wanted to ask you about Colonel Rushton."

Mrs Paulson held up her hands defensively and shook her head. "No, Miss Austen, I will not hear a bad word said about him. That man is a gentleman. A hero. He is above suspicion."

"You know him well, Mrs Paulson?"

"I do."

"He was a friend of your husband's?"

"No," Mrs Paulson said quickly and then glanced up at Jane. "That is not to say he did not get on with my husband, but he is my friend, not Mr Paulson's."

"How do you know him?"

Mrs Paulson sighed and smoothed down her dress.

"We are of a similar age, Miss Austen, although you would never believe it. A dashing colonel fresh out of the army and this old widow, haggard by life."

"You are not haggard," Cassandra said, placing her hand over the older woman's.

"I knew Colonel Rushton when I was young, before I met and married Mr Paulson, before I was even out in society. He was a friend during my adolescence, and then he went off to join the army and I married my husband."

Jane could tell there was much left unsaid and wondered if there had been a forbidden romance between the pair. It was difficult to imagine now, but twenty-five years ago many things would have been different.

"You kept in touch."

"Not at first. I suppose we were both too caught up in our new lives, but after a few years he bought a house in the area and we would see each other on occasion at various social events. Of course, he was away much of the time, but as he climbed the ranks he got to spend a little time in our corner of Hampshire." Mrs Paulson paused, considering her words. "There was nothing improper between myself and Colonel Rushton, Miss Austen. I do not want you to get the wrong idea. The colonel has always been a perfect gentleman, and I may not have liked how my husband acted, but I do respect the sanctity of marriage vows. I have never done anything that might invite scandal."

Jane cast her eyes down, feeling a little ashamed that she had made Mrs Paulson feel like she needed to explain herself and her morals.

"I'm sorry," she murmured. "I've been unforgivably rude. I fear I have become caught up in all of this and forgotten my basic manners. Can you forgive me?"

"Of course, Miss Austen. I can see your intentions and they are pure, but you must drop this idea about Colonel Rushton."

Jane nodded, a hundred more questions swirling in her mind, but she knew she had to swallow them for now and find the answers some other way. Her mother would never forgive her if she ever found out she had been pestering her good friend just a day after the death of her husband.

"While I have you, I thought I might make a list of where everyone was in the hour and a quarter that Mr Upton must have been killed."

"Such a shame about Mr Upton. He was a superior fellow but a jolly good butler. He'd been part of the household for years and was so efficient at getting it to run smoothly. Never missed a detail, never missed anything."

Cassandra's eyes came up to meet Jane's, and she could tell her sister was thinking the same as her. *That was probably what got him killed.*

Jane waited, hoping Mrs Paulson would volunteer the information without her having to press further, but the older woman just sat there, not saying anything.

"We think he was killed between half past nine — when Mrs Brown saw him in the kitchen — and a quarter to eleven this morning, when his body was found. I think you were in your room at the time, weren't you? With your maid, Mary."

"Yes, that's right, dear."

"Mary didn't leave?"

"No, I don't think so. She's been so good, a wonderful woman to have around in a crisis."

Mrs Paulson stood and smoothed down her skirts, smiling at Jane and Cassandra and then taking her leave. She looked exhausted despite spending much of the last twenty-four hours in bed, but Jane supposed shock could do that to you.

When they were alone, Jane threw herself back on the bed and sighed deeply as Cassandra came and sat next to her.

"Next time I complain about being bored, about nothing exciting ever happening, remind me of this moment," Jane said.

"It is a giant muddle, is it not?"

"I feel like I'm failing, Cassandra. If Lord Hinchbrooke were here…"

"Hush. If Lord Hinchbrooke were here, he would be at the same stage you are. Asking questions, testing theories. He is no magician, Jane; he has learnt to be tenacious and to accumulate information until everything fits."

"I suppose you are right."

"You know I am. You are in a slump, that is all. What is it you say to me when you are stuck with your writing, unable to work through a particularly challenging scene?"

"I have to approach from a different angle, look at it from another character's point of view."

"Then that is what you must do. Tell me about your top three suspects."

Jane closed her eyes for a moment and let all the information from the last few days wash over her.

"Our number one suspect has to be Benjamin Grout. He is the footman who has been dismissed. By all accounts he held Kitty in high regard and was not happy when Mr Paulson discarded her due to her pregnancy. Benjamin launched a verbal attack on Mr Paulson and was dismissed alongside Kitty. He has plenty of motive. There is revenge on the man who took advantage of the woman he loved; there is anger over the loss of his job. What is more, he was seen sneaking into the house and going into Mr Paulson's study on the day of the murder."

Cassandra listened intently, nodding along.

"But unless he is some sort of magician, I cannot explain how he, or anyone else, killed Mr Paulson and then escaped leaving the study door locked from the inside. No one saw him leave Melmont Hall after the murder, but it has been searched from top to bottom and there's no sign of him at all."

"He has motive," Cassandra summarised, "but if he is the killer, you cannot see how he executed the getaway."

"Exactly."

"How about suspect number two?"

"Peter Jones."

"He's a groom, isn't he?"

"Yes, he lives with his brother Gabriel in a cottage by the stables. He also was obsessed with Kitty, and had notions of marrying her before she got involved with Mr Paulson."

"That complicates things," Cassandra said, puffing out her cheeks and then collapsing on the bed beside Jane.

"He seemed a little shifty when Colonel Rushton and I visited, but that could just have been because the colonel implied that he thought Peter was untrustworthy. It would make me hostile as well."

"Surely it would be difficult for Peter Jones to access the study without anyone seeing him."

"Indeed. He had no reason to be in the house, and beyond motive the only suspicious thing is that he volunteered to go to the village to try and get a message to Lord Hinchbrooke when the roads cleared."

"Why is that suspicious?"

"On the surface, it is not, but Colonel Rushton is concerned he may flee."

Cassandra considered for a second and then shrugged. "Either he flees and that way you know he is guilty, or he doesn't and the evidence against him is scant at best."

"There is no evidence, just a weak, possible motive."

"How about suspect number three?"

Jane considered for a moment, wondering whether she was being foolish to rule out Mrs Paulson. Women could kill, and Lord Hinchbrooke had told her once that although most murders were committed by men, if women were going to kill it would often be their husbands who were the victims. Still, Mrs Paulson had been part of their mother's life for a long time, a friend. She may have hated how her husband treated the young women he had his affairs with, but unless something else had made her snap she couldn't see why she would kill him now, after all these years of putting up with his behaviour.

"Number three is Colonel Rushton," she said decisively. "He has tried to take over the investigation numerous times, and I feel he could be intent on misdirecting me, pulling my focus from what I really need to see. The butler wanted to speak to him, but he refused to do so publicly and could easily have arranged to meet him outside, alone."

"What would be his motive?"

"That is where the theory falls down. Perhaps he is still in love with Mrs Paulson and wanted to free her from her unhappiness."

Cassandra looked uncertain, and Jane knew it was probably just her dislike for the man that had made her put him so high on the list. It was difficult to remain impartial and not let her personal feelings cloud her perception.

"Then there's Mrs Paulson, of course. She has a lot of motive with Mr Paulson's affairs and secret children, all of this being conducted in her own house. It must have been heartbreaking for her, but I can't see why she would snap now. There doesn't seem to be a trigger, something that would mean she went from horrified but accepting to planning a murder."

"And you trust Mother's judgement."

"I do. I can't see Mama being friends with a murderer, not one who could plan out a killing so coldly."

"There's also Mrs Potter," Cassandra reminded her.

"Of course. The mysterious Potters. They turn up in the village and befriend Mrs Paulson, gaining an invitation to this house party. Perhaps it all could be innocent, but then what was Mrs Potter doing sneaking out of Mr Paulson's study?"

"Anyone else?"

"There's Kitty, but there's no hint that she returned to the house after she had been dismissed. She sent a note requesting that Mr Paulson meet her, but he was hardly going to arrange that whilst his wife was throwing a dinner party."

For a long time they lay on the bed, side by side, looking up at the ceiling. It was a decent list of suspects, some of them with convincing motives, but none of it felt right. Jane knew she was missing something.

"The worst thing is I can't move forward, can't do *anything* until I work out how he was killed inside a locked room."

"Perhaps Lord Hinchbrooke will have seen something like this before."

Jane murmured something incomprehensible and then pressed her lips together. She felt awful admitting it, but she wanted to be the one to solve this crime. Many people thought the idea of her, a woman of no particular renown, assisting the magistrate simply ridiculous. Just as time and again she had been told women did not write books, and they most certainly did not expect them to be published. Her family were exceptionally supportive, but the wider world looked for anything to set you apart from the crowd and then mocked you for it.

Allowing herself a few more minutes, she reached out and found Cassandra's fingers, and they lay there in silence, both contemplating the enormity of the task ahead.

"Come," Jane said, when she felt ready to face the world again. "The Potters will not question themselves."

Mr and Mrs Potter were nowhere to be found downstairs, and Jane felt a niggle of concern as she systematically entered each of the rooms.

"You haven't seen anyone leave?" she asked Fred, the young footman who was standing in the hall, ready to serve if anyone had need of him.

"No, Miss."

Jane ascended the stairs again, calculating which of the thick wooden doors led to the Potters' room and pausing outside. It was an invasion of privacy and against all social norms to call upon a married couple in their bedchamber, but Mr and Mrs Potter had proved elusive for much of the day and Jane didn't want to waste any more time. If Mrs Potter's trip into the study was important to the crime, she wanted to know about it now, not in another day or two.

With more confidence than she felt, she knocked on the door, listening for an answer.

The door was made of thick, dark wood, like most of the rest of the doors and panelling in the house. It was good quality, hundreds of years old, and worked well to stop inquisitive servants eavesdropping on their master. It also meant Jane could hardly make out the hushed voices inside the room. She certainly couldn't hear the words they were saying, but it did confirm the Potters were there.

After thirty seconds she knocked again, her hand drifting down to the handle. It would be unforgivably rude to burst into their room without an invitation, but Jane knew she would do it anyway to further the investigation. She might lose the respect of the Potters and anyone they told, but it would be worth it to question Mrs Potter.

Before her hand could reach the handle, the door opened a crack and Mr Potter's face peeked out.

"I'm so sorry to disturb you. I wondered if I might have a moment to talk to you about Mr Paulson and Mr Upton?"

Mr Potter looked back over his shoulder before answering.

"Can we arrange another time, Miss Austen? My wife has a headache."

"Oh, I am sorry, Mrs Potter," Jane said, inching forward and trying to catch a glimpse of the room beyond. Mr Potter was not a big man, but he was taller than Jane and filled the crack between the door and the frame.

Sensing she was about to lose the opportunity altogether, she placed her hand on the door and pushed a little, to Mr Potter's surprise.

"I can come back, of course, but it will likely be with Colonel Rushton beside me. I thought I would try and be more discreet than that, but if you are too unwell to talk now, Mrs Potter, I understand."

Jane turned, wondering if her ploy was going to work.

"What do you mean, more discreet?" Mr Potter asked sharply.

Counting to five before she turned around, Jane then looked the young man in the eye and held his gaze, noting the nervous expression he tried to hide.

"I saw you, Mrs Potter," she said and then looked over her shoulder. "I thought it better to do this in private, but if you prefer we can talk about it later in front of everyone."

"What did you see?" Mrs Potter was on her feet now, crowding behind her husband by the door.

"I saw you coming out of the study."

Mr and Mrs Potter exchanged a glance, and Jane could see the wealth of information they were trying to silently convey between them.

"I do not know what you mean," Mrs Potter said eventually.

"My wife has not been in Mr Paulson's study," Mr Potter agreed.

Jane gave a chuckle, a low, humourless sound and shook her head, turning away again.

"Miss Austen, you are mistaken," Mr Potter called, sounding desperate now.

Jane spun on her heel quickly and stalked back towards them.

"Do not think you can treat me like a fool," she said sharply. "I have exceptional vision and I know *exactly* what I saw. I thought I would give you the chance to explain, to offer any innocent justification for your being in the room where our host was murdered yesterday evening. A room that has clearly been marked as out of bounds."

The Potters stood frozen, neither answering, as if hoping the other would take it on themselves to make up a believable lie.

"I was in the study," Mrs Potter said eventually, "but only for a brief moment."

Jane waited, knowing that whatever came out of Mrs Potter's mouth next would be a lie. Her speech was too slow, too stilted to be relating the truth. It was clear she was choosing every word carefully as her mind ticked away, trying to spin a fallacy that Jane would accept.

"Come in, Miss Austen. My wife will explain."

The bedroom was another beautiful room, with wood panelling up to the middle of the walls and deep blue wallpaper above. There was a four-poster bed with blue drapes that matched the wallpaper as well as a writing desk and a couple of comfortable chairs. Mr Potter indicated Jane should take one of the chairs, and Mrs Potter sat down across from her in the other. Mr Potter remained standing, a little too close for comfort.

"I wanted to retrieve a letter," Mrs Potter said, biting her lip.

"A letter?"

"Yes. We brought a letter up to the house from the village. An acquaintance asked us to, and we didn't see any harm in it."

Jane thought of the letter from *K*, most likely from Kitty, requesting that Mr Paulson meet her to discuss her future.

"Who gave you the letter?"

"Our housemaid."

"Your housemaid?"

"She said it was from her sister. She used to work here, I believe, and wanted to send a note to Mr Paulson."

"And you agreed to bring it?"

"We couldn't see the harm."

"What is your housemaid called?"

"Anne."

"Do you know her sister's name?"

"Kitty."

Jane nodded. The connection was there, and it would explain how Kitty's letter had appeared amongst Mr Paulson's papers, but she felt it wasn't the whole story.

"Why did you sneak into the study to retrieve it?"

Mr Potter cleared his throat, looking at his wife.

"I went into Mr Paulson's study when we first arrived. He wasn't in there, so I left the letter on the desk." He swallowed and continued. "When the murder happened, I realised that if anyone had seen me creeping into the study, I may become a suspect."

Mrs Potter nodded vigorously. "I was so worried that someone might realise my husband was the one who delivered the letter from Kitty, especially as it is clear now that she left under less than ideal circumstances, and we might be tied to this whole mess. I thought that if I took the letter, it would solve the problem."

"So you risked being spotted for a second time and went into a room we had already searched to remove something we'd probably already seen."

Mrs Potter nodded, wide-eyed.

"I know it may seem foolish, Miss Austen, but my wife worries a lot. This awful situation is not good for her nerves."

Jane inclined her head, taking a moment to weigh up everything they had told her. It didn't feel cohesive. It was just believable enough that she couldn't call the story ridiculous outright, yet it was far-fetched to think someone would risk being caught entering a dead man's study to remove something that had no real link to them and had probably already been seen anyway.

"Thank you for explaining," Jane said, reaching out and taking Mrs Potter's hand. "What a terrible ordeal these past few days have been. I am sure you are eager to get back home when the snow clears."

"We are."

"Mrs Paulson tells me you have just moved into the local area. It is a beautiful part of the country to settle in."

"It is," Mrs Potter agreed effusively, refusing to be drawn into further conversation.

"Do you know the area well?"

"A little."

"Are you planning on settling here permanently?"

"Perhaps." She was giving nothing away, far more eager to get Jane out of the door than to continue with any pretence of politeness.

Within ten seconds Jane was back in the hall, and as she turned to try one last time to draw the Potters into conversation, the door was closed firmly in her face. For a long moment Jane did not move, contemplating how likely it was that the newlyweds would open the door if she knocked again.

Deciding there was no way she would gain an audience with them again right now, Jane retreated. They weren't going anywhere; they couldn't. Perhaps this evening she would be able to corner them on their way to dinner. It would be harder for them to swerve her questions with everyone else nearby, watching curiously.

Back downstairs Jane was surprised to see Mrs Paulson had re-joined her guests, looking hollow-eyed but with rosy cheeks thanks to the roaring fire. She was sitting with Colonel Rushton, Dr Histon and Cassandra, talking in a low voice.

"Was it helpful?" Cassandra enquired as Jane joined her on the sofa.

"No."

"You spoke to someone without me?" Colonel Rushton said.

"It was an impulsive decision to talk to the Potters," Jane said, not liking having to explain herself to the colonel. "Do not fear, you did not miss anything. They did not wish to talk to me."

Colonel Rushton tried to smother a little snort, and Jane felt the suppressed irritation from the last two days surging to the surface.

Cassandra must have sensed the impending eruption and stood quickly. "How about a game of cards?"

"What a marvellous idea," Mrs Paulson said, clapping her hands together. "The atmosphere in this house is dire. I think a little distraction is what we all need." She stood and began to arrange everything they would need, calling the young footman in to move a table they could sit at for the game. "You four play — it would please me to watch."

Initially Jane had thought it a little callous for the new widow to agree to a game of cards when her husband had not yet been dead twenty-four hours, but as she watched the older woman she saw the subtle signs of strain on her face. It was an unprecedented situation. With most deaths the bereaved would be able to hide away in private, to mourn without an audience, but here Mrs Paulson was trapped with her guests for the foreseeable future, unable to escape. No doubt the game of cards would provide a distraction from thinking about the horrors of the past day.

Or perhaps she really is that callous, the little voice in Jane's head said. The subtle shaking of Mrs Paulson's hands as she took the pack of cards from the footman seemed to go against the idea, and Jane felt awful for having it. Her mother would never forgive her if she caused Mrs Paulson any undue distress at such a difficult time by not being considerate and understanding.

"How shall we partner?" Dr Histon said, looking from person to person. Jane silently groaned at the thought of having to partner Colonel Rushton, and Cassandra seemed to sense this, for she quickly stepped forward.

"Colonel Rushton, shall we pair up?"

"Wonderful, Miss Austen."

"That leaves you with me, I am afraid, Miss Jane," Dr Histon said with a self-deprecating smile.

"A formidable team, I am sure," Colonel Rushton said. "Don't believe the man when he says he is a novice at cards. I have lost many a coin to him in a late night game."

"Playing whist is quite a different prospect."

"Do not fear," Cassandra said, leaning towards the doctor with a soft smile. "Jane is fiercely competitive and will soon tutor you in how to play with her methods if she is dissatisfied."

"You make me sound like an ogre," Jane murmured in complaint, but she knew it was at least partially true. With seven siblings, she had grown up in a house where all games fostered a gentle rivalry. She may not be able to climb the ranks in the navy or teach twenty sailors how to fire a cannon, but she *could* outfox her brothers at cards.

"You forget how many times I have partnered you," Cassandra teased.

"My sister was quite the same," Dr Histon said with a fond smile. "She was the most competitive and would choose her partner carefully, judging by who had been playing well in recent weeks."

"She sounds a sensible woman."

"She was," Dr Histon said, with a brief smile. "We lost her some years ago now, but she was wonderful and a superb card player."

"I'm sorry," Cassandra said, touching the doctor on the arm. He nodded in acknowledgement and then took his place at the table; clearly he did not want to talk about it anymore.

They played and Jane was surprised by how much she enjoyed the game. It was refreshing to think of something other than death and wrongdoing for an hour. She tried to focus entirely on the cards, to stop her mind from wandering, and for a short time it worked. Of course, the spectre of Mr Paulson was still there in the background, but for an hour at least it wasn't all-consuming.

Jane and Dr Histon won easily, and once it was clear there was to be no miraculous last-minute change in fortunes, Cassandra set down her cards for the last time. Mrs Paulson was sitting close by, watching them, but she hadn't said much throughout the game. Now it was over and attention turned back to her, Jane realised she looked very pale.

"Is something amiss, Mrs Paulson?"

"No, nothing. I am tired, that is all. I think I will go upstairs and rest."

"Can I get anything for you?" Cassandra asked.

"No, I will call for Mary. She will stay with me."

"Do you need anything to help you sleep?" Dr Histon enquired, half rising out of his chair.

Mrs Paulson hesitated for a moment and then shook her head. "No, thank you, Doctor. I will be fine. I just need a lie down, that is all."

She left without another word, and for a long moment everyone else was silent.

"What a strain this all is for her," Dr Histon said, shaking his head. "To be trapped here, probably with her husband's murderer and his dead body downstairs in the storeroom. It is unimaginable."

"Outwardly she seems to be coping admirably well, but every so often you can see a flicker of the turmoil she is in."

Cassandra stood as she spoke, tidying away the cards they had been playing with.

"We should press on." Jane stood too, smoothing down her skirt and wondering if after the trip out in the snow the colonel might be too exhausted to insist he accompany her whilst she questioned the servants.

"Good idea, Miss Austen, although you look a little tired yourself. If you would like me to proceed on my own, I would be happy to."

"No," Jane said sharply, standing. "I want to talk to Mrs Brown next. She has been here a long time, and as a senior member of the household servants she must have some insight she can offer us. She would have known Mr Upton the best, surely."

Colonel Rushton didn't argue. Instead, he held an arm out and motioned for Jane to step out of the room before him.

It was quiet downstairs in the kitchen, despite it being close to dinnertime. Pots were bubbling on the stove and a delicious aroma wafted from the oven. Mrs Brown was nowhere to be seen but after a moment Moll, the young kitchen maid, hurried into the cavernous room, head bowed as she carried a bunch of carrots. She almost barrelled into Colonel Rushton, looking up in surprise and exclaiming, before backing away and bouncing off the wooden countertop a few feet away. As always she looked excessively nervous, her eyes darting towards the door as if she were contemplating an escape.

"Good afternoon, Moll," Jane said kindly. "Whatever is cooking smells delicious."

Moll didn't answer; instead, she looked up at Jane with wide eyes.

"Where is Mrs Brown?" Colonel Rushton demanded, seemingly oblivious to the young girl's anxiety.

For a long moment Jane didn't think the kitchen maid was going to answer, but finally she found her voice.

"She's in her room, sir. She's having a rest. She's got one of her heads." Moll spoke in short sentences, blurting out the words as if in a hurry to finish.

It took Jane a moment to decipher the rapid speech, and next to her she felt Colonel Rushton shift impatiently.

"Come and sit down, Moll. We need to talk to you as well."

The maid did not move, her eyes widening even further at the suggestion.

"Sit!" Colonel Rushton barked, making Moll jump and then move to obey immediately.

There were six squat wooden stools tucked in under the long kitchen table and Jane pulled out two for her and the young girl. Colonel Rushton remained standing, looming like a malign presence.

"I don't know anything," Moll said, clutching her hands together to stop them shaking.

Jane reached out and placed a gentle hand on Moll's arm, waiting for the kitchen maid to look up at her before she spoke. "You are not in trouble, Moll, but we do need your help. There are questions that we need to ask everyone. All I need you to do is answer them honestly and openly. Can you do that for me?"

Moll nodded, her bun bobbing up and down at the back of her head.

Jane took a moment to organise the questions in her mind, wanting to start with something straightforward to put the maid at ease. "How long have you worked at Melmont Hall?"

"Two years, Miss."

"How old are you, Moll?"

"Sixteen, Miss."

Jane was surprised; the kitchen maid looked much younger. Her body was hidden under ill-fitting clothes, but her wrists were skinny and her face gaunt.

"Do you enjoy your position here?"

"Yes, Miss. Mrs Brown is kind."

Colonel Rushton let out a faint sigh somewhere behind Jane's right shoulder, and it took all of Jane's willpower not to turn and glare at the man.

"How about Mr Upton? Did you know him well?"

"Not really, Miss. I mean, he was always here, but I took my orders from Mrs Brown. He was a stickler for everything being done right."

"You must have taken your meals all together?"

Moll nodded but didn't elucidate.

"What about Mr Paulson? Did you come into contact with him much?"

Moll bunched her hands in her skirts, pulling at the material as she seemed to consider her answer.

"Good Lord, what is happening here? Those carrots won't chop themselves, Moll. It's only an hour until dinner, you don't have time to be sitting around."

Moll jumped up, but the look she flashed Mrs Brown was filled with gratitude, not guilt.

"I'm sorry, Mrs Brown. I'll get onto the carrots straight away." Without even looking at Jane or Colonel Rushton, Moll scuttled away.

Mrs Brown sat on the stool Moll had just vacated and gave Jane a warm smile.

"She's a sweet girl, obliging, but she doesn't know anything."

Out of the corner of her eye, Jane saw Colonel Rushton draw himself up to his full height. Mrs Brown glanced at him but didn't seem intimidated, bringing her attention back to Jane.

"Can I do anything to help?"

"Are you feeling better, Mrs Brown?"

"Yes, thank you. It is all the stress, I think. I've had a pounding headache since last night, but fifteen minutes in a dark room did me the world of good."

"It must be hard ensuring there is food ready for the guests without a set plan for the days."

Mrs Brown shrugged. "I have been doing this a long time, Miss Austen. It isn't ideal, of course, but I can feed a house full of people for a few days without too much trouble. The problems will start when our stores of fresh food get low, but we have a good few days yet before that happens."

"You've been working here a long time, then?"

"Oh yes. Twenty-two years. I started as a kitchen maid and learnt everything I know from Mrs Fellows, the old cook. When her health forced her to retire, I took over."

"Is that the hope with Moll, that you'll train her up?"

Mrs Brown looked over her shoulder in the direction the young maid had disappeared and smiled fondly.

"She's quiet, a nervous sort. Everyone underestimates her, but she is a hard worker and a quick study."

"Then she is lucky to have you as her mentor."

"We have to look out for one another in a house like this."

"A house like this?" Colonel Rushton said, pulling out another stool and taking a seat. "What do you mean?"

"Oh, nothing bad, sir. Just that in a large household the servants become a sort of family."

"You care for the younger maids, show them the way things are done, give them advice?" Jane enquired.

"Yes, at least some of them. The ones that will take it."

"How about Mr Upton? Did he feel the same?"

Mrs Brown snorted and then looked up quickly, realising she probably shouldn't be so derisive about a dead man.

"No. His loyalty was to Mr Paulson, not the servants."

"I got the impression he liked everything to be done completely right."

"He was fastidious," Mrs Brown said slowly, "although that isn't necessarily a bad thing in a butler. What he lacked was compassion."

"In this matter with Kitty, for example?"

Mrs Brown shifted uncomfortably but nodded. "Exactly. Of course Kitty had to go, Mr Paulson had been clear about that, and Benjamin lost control. Both of their departures were inevitable, but Fran was a good girl. Her only crime was overhearing something she shouldn't have."

"I don't quite understand why she had to leave," Jane said, realising this had been puzzling her for a while. "I know she overheard Kitty talking to Benjamin, but I don't think she was the only one who knew Kitty's secret."

"We didn't know about Kitty and Mr Paulson," Mrs Brown said, averting her eyes for a moment. "Of course, some of us suspected, but that isn't anywhere near the same thing. Fran was an innocent, too idealistic for the real world. She went to Mr Upton to tell him what she had heard and suggested they should tell Mrs Paulson, said it would be the right thing to do."

Jane nodded in understanding. Mr Upton, in a bid to protect his master who commanded all his loyalty, had decided to dismiss Fran rather than have her reveal a secret that in the end Mrs Paulson already knew.

"Luckily the mistress quietly intervened and secured Fran a job with a friend."

"You blame Mr Upton for her dismissal?"

Mrs Brown sighed a world-weary sigh and looked up to meet Jane's eyes. "There should be some loyalty between servants. Now, I'm not saying that bad deeds should go unpunished or crimes covered, but the maids and footmen are so young when they start — of course they are going to do foolish things and trust the wrong people. A good butler would have done as Mr Upton did; a *kind* one would have talked to Fran about why she should keep quiet and made her understand the way of things."

There was something about the cook's phrasing that made Jane pause. *The way of things.*

"You said you suspected what was happening between Kitty and Mr Paulson?"

"Kitty was hardly discreet. She would come from upstairs giggling and blushing, but I did not know it had gone as far as it had."

"Has this sort of thing happened before?"

Mrs Brown looked away sharply and didn't answer for a moment, her fingers moving to the table and clutching the edge of the thick, scarred wood.

"We know it has," Colonel Rushton said, his deep voice surprising Jane. He had remained largely quiet whilst she questioned Mrs Brown, and his interruption now was a shock to both Jane and the cook. "So do not think you need to betray your mistress. We merely want to know if it was common knowledge."

"There is a lot of talk between servants. Whispered rumours, snippets overheard. I think most have heard tales of Mr Paulson becoming entangled with some maid or other." She paused, choosing her words carefully before continuing. "I have worked here twenty-two years, and in that time I have seen a few maids with their heads turned, and it has not been difficult to work out what has happened."

"Any that have confided in you, told you openly?" Jane asked.

"No," Mrs Brown said quickly. "I do not wish to speak ill of the dead, and in many ways Mr Paulson was a fair master, but I want it to be clear he took advantage of those poor girls. Every single one was young and impressionable. He chose carefully and then pressed them into secrecy. Kitty was the most indiscreet. I think the silly girl thought there was something more than a casual affair between them."

Jane leaned back.

"Do you think Kitty could have hated Mr Paulson enough to want him dead?"

"From what I could gather, she still harboured hope she would be the one he upturned his life for." Mrs Paulson shook her head. "Besides, she isn't here, and she's certainly not cunning enough to plan out an elaborate scheme."

"You know the details of Mr Paulson's murder?" Colonel Rushton asked sharply.

Mrs Brown gave him a long, assessing look. "Our master died in horrific circumstances yesterday. No one has talked of anything else since."

"Do you have any idea as to who could be responsible for both deaths?"

"No."

"No insight at all, Mrs Brown?" Colonel Rushton murmured. "I find that hard to believe."

"I do not know the guests, sir," she said abruptly, "but I suggest you look there. Mr Paulson might have had wandering hands, but I cannot see why any servant here would want him dead. Kitty was gone, as was Benjamin, and death only brings uncertainty to those of us at the whims of our employers." She stood, turning as soon as she was on her feet. "Please excuse me. If you want dinner tonight, I need to get on."

"One more question, Mrs Brown," Colonel Rushton called, making the cook pause. "You've been here twenty-two years. Did Mr Paulson ever…" He trailed off, unsure how to finish the question politely.

Jane closed her eyes, feeling acute embarrassment for the cook, but Mrs Brown just turned back and gave Colonel Rushton a hard stare.

"Do you think I would still be here if he had?" She shook her head and walked away.

CHAPTER THIRTEEN

Dinner was a quiet affair. Mrs Paulson opted to eat in her room, as did the Potters. Miss Leveritt was still sitting with her mother and refused any food until the older woman recovered. Only Jane and Cassandra, Dr Histon and Colonel Rushton graced the dining room. The meal was simple, laid out on the sideboard for them to serve themselves, although the footman was hovering nearby in case anyone needed anything.

"Thank goodness there was not any more snow today," Cassandra said as they all sat down. "With luck, the roads will have cleared a little tomorrow and a rider will be able to get through to Lord Hinchbrooke."

Jane saw the exhaustion in her sister's face and knew what a relief it would be for Cassandra to have someone with authority come and take charge. Jane would also welcome the magistrate's arrival, but knew that despite the difficult circumstances she would not be in a hurry to rush home like her sister.

"Who do you still need to talk to?" Dr Histon enquired as he sipped a glass of wine. "I know you have made many enquiries now. You must have spoken to most."

"We have," Colonel Rushton said, leaning back in his chair and putting his fork down for a moment. "Miss Leveritt and her mother, although now is hardly the time. The Potters too, but I doubt they will know anything seeing as they are new to the area. I think we're better off focussing on the suspect we have."

"Mr Peter Jones?"

"That's right. One of the grooms. Shifty fellow. He went on to the village after we found Mrs Leveritt, ostensibly to arrange for a message to get to Lord Hinchbrooke, but he hasn't returned yet. I went to check before dinner."

"His absence doesn't prove his guilt," Jane said, pushing her chicken round her plate.

"If he is innocent, why would he have fled?"

"Fleeing and waiting out the snow in the village tavern are two very different things. Anyway, how do you propose he committed the murders? He is no master magician."

"You are looking at this wrong, Miss Austen," Colonel Rushton said, the hint of condescension in his voice again. "This whole time you have been fixated on the locked door, but I think to solve this crime we need to look at character and motive."

"Even the most suspicious person cannot be convicted without any evidence." Jane knew it wasn't strictly true. The courts were filled with people accused because someone didn't like the way they looked or how they conducted business. Sometimes a few damning statements about a man's character were enough to condemn him.

"We have people who will confirm he was in love with Kitty and as such had a dislike for Mr Paulson."

"He was never seen in the house."

"It is a big house, and I would wager it is not that difficult to slip by unseen."

"Why would he construct such a ruse with the locked door?"

"He may not have. You were the one who suggested Mr Paulson could have locked it himself. Perhaps you are right. Peter Jones goes into the study to confront Mr Paulson about his treatment of Kitty. In his anger he picks up the letter opener and stabs him in the abdomen. Thinking it is but a flesh wound and not wanting the rest of the guests to see his injury and ask the inevitable questions that would follow, Mr Paulson decides to lock the door and see to the wound himself. He sits down in his chair, perhaps preparing to pull out the knife, but then he feels faint and passes out before dying."

As a theory, Jane grudgingly had to concede it did have merit.

"It could have been that the act of starting to pull out the knife was enough to seal his fate," Dr Histon said, gesturing with his own knife. "Here, let me demonstrate."

He took a long piece of carrot and pierced it in the middle with his knife.

"Imagine this is a blood vessel and the knife has gone through the wall. At the moment, with the knife in place, the hole that has been made has largely been plugged. There may be a little seeping of blood, but not large amounts. As soon as you withdraw the knife, it reveals the hole and blood can pump out freely with nothing to stop it."

Jane watched, fascinated by the doctor's demonstration, but beside her she saw Cassandra shift, and when she glanced up her sister had gone pale. Dr Histon must have noticed too.

"Forgive me, Miss Austen, for my terrible lack of manners. Sometimes a doctor gets too caught up in the world of medicine, and we forget it is not normal to discuss these crudities at the dinner table."

"See, Miss Austen, I believe the crime is all but solved. Peter Jones is our culprit."

"And his reason for killing Mr Upton?"

"No doubt the butler saw him somewhere he shouldn't have been. As you say, we are light on evidence and I expect the butler's words were the ones that could condemn him. Mr

Jones knew it to be true and took the opportunity to kill the only possible witness."

Jane leaned back in her chair, wondering if Colonel Rushton was right. It didn't feel satisfactory, but perhaps that was just her animosity towards the man. The whole theory felt off, though, as if someone had forced a piece of jigsaw into a gap not intended for it and then declared the puzzle complete.

"What if Mr Jones returns? How does that affect your theory?"

"He won't," Colonel Rushton said, taking another long gulp of wine. Jane understood the urge to finish with the case, to declare it solved and pack it away ready to hand over to Lord Hinchbrooke when he arrived. It was mentally and emotionally exhausting, always considering people's words and motivations. To be suspicious of everything was more work than people realised.

"You may be right," Jane said quietly, feeling herself deflate a little. If she was completely honest, she didn't believe he was right, but she didn't have the words or energy to argue further right now.

Across the table, the colonel unconsciously puffed out his chest and Jane had to stop herself from rolling her eyes.

"What do you think will happen once the magistrate arrives? Will Lord Hinchbrooke mount a manhunt?" Dr Histon asked, his eyes meeting Jane's. Everyone around the table knew how easy it was for a fit young man to disappear if he was determined enough. Hampshire and the surrounding counties would be dangerous, but if he went to London he could easily get swallowed up by the crowds of people arriving from the countryside each day. A man could stay hidden for a lifetime in the streets of the capital if he was careful not to draw attention to himself. The risks came with homesickness, with those who struggled to leave their old lives behind. One slip, one visit to a family member or friend would be the thing that caught him.

"I expect so, if he is convinced Mr Jones is the perpetrator. He has some resources, although admittedly mainly in the local area."

"Some magistrates would see it enough to name the killer and issue a warrant for their arrest," Dr Histon said.

Jane shook her head. "Not Lord Hinchbrooke. He is a determined man, and he takes his responsibilities seriously."

"Let us hope tomorrow brings clear weather, melted snow and the magistrate, and we can all finally go home," Colonel Rushton said.

"That would be welcome." Cassandra smiled weakly as she pushed her food around her plate. Jane knew her sister was struggling tonight and wished there was something she could do, but the only thing that would make this better would be to get away from Melmont Hall and retreat to the safety of their home, and right now that wasn't possible.

"What about you, Dr Histon? Will you be returning home once the snow clears, or are you staying with Colonel Rushton a little longer?"

"I think after all the excitement of the last few days, I will return home. I had planned to stay a few more days, but I fear that by the time the roads have cleared enough to let us out of here, it will be time for me to journey home."

"Where is it you live, Doctor?"

"Kent, near Deal."

"That is a long way."

"Yes, and the roads that way are poor, unlike the journey from London to here, but there are a few good coaching inns along the route, and I do not plan to travel again any time soon."

"Is your family local to Kent?"

"They were. My father died a few years ago — that is when I retired from the army and took over his practice. Alas, I do not have any close family left alive, but Deal is like any small town; I am surrounded by people who have known me since I was a child. There is comfort in that."

Colonel Rushton reached over and clapped his friend on the back. "It is my turn to make the journey next to visit you. Perhaps in the summer, when there is less chance of this interminable snow or the roads being made impassable by floods."

"Arthur has many great qualities," the doctor said with a smile, "but one shared by many military men is that they do not mind a little travel. What is three days on horseback when you have marched across half a continent on the whim of a general?"

"What indeed?" Colonel Rushton said with a laugh.

They ate a little longer in silence before Cassandra placed down her knife and fork and carefully pushed back her chair.

"I hope you will excuse me. I am exhausted and I think I will retire for the night."

"Of course, Miss Austen."

Jane stood as well and silenced Cassandra's protests with a single look. She too felt a great weariness and thought she might sleep well for once.

"Sleep well, Miss Austen and Miss Jane," Dr Histon said, inclining his head as they turned to leave. Colonel Rushton stood as well, wiping his hands on a napkin and nodding to them before they left the room.

"You do not have to accompany me, Jane. I know the hour is yet early."

"I was sitting at dinner finding it hard to keep my eyes open."

It was the truth. Jane had a sudden desire to be tucked up in bed beside her sister, the door to their room securely locked.

"You do look tired," Cassandra said, regarding her with concern.

They undressed silently, slipping into bed with just a single candle still flickering on the bedside table whilst they settled. Neither of them felt like conversing that night, and after half a minute Cassandra leaned over and blew out the candle, plunging the room into darkness.

Jane woke whilst it was still dark, something rousing her from sleep suddenly. It wasn't a gentle awakening, and she felt a little disorientated at first, her body on edge as she tried to work out what it was that had woken her.

She was about to settle back on the pillows when she heard a noise, a slight scrape followed by hurried whispers in the hallway outside the door. For a moment Jane was frozen with fear, wondering if someone was trying to gain access to her room, but the door handle didn't move and the key was still safely in the lock on the inside. When she was certain it wasn't anyone coming for her, she felt a little more confident and rose from bed, searching for her slippers and pulling on her dressing gown over her nightgown. Even with the extra layer she could feel the chill and wished there was some residual warmth from the fire that had been glowing in the grate when they had retired to bed.

With a trembling hand, she reached out for the key and as quietly as possible turned it in the lock, opening the door quickly.

Out in the hallway there was an exclamation of surprise as Jane came almost face to face with Mr and Mrs Potter. Mr Potter was carrying a small trunk, no doubt containing their clothes for the weekend stay, and it was this that Jane must have heard clattering to the floor.

"What on earth are you doing?"

Neither Mr nor Mrs Potter replied, looking at each other as if willing an answer to appear out of thin air.

"What time is it?" Jane asked, feeling dazed. "And where are you going? Surely you don't mean to leave at this hour."

"We cannot stay here any longer," Mrs Potter said eventually. "Not after everything that has happened. It is bad luck to stay in a house where there has been a murder."

"Undoubtedly," Jane murmured, although she didn't believe for a moment that was the reason they were leaving. "What about the snow?"

"We will take our chances. It has not snowed any more and looks to have melted some."

"You will take your chances in the snow, in the dark?"

Mr Potter moved to take a step forward, but emboldened by the realisation that the other guests were sleeping nearby, liable to be roused by a loud shout, Jane stepped to block his way.

"Move aside, Miss Austen."

"Mrs Leveritt still lies fighting for her life, and you think to repeat her foolhardiness?"

"I will not ask again, Miss Austen. You have no authority to keep us here."

"What could have spooked you so much that you would put the life of your new wife at risk to flee Melmont Hall?"

Mr Potter stepped forward and Jane saw a flash of maniacal desperation in his eyes, but Mrs Potter laid a hand on his arm.

"Rupert, stop."

Jane frowned at the name, feeling something wasn't quite right. She trawled through the hours of interviews and discussions she had conducted and finally settled on the day they had arrived at Melmont Hall. That first evening in the drawing room, before tragedy had struck. Cassandra had been sitting with the Potters, making conversation, and Jane could distinctly remember Mrs Potter leaning in and saying something about her *dear Thomas*. The name had stuck in Jane's mind, for it had momentarily conjured unwanted thoughts of Tom Lefroy.

"Who are you?" she asked, taking a step back.

For a long moment Mr Potter stared at her, and Jane could see he was contemplating his options. They could push past her and take their chances in the snow as they had planned, but now she knew they weren't who they claimed. It would make them the first people to track down on the magistrate's list when he arrived.

Mrs Potter was still holding her husband's arm, exerting a firm pressure, until he yielded and turned to look at her.

"We should explain, Rupert," the young woman said gently. "Then perhaps Miss Austen can put in a good word with the magistrate."

Mr Potter still seemed ready to stalk past Jane, but after a moment he deflated and nodded, smiling sadly at his wife.

Jane felt a frisson of excitement spark within her. Their reason for trying to flee in the middle of the night must be serious indeed. She knew Cassandra would caution her to have a care for her own safety, to consider what this couple might be planning if they were responsible for killing Mr Paulson and Mr Upton. For a moment she hesitated, wondering whether to wake Colonel Rushton or even her sister.

"Shall we find somewhere a little more comfortable?" Mrs Potter suggested, signalling for her husband to take the trunk back to their room. "Fetch a candle whilst you are there, my love."

Mr Potter obeyed, moving slowly, his shoulders slouched.

"Perhaps the drawing room?" Mrs Potter said, stepping towards the stairs without waiting to see if Jane would follow. "I know it will be cold with the fire long out, but at least we can sit comfortably."

Jane followed the young woman to the stairs, hesitating as she heard Mr Potter returning from the bedroom behind her. She tensed, wondering if she was about to feel a firm hand in the middle of her back, pushing her, forcing her to tumble down the stairs, no doubt to land at the bottom with a broken neck or shattered skull.

A push never came and Mr Potter slipped past her to join his wife, clutching her hand as if it were a lifeline.

The drawing room was cold and dark, the thick curtains shutting out any natural light, but Jane was loath to open them and let what residual warmth there was in the room out of the large windows. Instead, Mr Potter fiddled with a tinder box for a minute until he had a spark to light a candle. It didn't do much to illuminate the large room, instead giving the shadows a sinister quality, the flickering light on the Potters' faces making them look more ominous.

"You mustn't think the worst of us, Miss Austen," Mrs Potter said, settling herself on a sofa next to her husband. They held hands and her body was angled towards his, the ultimate show of unity.

"Right now, I cannot help but think the worst. You were planning to flee in the dark and take your chances in the snow. Surely only guilty people would do so. In addition to that is the fact I saw you sneaking out of Mr Paulson's study. It is all highly suspicious."

"It is suspicious, and we do not claim to be completely innocent, but we had nothing to do with the terrible murders."

"Perhaps you had better tell me everything," Jane said, feeling a knot of anticipation in her belly. *This* was the thrill Lord Hinchbrooke spoke about, that wonderful feeling when you had thought everything was tied up in a mass of knots and you suddenly find the end of the thread that would start to unravel it all if you pulled. "Starting with who you are."

"My name is Mr Rupert Williams and this is my wife, Lilith Williams."

The names didn't mean anything to Jane and she sat, waiting for more.

"Mr Paulson was my uncle," Mr Williams said after a quick glance at his wife for reassurance.

"Your uncle?" Jane remembered the information Mary Wright had given her about an estranged nephew who would be the one to inherit Melmont Hall and much of the fortune.

"Yes, he was my mother's brother, although before this weekend I had never met him. When my mother married my father, they moved to America before I was born. From what I can gather there was already a family rift, and she did not keep in contact with her brother. We returned to England when I was seven, but there was no contact with my uncle, no visits, no letters, no presents sent at Christmas."

Jane was astounded and sat back in her chair, trying to work through the implications of the revelation. It certainly gave the young couple a motive for murder. Melmont Hall was in itself a substantial inheritance, and if rumour was to be believed Mr Paulson had been an astute investor, buying land at the right time and managing it carefully. The fortune the nephew would inherit was more than enough to keep a young couple comfortable for their entire lives.

"Mr Paulson did not know who you were, then?"

Mr Williams grimaced and shook his head. "No. I wrote to him soon after Lilith and I were married, requesting a little assistance."

Jane saw how the young man squirmed in his seat at the memory and concluded that it had been financial assistance he had sought.

"You wrote to your uncle?"

"Yes. I wasn't looking for a handout, you understand, but my father died in debt a few years ago and many of his creditors were not the sort of people who were willing to forget a debt owed just because the man they initially lent the money to was dead."

"It was a terrible time," Mrs Williams said, looking away for a moment. "You never knew when the next knock on the door would come. I was forever peeking out from behind the curtains, trying to work out if the caller was friend or foe."

"We struggled along alone for a while, and then I thought I would contact my uncle. I had always been told I was his heir and I thought he might be sympathetic, especially seeing as the debts were not of my making." Mr Williams looked up, meeting Jane's eye. "I thought he might help us. A loan, perhaps, or an introduction to someone who might offer me a position."

"Do you work, Mr Williams?"

"Yes. I am an architect. I love my work, but it does not pay particularly well."

"Mr Paulson was not sympathetic."

"I received no answer to my first letter and thought maybe it had got lost somewhere, so I wrote again. I waited two months for a reply, and when it arrived it was a curt dismissal, informing me he didn't like people who begged for charity."

"I read my husband's letters, Miss Austen. There was no begging, just a truthful outlining of our situation and a request for Mr Paulson's help. Rupert did not ask for a gift of money, not once. He asked for introductions, for connections, the sort of thing that family normally are keen to assist with."

"A week later, another letter arrived stating he was considering changing his will and we would do well not to rely on the promise of that money in the future."

It seemed cruel and unnecessary, but from the picture Jane was building of Mr Paulson he wasn't the most pleasant of men.

"How did that bring you here? Under assumed identities, no less."

"We were desperate," Mr Williams said, closing his eyes. "*I* was desperate. Some of the creditors I had managed to hold off by telling them of my inheritance one day. Some allowed me to negotiate more favourable repayment terms because they knew I had the backing of family money, money that one day would be mine. When Mr Paulson said he might disinherit me…" He trailed off, shaking his head.

"Coming here was my idea. I thought if we found out a little more about him from the locals, it might give us an advantage, allow us to approach him on more favourable terms. Then Mrs Paulson came barrelling into our lives, insisting we come to dinner, offering friendship when we were deceiving her. Rupert wanted to flee, to cut our losses, but I insisted we come. Now we were here, I thought we might try and talk to Mr Paulson, reveal our true identities and throw ourselves on his mercy."

Jane glanced at Mr Williams and saw him bury his head in his hands.

"We should have just gone home," he said quietly. "You have too much faith in people, my darling. That man was never going to react with empathy; he was never going to show us mercy."

They looked hopeless sitting there across from her, and Jane took a moment to contemplate their story. It had the ring of truth about it, silly decisions made in desperation, a foolish plan that had gone wrong.

"Did you talk to him?"

"No, I slipped away and knocked on his study door about half an hour before dinner. I thought he was hardly going to throw out an invited guest of his wife's when there was a house full of people, but the door was locked and there was no answer."

"He was probably already dead," Jane said, thinking about when Mr Paulson had last been seen.

"What a mess this whole affair is. Do you see why we couldn't say anything? We'd lied to our hosts and gained an invitation to the house under false pretences. Even the names we gave were not our own."

"What were you doing coming out of Mr Paulson's study yesterday, Mrs Williams?"

"Searching for Mr Paulson's will." She glanced at her husband and bit her lip. "Rupert told me not to. He said we needed to wait until the snow melted and then leave."

"It was too risky, admitting who we were. I thought if there was an inheritance I could send an agent to claim it, settle my debts and then worry about taking possession of the house at a later date."

Mr Williams sank back into the sofa, seeming to relax a little now his story was told and the truth was out there for Jane to examine. She wanted to believe them; they told their story with fluency and the right amount of self-deprecation and regret for poor decisions. Still, she knew Lord Hinchbrooke would caution her to weigh the tale for merit, to probe at it and see if it withstood questioning.

"The story you told me about taking a letter to Mr Paulson, was that a lie?"

"Yes," Mrs Williams said quietly. "We do know Kitty, she is the sister of the maid we paid to see to our lodgings whilst we stayed in the village. I overheard her saying to her sister that she was going to get someone to take a letter to Mr Paulson, that it would remind him of all they had shared and he would change his mind and help her. We never had possession of such a letter, but I thought it a good excuse when you questioned me, since it must have existed and may have found its way to Mr Paulson."

Jane closed her eyes and allowed her head to fall back against the chair, wondering if this was what Benjamin Grout had been doing when he had been seen sneaking into the study on the morning of the murder.

"What will you do now?" she asked eventually. They could still leave; she had no power to detain them. Their actions had been misguided, suspicious even, but there was no evidence they had harmed Mr Paulson or Mr Upton. If they decided to risk a journey in the snow, there wasn't much she could do.

Mrs Williams shrugged and looked at her husband, watching as he took a moment to review their options.

"Your magistrate is a fair man?"

"He is."

Another pause as Mr Williams looked at his wife.

"I suppose it would be foolish to risk the journey in the snow now, seeing as you know our names. We shall stay until the road clears and speak to your magistrate, throw ourselves upon his mercy."

Jane cleared her throat, nodding. "I'm glad. What about Mrs Paulson? Will you tell her your true identities?"

"No," Mrs Williams said quickly. "At least, not yet, not while she is forced to provide us with hospitality. She has so much to cope with that I do not think this is a purely selfish decision on our part. We will tell her when we no longer have to impose on her, when we can leave."

"I will try not to let anything slip until you have spoken to her yourselves. I think this revelation has to come from you."

"Thank you, Miss Austen."

Jane stood. Mr and Mrs Williams were right; there was no point in them fleeing now, not when she knew their names and their story. She would leave them to discuss their next steps and contemplate herself what this new revelation meant for the tangled web that this affair had become.

CHAPTER FOURTEEN

It was still early, and apart from Mr and Mrs Williams the rest of the household was asleep. Even the servants weren't stirring yet. Jane knew she should return to bed, but if she climbed between the sheets she would toss and turn so much that it would certainly disturb Cassandra.

What she needed was to clear her mind entirely of the murder and all the facts she had accumulated over the last couple of days. At the moment she felt lost in a maze, as if all the conflicting ideas and statements from people had wrapped themselves around her and she couldn't find a way out.

Making her way back to her room in the darkness, she had to move slowly, to feel her way along the hall until she reached the correct door. She wished she had lit a candle of her own from Mr Williams's flickering one, but she didn't want to return downstairs to ask to use his flame. No doubt the couple had their heads bent together, discussing what to do next now their deception had been unveiled.

Jane sat for a long time in the chair by the small writing desk in her and Cassandra's bedroom. Cassandra's breathing was regular and even, and listening to it soothed Jane. She had pulled back the curtain to watch the lightening of the night sky and was mesmerised by the peaceful scene, still covered in snow. It was impossible to tell in this light if it had melted at all, but Jane didn't see any evidence that fresh snow had fallen in the night.

As the light increased a little, she took a piece of paper from the desk and set up her pen and ink, arranging the little table as she did at home, liking the familiarity this small act brought.

Then she wrote, the pen scratching across the paper at great speed. Since the matter with Tom Lefroy she hadn't written much, or at least not much of use. She'd spent hours in her room, at her desk, toying with sentences, trying to get them to sound right, but she had found it difficult to concentrate. Everything she wrote she was dissatisfied with, everything was just a little *off*, but suddenly she felt a great calm descend over her, a clarity she hadn't had for weeks.

In her manuscript she had struggled with the circumstances of Elinor and Marianne's downturn of luck, flipping from the death of a family member to a scandal that forced the two sisters out of society. These last few days had got her thinking about inheritance. Here Mrs Paulson would be forced out of the home she had lovingly run for the last thirty years to make way for a young couple her husband had never met. She was provided for, but it would not be to the same degree of luxury she was used to. It felt exquisitely unfair that she could devote her life to marriage, put up with so much from her husband, and still be treated in this way on his death.

Jane played with different scenarios, her pen scratching furiously across the paper. She thought of all the ways a woman could be wronged on the death of her spouse or her father. She thought of the women she had known who had acquired unwanted guardians, or had been forced to accede to a strange man's wishes; she thought of young women at the mercy of *the heir*, unsure if they would receive a small stipend, let alone a dowry. The death of the head of a household was a far-reaching thing indeed.

It was getting light by the time Jane set down her pen, her fingers stained with ink and the paper now filled with tiny writing. She had let the words flow, allowed idea after idea to be committed to paper, but finally she had settled on one.

Sitting back with a small smile, she felt the first flicker of satisfaction she had had in a long time. Perhaps Cassandra had been right; perhaps she had needed to come away, to clear her head of all that had happened over the festive period. A murder wasn't the most conventional way to do it, but it certainly helped to put all other woes into perspective.

As she sat back, looking out of the window, she realised how cold she had become. Her feet were stiff, as if she had slipped them into a bucket of ice.

She had two options. Either she could slip back into bed beside Cassandra, stealing some of her sister's warmth, or she could dress, add another couple of layers and hope eventually she would shed the chill she felt.

It was too difficult to ignore the warmth of the bed, so she shed her dressing gown and climbed in beside her sister, and for the first time in three days she allowed herself to relax.

"Miss Austen?" The gentle voice was accompanied by a light hand on her shoulder. "I'm sorry to wake you, Miss Austen."

Jane stirred groggily, taking a moment to realise where she was and what was happening.

The room was light now, the sun shining in through the open curtains, illuminating a rectangular patch on the floor. Charlotte was standing over her, looking worried and almost hopping from foot to foot. Jane hastened to sit up and shake off the sleep that still clung to her.

"Is something amiss, Charlotte?" she asked with a sinking feeling. Surely no one else could be dead. Two deaths were far too many; she would feel responsible if there was a third purely because she had taken too long to unmask the killer. "Is someone dead?"

"No, Miss, but Gabriel Jones is downstairs and he's in a state, Miss. His brother didn't return home yesterday after walking to the village."

"Surely he has just stayed somewhere. At the inn, perhaps, or with a friend?"

"That's the thing Miss, Gabriel assumed so, but the snow has cleared quite a lot this morning, so he walked into the village to find Peter and he wasn't there."

Jane felt her heart sink. She hadn't wanted to believe Colonel Rushton's assertation that the groom was guilty. She had liked the brothers, cloistered away as they were in their cottage, and had hoped for another explanation, but if he had disappeared there had to be a reason for it, and the only one she could see was guilt.

"I will get dressed, Charlotte, and come downstairs to see Mr Jones."

"Thank you, Miss. I'm sorry for waking you, but I knew you would sort everything out. Shall I help you dress?"

"That would be very helpful, Charlotte, thank you."

Jane was ready in a few minutes, smoothing her hair down before she straightened the sheets over her still sleeping sister. She followed Charlotte out of the bedroom and downstairs, hearing the house stirring around her. The servants may have been up a while, but most of the guests were likely still tucked in their beds.

They descended the stairs to the main hall and then continued on down to the kitchens, where Mrs Brown was just handing over a cup of tea to Gabriel Jones. She gave Jane an assessing look and then, deciding she was friend not foe, passed her a cup of tea as well.

"To warm your bones, Miss. The house still has not heated up yet."

"Thank you, Mrs Brown."

"Why don't you use my sitting room to talk? It is private there, away from the bustle of the kitchen." The cook made the offer with a kind smile at the groom, and Gabriel nodded morosely.

The cook's rooms were comfortable and spacious. There was a large sitting room with two high-backed chairs arranged to face the fire as well as a small table with a single chair. A door led off this room into what Jane presumed was a bedroom, but it was completely shut, allowing no glimpse of the room beyond.

"I'm worried about my brother, Miss Austen," Gabriel said without any preamble.

"He hasn't returned home?"

"No, but that in itself would not concern me. Peter has friends in the village. We have lived in the area since we were young."

"What has given you cause for concern, Mr Jones?"

"The snow has melted somewhat this morning. I was up early seeing to the horses and I realised it would be relatively easy walk into the village today. Once I finished my duties, I thought I would walk there and bring Peter home with me." He paused, running a hand through his hair. "When I reached The Black Horse, the innkeeper told me Peter had been there but he'd left early that morning. He had taken a horse and ridden off before sunrise, even though the roads were far too treacherous on horseback."

"Did the innkeeper know where your brother was planning to go?"

"No." Gabriel glanced up, his shoulders still hunched. "I know my brother better than I know myself, Miss Austen. He makes a bad impression sometimes, I am aware of that, but he is a good man. He is not a murderer."

Jane nodded without speaking. Gabriel was an astute man. He had come to the conclusion that his brother's disappearance would cast him in a guilty light and was here ostensibly to throw them both on her mercy.

"Why would he flee if he was innocent?"

"We do not know that he has fled," Gabriel said slowly, grimacing and shaking his head as if he knew that argument did not hold much sway. "He has probably gone to visit someone I do not know about, a friend or perhaps someone he admires. He does not tell me everything."

"He may have ridden for the magistrate," Jane said, watching Gabriel's reaction to the suggestion.

"Perhaps," he said, seeming to sag even more in his chair. Jane could see he didn't believe Peter was currently battling the elements to be the hero of the day, putting himself in peril to fetch the magistrate.

"Why did you come in to tell me this, Mr Jones?" Jane said quietly. "You are an intelligent man. You know how this looks."

"I do. That is why I wanted to be the one to tell you. Peter has strong opinions; he makes enemies easily. There will be some who are eager to tell you he has left and should be condemned for it."

"You ask me to keep an open mind."

"I do."

"I can do that, Mr Jones." Jane paused, wondering whether to say any more. She wanted to probe this man's relationship with his brother, to work out how far he would go to protect him, but she saw the ashen face and concerned frown and knew she had to tread carefully.

"The good news is a boy from the village will ride to Lord Hinchbrooke as soon as he judges the road to be clear. His name is Christopher Cunningham, and he works for the local tailor. He often will ride long distances with a delivery, even in poor conditions, so he is well suited to the task. His master was happy to spare him as a favour to Mrs Paulson; he told me he has done much business with the house over the years."

"I am glad," Jane said, wondering if the magistrate would arrive later that day. She prayed so but held out little hope, even if the sun continued to melt the rest of the snow. It was fifteen miles to Lord Hinchbrooke's estate. It would take a messenger hours to cover that distance if the route was not clear. Then Lord Hinchbrooke would have to organise his household for his absence and pack for a few days away from home. She knew on his good days he was capable of riding fifteen miles, but if his limbs were feeling particularly stiff or his hands were shaking badly, he could be forced to wait for the roads to clear enough to allow a carriage to pass. It was far too optimistic to think he might arrive today. "You said sometimes people judged your brother harshly, Mr Jones," Jane went on. "Was there an incident in particular you had in mind?"

Gabriel looked surprised by the question. He had placed his hands on the table as if about to get up and take his leave, but he dutifully settled back into his chair and considered his answer.

"There was a brawl a few months back. Peter and I are very much separate to the household servants. It suits us better that way. We are careful not to take advantage of our situation, but we used to be afforded a modicum of freedom once our duties were done. One or other of us used to visit the village tavern on occasion, play a few rounds of cards or dice."

Jane nodded, knowing this probably wasn't strictly allowed but as long as the brothers were discreet, there would be no one checking up on them.

"There was an argument. Peter was convinced his opponent was cheating and called him out. His opponent did not take kindly to the accusation and thumped Peter. Naturally my brother sought to defend himself and hit the other man. Peter is a big lad, and I think he did more damage than he was expecting. The other man was knocked unconscious for a few minutes, but ultimately he did recover."

Jane raised her eyebrows, imagining the force of a punch from the large man.

"The other patrons of the inn hustled Peter home and saw to it he didn't find any more trouble along the way, and at first it seemed like he had come away unscathed by the whole thing. The other man recovered, and although I doubt he will ever walk past Peter without hurling an insult, he didn't seem keen for any immediate retribution." Gabriel shook his head and sighed, rubbing a hand across his eyes. "Then Mr Upton got wind of the whole thing. Called both of us in to see him like some puffed-up official. He spent twenty minutes lecturing us on conduct and responsibility, holding the threat of losing our jobs over us. In the end he said he had conversed with Mr Paulson and they had agreed to give us one last chance, but that he would be watching out for any misstep." He let out a short, barking laugh that had no humour in it. "He said he had his spies and he would be constantly watching us, waiting for us to fail."

"But you didn't?"

"No. We were careful to do everything properly, and sometimes I did feel the old man's eyes on me, willing me to do something wrong. I am sure he had allies in this house, those he set to watch us. It is them I fear would poison your thoughts against my brother."

"Now you do not need to worry what the butler might do, not now he has been killed."

Gabriel's jaw set and he shook his head. "No one should suffer a violent death, but I find myself unable to mourn that man. He was cold and unfeeling. I never liked Kitty, but the way Mr Upton marched her off the estate, all the time with that smirk on his face, was terrible. You could tell he took pleasure from her distress."

"Surely he was just a man carrying out his master's orders?"

"No," Gabriel said sharply. "There are ways to do things, even if you must follow orders. There was no need to make Kitty suffer in that way, no need to humiliate her alongside dashing all her ridiculous hopes and dreams. Mr Paulson may have given the instruction to get rid of Kitty, but the manner in which it was done, that was all Mr Upton."

It matched what Jane had seen of the butler before he was killed. He had been officious, obstructive, and harsh to the servants.

"I have said more than I should, but I wanted to be the one to tell you, to explain. I expect Peter has become distracted and used the chaos to quit the estate for a while, but please judge him as imprudent, not malicious. He may be a foolish young man, but he is not a murderer." Gabriel stood and bowed his head and then turned to leave.

"Thank you for ensuring someone will ride for Lord Hinchbrooke today when the roads clear," Jane called after him. Gabriel raised a hand in acknowledgement and then disappeared out the door.

For a long while Jane did not move, contemplating this new information. She examined the idea of Peter Jones as the murderer from every angle and was disappointed to find he was a perfectly rational suspect. He had a motive to kill Mr Paulson, with his infatuation with Kitty and the older man's treatment of the woman he loved. There was a chance he could have snuck into the study unseen to commit the murder, and he had ample motive for killing Mr Upton.

For many magistrates it would be enough to haul the young groom off to jail and see if a confession could be extracted with the promise of more comfortable conditions. Jane knew Lord Hinchbrooke was one of the few magistrates who was actually interested in justice. Most saw the post as an inconvenience when it required them to do something, preferring to preside over cases at the courts that were neatly presented, often siding with popular opinion rather than examining the cases too thoroughly.

Luckily for Peter Jones, Lord Hinchbrooke was much more exhaustive in his methods and would not take the groom into custody simply for having a motive and disappearing for a day or two. If he didn't reappear, that, of course, would be a different matter.

Jane stood and left the cook's room, wandering back through the kitchen. It was bustling at this time in the morning, with Mrs Brown and Moll busy preparing breakfast and Fred and Charlotte coming and going to take various plates upstairs and bring the used cutlery and dishes back down.

"Miss Leveritt is asking for a tray for her mother," Charlotte said as she picked up a steaming plate of bacon. Jane felt her mouth watering and had the urge to take the plate from the maid, find herself a quiet spot in the kitchen and eat.

"I'll get to it straight away. Poor woman must be ravenous after being out in the snow all that time yesterday," Mrs Brown said, taking a tray and starting to make it up.

"Would you like me to take it up to her, Mrs Brown?" Jane asked over the noise of the kitchen. "I was planning on going to check how she is feeling anyway, so it would be no trouble."

"That would be kind, Miss Austen. We are a little run off our feet, as you can see, with so few staff and everyone wanting different things."

Jane waited for the tray to be ready and then picked it up, moving slowly so she wouldn't spill anything. She went up the servants' stairs, knowing it was the most direct route to the Leveritts' room on the first floor.

As she knocked on the door she heard movement from within and quiet voices before Miss Leveritt appeared, looking tired but not unhappy. It must have been a relief for the young woman to have her mother awake and recovering.

"Miss Austen, they have you doing the servants' work now?"

"I volunteered to bring up the tray. I wished to enquire how your mother is this morning and thought it the perfect opportunity."

"Miss Austen is at the door, Mother. Are you feeling up to her visit?" Miss Leveritt called back over her shoulder.

"Yes, send her in."

Jane entered, still carrying the tray. She set it down on the little table in front of the window. The room was gloomy with the curtains not yet drawn back, and the only light came through the cracks where the fabric didn't quite meet.

As Jane's eyes adjusted she saw Mrs Leveritt propped up in bed, the covers neatly folded back and her pillows lovingly plumped. She looked rested and rosy-cheeked, with no obvious ill effects from her disastrous trip out in the snow the day before. Her daughter, by contrast, looked exhausted, and Jane could tell she had been sitting up all night, seeing to her mother's every request. She wondered what it must be like, to live as a family of two. Her own family was smaller now, at least the core of it. Her brothers had struck out to find their own way in the world, and now it was normally only her and Cassandra at home with her parents, although often there would be someone visiting, someone making the house feel full of life. That was the way Jane imagined the rectory when she pictured it in her mind, bustling with her siblings, never quiet. The idea of being just a mother and a daughter was foreign to her, and she could imagine it would get very claustrophobic, always being reliant on one another.

"Come closer, my dear. It is kind of you to check on me. Annabelle, get Miss Austen a chair."

"Yes, Mother," Miss Leveritt said, lifting one of the upright chairs over to the side of the bed.

Jane perched on the edge, wondering if they were going to sit in the darkness.

"Dr Histon prescribed complete rest," Mrs Leveritt said, seeming to read Jane's thoughts. "He said to keep the room dark and sleep as much as I could to allow my body to recuperate. My darling Annabelle has been wonderful, tending to me. I am fortunate to have such a devoted daughter."

"How are you feeling, Mrs Leveritt?"

"Sore. My ankle hurts if I move it. It has ballooned to quite a size, but all my muscles ache too. Dr Histon tells me that is normal after being out in the snow for so long. He said I was lucky I did not suffer any more ill effects."

"We have all been very worried about you."

Jane couldn't see every expression, but she thought the older woman preened at that and realised she was enjoying being the centre of attention. Jane thought back to Miss Leveritt's revelation that Mrs Paulson had planned to sponsor her for the season with the hope of attracting a wealthy and influential husband. She wondered how much the daughter wanted this. No doubt Miss Leveritt was keen to secure an offer of marriage, to find someone who would take care of herself and her mother financially, but Jane suspected it was Mrs Leveritt who had set her sights so high for her daughter, eschewing the suit of respectable but middle-class professionals for a chance at someone titled and wealthy.

"It was ever so valiant, all the gentlemen rushing out like that to save me," Mrs Leveritt said with a little smile. "I thought myself abandoned, close to death, and then suddenly strong arms lifted me up."

"Dr Histon said she was lucky to not lose any fingers or toes. Her boots were soaked through and her hands icy when she first was brought back in."

"It took me so long to warm up. I was shivering for hours. It is only this morning I feel more like my normal self."

"You must stay in bed, though, Mama."

Jane stood up. "I will leave you to rest. I only came to enquire as to how you were. I wish you a quick recovery, and please let me know if there is anything I can do."

"Farewell, Miss Austen."

Miss Leveritt walked with Jane to the door, looking sombre as Jane paused on the threshold, turning back and lowering her voice.

"How are you, Miss Leveritt? You too must be exhausted from your trip out yesterday, and I fear you have sat up all night tending to your mother."

"I do feel a little weary, Miss Austen, and I long to be away from here in my own bed. I wonder if Lord Hinchbrooke will allow us to go as soon as the snow has cleared and Mama is well enough to travel."

"I expect so. You are local and he knows where to find you if he needs to talk to you again. There is no benefit in keeping you all cooped up here." *Quite the opposite*, Jane thought. Although she expected he would ask a few people to stay whilst he established the facts of the case, most people were local and he could hardly detain them without good cause. Jane took a step out of the room and lowered her voice so Mrs Leveritt would not be able to hear. "I am compiling my notes to help Lord Hinchbrooke when he does arrive, and I am trying to put together a timeline of where everyone was when the murders were committed. We think Mr Paulson was likely killed between six and half past six. Mr Upton was found outside at a little after half past ten the following morning, so his death must have occurred in the hour before then."

"You want to know where I was?"

"And your mother."

Miss Leveritt looked a little surprised but rallied quickly, giving a sharp nod and then looking off into the distance for a moment.

"I was in the drawing room, playing the pianoforte. I think we came down from our room just before six because I heard the hour strike as we entered the drawing room."

"Your mother was with you?"

"Yes."

"Did either of you leave in that half an hour?"

"No," Miss Leveritt said and then corrected herself quickly. "Actually, yes. I was cold, so my mother went to get my shawl from upstairs. She was only gone for a few minutes, though."

"What time was this?"

Miss Leveritt frowned as if she couldn't understand Jane's persistence.

"She may have seen something she didn't realise was relevant," Jane said with a soft, reassuring smile.

"Perhaps twenty past the hour. I am not sure entirely. I spoke with Dr Histon and Colonel Rushton for a while, and then Mama suggested I take my place at the pianoforte. It was whilst I was playing the first piece that I felt cold, and she offered to get the shawl so I wouldn't have to interrupt my performance."

"Thank you Miss Leveritt. How about around the time of Mr Upton's death?"

"I had breakfast with my mother and then you and I conversed, I think. After that I spent some time in my room alone."

Leaving the Leveritts to their peace, Jane wandered back along the upstairs hallway to the main staircase. The smell of breakfast from the kitchen was too enticing to ignore, and she made her way downstairs to the dining room.

Colonel Rushton was inside, standing by the window and looking out at the snow. Cassandra was sitting at the table and gave her sister a warm smile as she entered, reaching out her hand for Jane's.

"I hear the groom still isn't back. The servants are saying he's fled," Colonel Rushton said as he noticed Jane. "What do you say, Miss Austen? Surely that must be an end to it."

"We do not know he has run away," Jane said quietly, ignoring the self-satisfaction Colonel Rushton was trying, and failing, to hide.

"Come now, Miss Austen, you cannot deny there is much to condemn him."

"Tell me, Colonel Rushton, how did Mr Jones commit the crime? How did he stab Mr Paulson and leave the study, with every door and window locked from the inside?"

"As I said yesterday, Mr Paulson must have locked it himself, perhaps unaware of how badly he'd been injured."

"If Mr Jones had stabbed him, why would Mr Paulson not cry out? There were plenty of people who could have rushed to his aid and detained the groom. Why would he let the man walk away with no repercussions and then lock himself in his room to die?"

"You are picking at a scab that does not need to be examined, Miss Austen. I understand you wanted to be the one to solve this crime, but sometimes things do not go our way. When the magistrate arrives, *I* will lay out the evidence we have and he will see it is the only sensible theory."

Jane sank into a seat beside Cassandra and considered telling Colonel Rushton about Mr and Mrs Williams and their deception, but she quickly decided against it.

"Please do," Jane said, taking a slice of toast and starting to spread the butter across it more violently than she meant to. Cassandra laid a hand on hers and took the knife from her before she could butcher the entire slice. "I am sure Lord Hinchbrooke will be delighted to hear your theory."

"I am glad the matter is closed. Now, we simply have to wait for the roads to be clear enough for a rider to get through," Colonel Rushton said, taking a seat at the table. "At least now we know there is no longer a murderer in our midst."

Jane's reply was cut short by a scream so loud and desperate that for a moment it sounded like the world itself was coming to an end.

CHAPTER FIFTEEN

Jane ran, pushing past the colonel in her haste to get to where the scream came from. In her mind, she was ticking off people she knew were unlikely to be involved. She knew Cassandra and Colonel Rushton were safe, and she had just been with the Leveritts and they both seemed in good health. Mrs Brown, Moll, Charlotte and Fred had all been bustling about in the kitchen together whilst breakfast was being prepared, and Gabriel Jones had no doubt left for his duties in the stables or the warmth of his little cottage.

She took the stairs two at a time, gathering her skirts in one hand and lifting them higher than her mother would have approved of. Behind her there were footsteps as the rest of the house responded to the scream.

Jane felt an icy chill settle over her as she saw Mary Wright backing out of Mrs Paulson's room. As she watched, all the colour drained from the maid's face and she stumbled, clutching at the wall.

Lunging forward, Jane managed to catch Mary under the arms, but the woman was tall and well built, whereas Jane was relatively petite. Feeling her knees begin to buckle, Jane looked around wildly, thankful when Dr Histon stepped in and took much of the maid's weight, lowering her gently to the ground.

"Miss Wright," he said, shaking her shoulder and then looking up. "She has fainted. Someone ask the cook for smelling salts."

Cassandra turned and made her way back downstairs, no doubt pleased to distance herself from whatever had elicited such a reaction from the normally stoical lady's maid.

Jane stood, taking a deep breath to steel herself. Her hands were shaking and she wished her heart would stop pounding, but the anticipation of what she would find was keeping her whole body on edge.

The room was dark with the curtains still drawn together, but there was just enough light to make out the scene in the room.

Mrs Paulson lay on the bed, sheets pulled up to her chin, looking at first glance as though she were sleeping peacefully. Her eyes were closed and her hands folded on top of the bedcovers. It was only as Jane stepped closer that she noted the waxy sheen to her skin and the unnatural pallor in her cheeks. Her mouth was slightly open, and as Jane leaned closer she had horrible visions of the woman suddenly exhaling and reaching up to clutch at her.

There was no movement, no sudden breath. When Jane reached out and placed a tentative hand on hers, the body was stiff and cool despite the bedcovers.

Feeling a presence behind her, she turned to see Colonel Rushton and quickly moved to urge him out of the room. It might have been a long time since he and Mrs Paulson had been close, but there would have been a lingering affection. He shouldn't have to see someone he had once cared for deeply like this.

"No," he whispered, unable to tear his eyes from the unmoving form of Mrs Paulson in the bed.

"Leave, Colonel," Jane said, more harshly than she had intended. With an effort, she softened her tone. "You do not need to see this."

For a long moment he did not stir, and then with a curt nod he spun and left the room, hurrying away down the corridor.

It was a few seconds before anyone else entered the room, and Jane was pleased to see it was the calm Dr Histon. She stepped back, allowing him to get closer to the bed.

"Open the curtains, please, Miss Austen," he said. She remembered his hesitation the first time she had asked him to examine a dead body just a few days ago. He had performed admirably given the circumstances, but now he stepped up without prompting and allowed his eyes to roam expertly over the late Mrs Paulson. First he checked her pulse, standing with his fingers on her wrist, and then he gently folded back the bedcovers.

"There is no sign of violence," he said eventually. "She is cooling rapidly, even tucked up under the sheets and blankets, so I think she most likely passed away in the earlier part of the night."

Jane's eyes roamed around the room and landed on a cup and the little brown bottle beside the bed. Reaching out, she picked it up and read the label.

"Laudanum."

Dr Histon turned to Jane with a frown. "Let me see."

She handed the bottle over and watched as he popped out the stopper and peered inside. His reaction was subtle but heartbreaking to watch. Dr Histon closed his eyes and inhaled sharply. His hand was shaking as he placed the bottle on the bedside table.

"I measured Mrs Paulson a dose the night before last to help her sleep. There was almost a full bottle at the time. The bottle is now empty."

"Empty? How many doses would that be?"

Dr Histon hesitated, squinting at the little bottle. "Fifteen, perhaps twenty."

Jane felt a queasiness come over her and wondered if Mrs Paulson had taken the rest of the bottle of laudanum herself. It seemed unlikely, going against everything she knew about the woman. Certainly she was in mourning and the next few months would be a time of change, but the marriage had hardly been a happy one, and although she may have had to vacate Melmont Hall, she would not be destitute. It made no sense.

"Do you think she took it on purpose?" Jane asked quietly.

"Perhaps. I can hardly see it would have been an accident. Patients sometimes take double the recommended dose or even triple, but they know not to take the whole bottle. Even those in pain are not foolish enough to do that."

"So either she took the laudanum with the intention of killing herself, or someone else poisoned her with it."

"Yes." He sounded unsure. "Have you ever taken laudanum, Miss Austen?"

Jane grimaced, remembering the horrible light-headed sensation she had experienced on the couple of occasions she had required the drug.

"It has a very distinctive taste and odour. It is not something you can mix into a cup of tea and induce someone to drink without their knowledge, at least not a full bottle."

Hating the implication, Jane closed her eyes for a moment. Her mother would be devastated at the loss of her friend. Any death was terrible, but death by suicide was a particular tragedy.

"Mrs Paulson." Mary's voice came from the hallway, and Jane felt a pang of sympathy for the devoted lady's maid.

"I must see to the living, Miss Austen," said Dr Histon. "Will you excuse me for a moment?"

Jane nodded, distracted, unable to tear her eyes away from the little bottle on the bedside table. How could such a small amount of innocuous-looking liquid cause so much devastation?

Feeling suddenly light-headed Jane took a few steps back, her hand finding the back of the chair tucked in under the writing desk. She pulled it out and sank down into it, hanging her head low and trying to push away the darkness that threatened to consume her.

"Jane." Cassandra's voice sounded like it was coming from a long way away, and she was surprised when her sister gently placed a hand on her shoulder. "Come, let us get you out of here."

"No," Jane said, feeling the tears begin to fall from her eyes. They dripped onto her dress, darkening the fabric.

"Come, Jane, you've had a shock. Everything will still be here in half an hour. You must look after yourself."

Shaking her head Jane tried to stand, clutching at the edge of the desk as the world swayed around her. Reluctantly she allowed Cassandra to take her arm and guide her towards the door.

"Wait," Jane said, turning back towards the desk. A scrap of paper had caught her eye, and now she could not leave without making sure what she was seeing.

Sitting in the middle of the desk, the white of the paper contrasting against the dark mahogany of the wood, was a small scrap torn from a larger sheet. It was written in a fancy hand, neat and precise, the blue ink a little faded against the background of the paper.

I am sorry. That was all it said. No other explanation, no other claim, no confession. Jane picked it up, her vision blurring for a minute and the letters mixing into one before she blinked and the words formed again.

"What do you mean?" she whispered.

Jane closed her eyes and remembered Mrs Paulson from the day before. She had been shaky in the morning, still in shock, but had emerged with an air of fortitude about her in the afternoon. Jane wouldn't go so far as to say she enjoyed watching her guests play cards, but she certainly didn't seem as if she were contemplating suicide.

Perhaps it had been a last foray into the world, a test to see if she could truly leave it all behind.

"Why would she do this?" Jane said, leaning towards her sister as Cassandra's arms wrapped around her.

"Don't think of it right now," Cassandra said, taking the piece of paper from Jane's hands and placing it back on the table. Slowly but firmly, she guided Jane from the room.

"How many more are going to die before this damn snow melts?" Jane said, surprised by the vehemence in her words. She had the urge to flee, to throw open the front door and escape from this house of death.

In the hall Mary Wright was sitting propped up against the wall, looking as pale and drained as Jane felt. Her eyes were red-rimmed and her tears were still flowing freely onto her cheeks.

"Tell me it isn't true, Miss Austen," Mary said, looking up at her with pleading eyes.

It struck Jane that although there had been two other deaths this weekend, this was the first true display of grief she had seen. Mrs Paulson had been shocked and unsettled by her husband's death, but she hadn't seemed to grieve him.

"I'm sorry," Jane said, feeling her legs wobble.

"No," Mary whispered, the anguish filling that single word as fully as if it had been a complete eulogy.

Cassandra began to lead Jane away, looking back over her shoulder to where Mrs Brown was trying to help Mary up.

"Get her somewhere comfortable, Mrs Brown, and give her a tot of brandy for the shock."

"Yes, Miss."

Everyone else was gathering downstairs. The servants were huddled in the entrance hall, looking up the stairs, but none of them were venturing up. Mr and Mrs Williams were huddled together in the drawing room, heads bent, with serious expressions on their faces. Miss Leveritt was standing by the fireplace, shaking her head and murmuring to herself. Dr Histon followed Jane and Cassandra into the room, flopping down into a chair and burying his head in his hands.

Jane sank down into a chair and felt Cassandra sit beside her, and for a long while everyone in the room was silent. Mrs Paulson was the reason they were all here, the social glue that held everyone together. She had been bright and vibrant and in the prime of her life. Jane felt the lump in her throat as she thought of all the times she had listened to her mother exchange news with Mrs Paulson over a cup of tea, both women eager to hear of what was going on in the little corner of Hampshire they occupied. She thought of all the times the older woman had turned to Jane and enquired about her health and her happiness. Jane felt her shoulders sag and the tears began to flow from her eyes again.

There were three loud thumps on the door that made everyone look up, startled by the interruption to their grief. For a long time no one moved and there was silence from the hallway, but eventually one of the servants must have roused themselves enough to get to the door.

There were low voices outside the drawing room, too quiet for Jane to hear what they were saying. She didn't make much effort to distinguish who it was, thinking perhaps it was Gabriel Jones with news from the village, or perhaps a messenger come from the inn to let them know someone had been able to set off on the road to fetch Lord Hinchbrooke.

The door to the drawing room opened and Jane almost cried out with relief when the solid form of the magistrate walked through the door.

"Miss Austen," he said softly, "I came as soon as I could."

"How did you know to come? How have you got here so quickly?" Jane said.

"Mr Jones set out from the village at first light," Lord Hinchbrooke said. "It took him three hours to reach me. He must have ridden hard, for the roads are still dangerous. When I heard what had occurred, I knew I had to come at once."

"You rode in the snow?"

He smiled at her indulgently. "I couldn't leave you here on your own to deal with this. As capable as I know you are, sometimes these matters need two heads rather than one."

Jane leaned in, knowing all eyes and ears were on them, lowering her voice as much as possible. "I have never been so glad to see anyone in my entire life."

"I am flattered, Miss Austen. Let me introduce myself, and then we should find somewhere quiet to talk. I am sure you have much to tell me."

Lord Hinchbrooke turned to the room and gave everyone a warm smile.

"Ladies and gentlemen, I am Lord Hinchbrooke, the local magistrate. I was informed this morning of the terrible events that happened here a few days ago, and I want to assure you that together we will find out exactly what happened."

"There has been another death," Jane murmured in his ear.

She saw his eyes widen and he took a moment to consider the implications.

"Mrs Paulson, our hostess."

"I am sorry to hear that. I knew Mrs Paulson; she was a woman of great warmth and charity."

Lord Hinchbrooke surveyed the room for a moment, and Jane could see he was committing each face to memory so that when she told him about each of them he would know who to match with the description.

"Please excuse me. It seems there is much to hear about. I will speak to each of you in turn shortly."

CHAPTER SIXTEEN

They were ensconced in a cosy room at the back of the house with lovely views over the formal gardens. Lord Hinchbrooke had asked Charlotte to light the fire and he had pulled two armchairs close to the blaze.

Jane felt like a great weight had been lifted from her shoulders now that Lord Hinchbrooke was here. She could question people and piece together evidence, but without the magistrate she had no authority to go any further.

From under her dark eyelashes she watched him. He'd managed to conceal the stiffness of his movements in the drawing room, but she could see the toll the dash across the county in dangerous conditions had taken on him. Lord Hinchbrooke suffered from a shaking palsy. His hands trembled uncontrollably at times, and he had confided to Jane that his doctors had told him it was likely to get worse. Alongside that there was the stiffness, muscles not responding to commands, making it difficult sometimes for him to ride or climb the stairs or even use a pen. He hid it well, found ways to compensate for his difficulties, but Jane knew the future weighed on him heavily. Soon he would not be able to conduct his duties as magistrate, at least not in the active way he had done so for the last few years. He might be reduced to sitting at the bench during trials, giving his verdicts without becoming actively involved in the investigation before that. Then one day, even that would become too difficult.

"Tell me everything, Miss Austen."

Jane closed her eyes, wanting to collect her thoughts before she launched into a recital of everything that had occurred. She didn't want to miss anything out, and she also knew this was a wonderful opportunity to get the facts straight in her own mind.

"My mother received an invitation for the house party two weeks ago," Jane said slowly, stretching her feet out towards the fire. She had kicked off her shoes and the heat felt wonderful on her toes. "I expect it was the same for the rest of the guests. We arrived in the snow. There was a layer already settled, but it came down heavily in the hour after we arrived but before dinner."

"Who was in attendance?"

"Cassandra and I were the last to arrive. Mrs Paulson greeted us and took us upstairs to freshen up. When we came downstairs again, Mrs Paulson and the rest of the guests were in the drawing room." Jane started to count people off on her fingers. "There is Mrs Leveritt and her daughter Miss Annabelle Leveritt. They were friends of Mrs Paulson, and there was a hope Mrs Paulson might sponsor Miss Leveritt for a season in London."

"A good friendship, then. A London season is no small undertaking, and expensive too."

"Indeed. There is also a young married couple; they were introduced as Mr and Mrs Potter, but I have since discovered they are in fact Mr and Mrs Williams."

"How intriguing. What was their reason for hiding their true identities?"

"Mr Williams is Mr Paulson's heir, although they have never met. He seems to be in quite a lot of debt, apparently inherited from his father. He had contacted Mr Paulson asking for help, and the old man had brushed him off and even threatened him with disinheritance. The Williamses say they came to

202

Hampshire to learn a little more about Mr Paulson and hopefully find some way to mend the rift."

"They have a solid motive for the murders, then. Mr Paulson was a wealthy man, and Melmont Hall is a fine residence."

"Yes, and yesterday I saw Mrs Williams sneaking out of the study where Mr Paulson was killed. She says she was looking for the will, but we only have her word for it."

"Who else is there?"

"The final two guests are Colonel Rushton, a retired army officer, and his friend Dr Histon, who was invited because he was staying with Colonel Rushton for the week."

"Not how you would hope your holiday would proceed," Lord Hinchbrooke said dryly.

"Colonel Rushton has not been keen on my involvement in questioning people, hinting strongly that I should keep to a womanly role."

"I cannot imagine that has sat well with you."

"No. I knew him a little before, but I cannot say I like the man any more." Jane sighed and shook her head. "He used to know Mrs Paulson, before she was married. I think there was a fondness between them, although it was a long time ago."

"And what about the doctor?"

"He is a friend of Colonel Rushton's from the army. He lives in Deal in Kent, and that is where he is from. He does not seem to have a prior connection with the Paulsons."

"So are we thinking money is the motivator for everything here? The Williamses were concerned with losing their inheritance and decided to hurry the old man into the afterlife?"

Jane grimaced. She didn't quite believe it.

"There is another possibility," she said, looking at the flames and tapping her fingers on the edge of the chair. "Mrs Paulson revealed her husband had a penchant for conducting affairs with younger women. These were almost exclusively young girls who worked as servants in the household. Over the years there have been dozens of affairs, and inevitably it follows the same course."

Lord Hinchbrooke shook his head in disgust. "Let me guess: he uses his position and wealth to dazzle them, promises them the world and then when they get with child he abandons them."

"Yes. Mrs Paulson has been aware of this for a very long time and unbeknownst to her husband had set up a charitable organisation to provide aid to these women and their children."

"Interesting," Lord Hinchbrooke said, rubbing his chin.

"There has been a recent affair just ended. A maid called Kitty. She was a favourite amongst some of the male servants as well. From what I can tell, the groom who came to fetch you, Peter Jones, was in love with her, as was a footman by the name of Benjamin Grout."

"Are they still here?"

"Peter is, but Kitty and Benjamin were dismissed a couple of weeks ago. Kitty went without too much of a fuss, I think, still believing Mr Paulson would provide for her. Benjamin Grout confronted his master and was thrown out the same day."

"So three more possible suspects, this Kitty and the two men who fancied themselves in love with her."

"And Mrs Paulson," Jane said quietly.

"Of course, we mustn't forget her."

"It gets more complicated," Jane said, closing her eyes for a moment and forcing herself to recall the scene she had been faced with immediately after Mr Paulson's murder.

Lord Hinchbrooke motioned for her to continue but didn't pepper her with a dozen questions. This was one of the things she admired about the man. He didn't mind taking his time. Sometimes Jane felt like she was being propelled forward at high speed, never able to pause to catch her breath, but Lord Hinchbrooke extolled the virtue of slowing down, of considering things from different angles.

"Mr Paulson was in his study all afternoon. At six o'clock the maid, Charlotte, took him a glass of whiskey, something of a night-time routine, I believe. At seven o'clock we all went in for dinner and Mr Paulson did not appear." Jane tried to remember the exact order of events, knowing accuracy was vital. "Mrs Paulson asked Mr Upton, the butler, to go and tell her husband everyone was waiting on him for dinner. After a minute or two, Mr Upton reappeared and whispered to Mrs Paulson that he could not get into the study and Mr Paulson was not responding."

Lord Hinchbrooke was leaning forward in his chair, engrossed in her re-telling of the murder.

"Mrs Paulson excused herself and I followed. Colonel Rushton came soon after and banged on the door loudly. He suggested we break it down when there was no response."

"Was he the man to put his shoulder to the door?"

"No, Dr Histon stopped him. I think the colonel has an old injury, so Dr Histon was the one to break the door down. He entered the room and immediately it was clear Mr Paulson was dead. We could all see that from the doorway." Jane shook her head at the memory. "He was slumped in his chair behind his desk. At first I thought perhaps his heart had given out, but when Dr Histon got closer he saw the knife and informed us he'd been stabbed."

Jane recalled the flurry of activity that had followed — Mrs Paulson almost collapsing in shock, Cassandra taking the newly bereaved widow away, herself, Colonel Rushton and Dr Histon surveying the room, dazed by what had just happened.

"The door was locked from the inside, the key still in the lock. The windows were all fastened from the inside and we searched the room thoroughly. There was no place anyone could have concealed themselves."

"What did the doctor have to say about the death?"

"He thinks the knife probably nicked the superior mesenteric artery and he died of internal bleeding. There was a little blood on his shirt around where the knife went in, not a huge amount, but Dr Histon didn't seem to think that was too unusual for an injury such as this."

"A man stabbed in a locked room. That certainly is no straightforward crime."

"Colonel Rushton and I also took a walk around the house soon after the body was discovered. The snow was thick by that point and there were no footprints to or from the house, nothing by the study window suggesting someone had come from outside."

"So we have a closed pool of suspects."

Jane nodded. "We are fairly sure there is no one hiding anywhere. We searched the house from top to bottom and all the outbuildings."

"Tell me about the second death."

"Mr Upton had been the butler here for many years. He was efficient but not particularly well liked. He pulled Colonel Rushton aside and asked to speak to him the morning after Mr Paulson's death. Colonel Rushton was busy doing something else and asked the butler to wait. Before they could talk, Mr

Upton had been hit over the head with a blunt object just outside the front door."

"Does anyone have an alibi?"

Shaking her head, Jane tried to recall where everyone had been. "We don't have an exact time of death, and people were coming and going. It would only have taken a minute or two to slip out the front door and hit Mr Upton over the head."

"So we're thinking Mr Upton knew something about his master's death, something that put him in danger."

"I think that is the most likely scenario," Jane said, drumming her fingers on the arms of the chair. "Mr Paulson was murdered first, so it feels like he is the primary victim here. Mr Upton was just unlucky enough to see something or hear something, or perhaps he had deduced something that could be damaging to the killer."

"How about the third death, Mrs Paulson?"

Even though it was less violent than the other two deaths, Jane found Mrs Paulson's was the one that shook her the most. She had known this woman, drank tea with her, enjoyed her hospitality.

"I last saw Mrs Paulson yesterday afternoon. She had spent much of the last few days in her bedroom but came out for a few hours yesterday. She urged us to play cards, to have a little normality in this terrible time."

"She played?"

"No, she watched. Towards the end she excused herself, seeming a little overwhelmed. I didn't think any more of Mrs Paulson until this morning when Mary Wright, her lady's maid, went into the bedroom and screamed upon finding Mrs Paulson dead."

"How did she die?"

Jane remembered the peaceful pose the older woman had been lying in, the waxy sheen to her skin the only clue that she wasn't merely asleep.

"An overdose of laudanum, it would seem. There was a scrap of paper on her writing desk that said *I am sorry*." Jane leaned forward, feeling suddenly on edge and needing to move. "This was discovered only minutes before you arrived, so I haven't done anything more than take a perfunctory look at the scene."

Lord Hinchbrooke exhaled and gave her a warm smile. "You have done well, Miss Austen, in a very difficult situation." He reached out and patted her hand in a fatherly gesture. "I know too well how painful this can be when you know many of the people involved. I have no doubt it has weighed heavily on you."

"I cannot deny it."

"It would be callous of me to insist you stay," he said quietly, looking at her intently and holding up a hand to still the protest that immediately formed on her lips. "Do not think that means I want to send you home, Miss Austen. More than anything I want to keep you here, to learn from your investigation these last few days, to hear your insights into the characters of our suspects, but I am acutely aware that you will be traumatised by these events and it is my duty to offer to release you."

"I want to stay."

He nodded as if he hadn't expected any other answer.

"I would not want you travelling on the roads whilst there is still snow and ice anyway. Perhaps your mother and father might forgive me for not sending you straight home if they think we are mainly considering your safety." He stood, shuffling stiffly towards the fire for a moment. He must have seen her gaze on him, for he turned to her with a wry smile.

"The cold does not improve my condition, alas. I do not know how much longer it will go unnoticed, but I am hopeful to push on for a while more."

Jane stood too and placed a hand on his arm. It was a fleeting gesture, but one she hoped conveyed some of the warmth she felt for Lord Hinchbrooke. She couldn't embrace him as she would Cassandra or a close friend — the rules of society would render that far too scandalous — but she wished him to know how much she cared for him.

"Come, Miss Austen, we have much work to do. On the way, you can tell me about the servants."

CHAPTER SEVENTEEN

It was a peculiar sensation, stepping into a room with a dead body in it. The space felt empty and cold, and Jane shuddered despite trying her hardest not to.

"Thank you for coming in here, Mary," Lord Hinchbrooke said kindly.

The lady's maid couldn't keep her eyes off Mrs Paulson but managed a shaky nod.

"I know it is distressing but I want you to look around, to tell me if anything looks out of place."

Mary did, taking her time to survey the bedroom.

"What time did you last see Mrs Paulson?" Jane asked, keen to establish a timeline in her mind.

"Ten o'clock, Miss. She couldn't sleep, despite retiring to bed much earlier. I offered to fetch Dr Histon but she declined, telling me she would settle on her own eventually. She asked me for a cup of warm milk and after that sent me away."

"Had she taken any laudanum at that time?"

"No, Miss, and this bottle wasn't here either. Mrs Paulson was aware of how strong the drug is and was careful always to keep it under lock and key."

"Where is it kept normally?"

"In here."

Mary sidled past the bed and led the way into a spacious dressing room. There was a shelf on one wall and on that shelf there was a box. A key sat in the lock, the lid shut but not locked.

"She kept the key on her; she was very particular about it."

"It is strange to have the household medicines kept here in her dressing room, is it not?" Lord Hinchbrooke said, peering in.

"Yes, my lord. Years ago I think they were kept downstairs in one of the storerooms off the kitchen. There was a tragedy; the governess to Mrs Paulson's son requested the key for some innocuous reason and then took a huge dose of one of the medicines. It killed her."

"How terrible," Jane murmured. "Was it intentional?"

"Difficult to say, Miss, but the governess was one of the young ladies Mr Paulson was involved with. It was how the mistress became aware of his liaisons. Ever since, I believe Mrs Paulson has kept the medicines in here, and if someone comes asking for something she will give them just what they need, never the entire bottle."

"Where did she keep the key?"

"On a chain around her neck. She would take it off before bed and put it on this little bedside table here." Mary paused, seeming to consider her words before continuing. "I don't think she was worried about people stealing from it, more that she wanted to be in control of the amount people took."

"To prevent another tragedy."

"Is the laudanum bottle on the bedside table from this chest, Mary?" Lord Hinchbrooke said, prompting the maid to look inside.

Mary peered in, counting the bottles and picking up a few.

"Yes, my lord."

"Then either Mrs Paulson got up in the night and took the bottle or someone used her key whilst she was sleeping," Jane said, trying to work out if an unknown assailant could creep past Mrs Paulson whilst she was asleep, take the key from the bedside table and find the bottle of laudanum all without waking the older woman up.

"You weren't summoned in the night at all?" Lord Hinchbrooke said as they all backed out of the dressing room.

"No, Charlotte would have come to set the fire about seven o'clock and I came in shortly after. The room was dark and Mrs Paulson had asked to be left to sleep this morning, so I did not attempt to rouse her." Mary choked back a strangled sob and then managed to compose herself. "I returned at eleven, thinking I would check again as I had not been summoned, and this time there was a little more light. I had this sense something was wrong, so I went over to the bed and touched her hand."

"She was cold," Jane said softly.

"Yes."

"Thank you," Lord Hinchbrooke said, still surveying the scene. "One more thing before you go, Mary: is this Mrs Paulson's handwriting?" He handed her the scrap of paper Jane had found on the desk, scrutinising the maid as she looked at it carefully.

"Yes, my lord."

"Thank you, Mary. That will be all for now."

Mary turned to leave but paused at the door, turning back with tears streaming down her face. "She wouldn't do this. She wouldn't kill herself."

"People can act unpredictably in the face of grief," the magistrate said.

"No." Mary was insistent. "I'm not saying she was happy Mr Paulson was dead, but she was unhappy when he was alive. She was strong. If she didn't kill herself when her son died, she wouldn't kill herself now."

"Thank you for your insight," Lord Hinchbrooke said in that grave voice of his. Jane saw Mary respond to it, saw her back straighten as she realised her concerns had been heard and noted.

Lord Hinchbrooke quietly closed the door once they were alone and turned to Jane.

"Tell me, Miss Austen, what do you see? What sparks your curiosity?"

This was the sort of question he would ask her when they were ensconced in his library, sitting by the fire, talking of his old cases or discussing matters he would preside over in the courts.

"First, there is the matter of the laudanum. The simplest explanation is that Mrs Paulson decided to kill herself and took the bottle from the locked chest." She paused, stepping closer to the bed, trying to ignore the cold corpse. "Of course, there are a few things that go against that."

"Go on."

"First, this protestation from Mary that she wouldn't kill herself. Perhaps it is wishful thinking, but I did not see any reason or desire to stop living in her mind."

"What else?"

"The cup," Jane said. "I bent over it and it smells of laudanum. If I were to take a lethal dose of laudanum, would I bother mixing it in with my cup of milk, or would I drink it straight out of the bottle?"

"The milk would hardly disguise the taste of a whole bottle of laudanum."

"No, so why put it in there?"

They both remained silent for a moment.

"What else is bothering you, Miss Austen?"

"The note."

Looking over to the writing desk, Lord Hinchbrooke nodded.

"It is curious, is it not?"

"Why would she write it on a scrap of paper? Why is it so faded? Where is the rest of the paper that this scrap was torn from?"

"I think our perpetrator might be beginning to panic," Lord Hinchbrooke said quietly. "I have seen it before, on the rare occasions someone is involved in multiple deaths. The first is planned meticulously, every detail accounted for, but eventually they slip up, they panic, they can tell the end is drawing close. They make a mistake and then another to try and cover up the first. It is their undoing."

"You think this was a mistake?"

"Oh yes. It is meant to steer our minds towards Mrs Paulson as the perpetrator. Sick of her husband's affairs, she somehow managed to kill him whilst her dinner party guests were gathering in the drawing room. Mr Upton was either privy to her plans or worked out what had happened and she killed him too. Overcome by remorse, she then decided to take her own life."

"I suppose it does all hang together rather nicely," Jane said.

"You know these people. Do you believe it?"

"Not for a moment."

"No, nor do I."

They fell silent, both still staring at the scrap of paper with the scrawled blue handwriting.

"Mary Wright confirmed the writing was Mrs Paulson's," Jane said slowly. "So whoever planted it here must have the rest of the piece of paper."

"That is true, unless they have already destroyed it. People are foolish, but surely not foolish enough to keep something that would tie them so directly to the crime." He shook his head. "Of course, there is a possibility."

"But we can't go rifling through everyone's private papers without an idea of where to direct our search."

"No. Come, Miss Austen, I think we have done all we can here. I would like to meet the guests and servants properly and take a look at the study where Mr Paulson was murdered."

"The other two bodies are being kept in a cool storeroom downstairs in the hope it will keep their flesh from putrefying. Shall we ask the servants to remove Mrs Paulson's body too?"

"Yes, good idea."

They emerged from the bedroom into the hallway to find Cassandra waiting for them, arms crossed and a determined expression on her face.

"Miss Austen," Lord Hinchbrooke greeted her formally, bowing as he said her name. "It is a pleasure, as always."

"It is a pleasure to see you too, my lord, a pleasure and a relief."

"I am sorry my arrival was held up by the snow."

"These things are sent to challenge us. I wondered, my lord, what the plan is now you are here." She flashed a warning look at Jane. "The events of the last few days have been exhausting, both mentally and emotionally."

"I am sure they have." The magistrate cleared his throat and glanced at Jane, but she was too busy frowning at her sister to notice. "Miss Austen is letting me know where we are in the investigation so far. She has done an admirable job in my absence."

"But you are here now."

"Yes, I am."

"Cassandra," Jane said, a note of warning in her voice.

"I must advocate for you, Jane, for often you do not know what is good for you. After that last awful affair with Miss Roscoe you were a wreck. Don't think I don't know you haven't slept properly for weeks, that you cry into your pillow when you think I am asleep. Even your writing no longer brings you solace."

"Stop," Jane said, not wanting Lord Hinchbrooke to know any of this. He was a kind man who saw something in her, but she knew he wouldn't hesitate to cut her loose if he thought it was the better thing for her.

"You will make yourself ill, shouldering this burden on top of everything else. You think you have to be strong, to cope with everything yourself, to be the one who solves every problem."

Jane took a step towards Cassandra and tried to take her arm, but Cassandra shook her off.

"You do not have to be strong, Jane. *This* is not your responsibility."

Jane glanced over her shoulder and lowered her voice, knowing Lord Hinchbrooke would still hear her but wanting Cassandra to be sure that her words were directed at her.

"I know it is difficult for you to understand, I know I often seem pig-headed and as if I will not listen to reason, but I feel this compulsion inside me, Cassandra. I want to strive to do better and better. I feel like there is some great wheel inside me, forever turning, forever pushing me on."

Cassandra looked at her, studying her eyes and shaking her head softly.

"You will be great, Jane. I know this. I've known it since we were little girls, but you do not have to endanger yourself to get there."

"I am in no danger. I am with Lord Hinchbrooke, and I promise I will not leave his side. I have no desire to rush out on my own, to be the one grasping at glory."

Cassandra released her sister. "I know I am not going to get through to you, Jane, but please be careful. My world would crumble without you."

Without another word, Cassandra turned and walked away. Jane watched her, not wanting to turn round and have to dissect what had happened with the magistrate.

Eventually she turned and felt a flood of relief as Lord Hinchbrooke merely held out his arm for her to take.

"You're not going to lecture me on my safety or reckless decisions?"

"No," he said, "because I know it would be futile, but do understand how deeply your safety matters to me, Miss Austen."

"I understand," she said, thinking of the treacherous conditions he had ridden through to get here. She was in no doubt that if she had not been present, he would not have rushed so.

"Good. Now, shall we proceed?"

Together they walked along the hallway, pausing outside one of the doors at the sound of loud sobs coming from inside.

"Mrs Leveritt's room. She is sharing with her daughter, Miss Leveritt. Mrs Leveritt became hysterical yesterday morning and insisted she and her daughter leave. They almost got to the village before Mrs Leveritt slipped in the snow and hurt her ankle. Thankfully, Miss Leveritt made it back to the house and was able to summon help."

"It has been an eventful few days," Lord Hinchbrooke murmured and then knocked loudly on the door.

There was a rustling inside and then Miss Leveritt's face appeared at the door, her eyes red but her cheeks free from tears. The sobbing continued from inside the room.

"This is Lord Hinchbrooke, Miss Leveritt," Jane said, stepping back so the magistrate could appraise the young woman.

Miss Leveritt lowered her eyes and dipped her head.

"I am pleased to make your acquaintance, Miss Leveritt."

"Who is it?" Mrs Leveritt's voice came from inside the room.

"The magistrate, Mama, and Miss Austen."

"Don't dally, show them in."

Mrs Leveritt was in much the same position Jane had left her in earlier, propped up on her pillows in the darkness.

"You have heard the news about Mrs Paulson?" Jane asked as kindly as she could.

"Terrible affair. I cannot believe it. She was in the prime of her life. What anguish she must have felt to commit such a sin."

"We do not know what happened yet, Mama," Miss Leveritt said quietly.

"Laudanum, that is what the maid said. A whole bottle of laudanum. Is that true, my lord?"

"I am still gathering all the facts, Mrs Leveritt. Did you know Mrs Paulson well?"

"Yes. We were dear friends, had been for years. She was going to take my darling daughter to London for the season. Mrs Paulson was such a kind woman, such a generous soul. Last night when she came to see me, I never imagined…" She trailed off, shaking her head.

"Mrs Paulson came to see you last night?" Jane asked sharply.

"Yes, what time was it, my dear? A little after ten, I suppose. She knocked on the door and said she thought she had heard me cry out."

"Had you?"

"No, I am in pain but I am quite stoical," Mrs Leveritt said without even a hint of irony. "We were settling down for sleep. I asked Mrs Paulson to come in for a few minutes and we talked. She was a little maudlin, reminiscing about the past, but I never thought it would lead to this."

"What was she reminiscing about?"

"Oh, our younger days. Those carefree times past when my husband was alive and her little Charles was running around, causing mischief."

"Mrs Paulson's son died when he was four," Jane said, leaning towards Lord Hinchbrooke.

"After about fifteen minutes, she said she had better return to her room and try to sleep," Miss Leveritt said, taking a seat beside her mother. "We blew out the candles a few minutes later."

"Did you hear anyone cry out, someone Mrs Paulson could have mistaken for you?"

"No."

"Thank you, Mrs Leveritt. Is there anything else you wish to tell me?"

"I want to know when we are permitted to leave?"

"I cannot keep you here against your will, although I would caution against riding just yet. The roads were icy when I made the journey. Perhaps tomorrow might be safer."

Outside the room, Lord Hinchbrooke waited for the door to close before he turned to Jane with a raised eyebrow.

"Well, what did you make of that?"

"It is possible," she said slowly, "that someone lured Mrs Paulson out of her room with the cry, knowing she would go and check on her injured friend. They could then have taken the opportunity to slip into her room, retrieve the key from her bedside table and select the laudanum from the box, before dropping the contents of the bottle into her evening cup of milk."

"It would have been risky," Lord Hinchbrooke said.

"Risky, but possible."

"The perpetrator would have had to have known about the box of medicines and the key."

"It doesn't explain why Mrs Paulson drank her milk when the smell and flavour would have been overwhelmingly that of laudanum."

"Lord Hinchbrooke, I presume," Colonel Rushton said, marching along the corridor and interrupting their conversation.

"Glad to make you acquaintance, Colonel."

"Thank goodness you are here. It has been a nightmare these last few days. I want to know if you have detained the man?"

"What man?"

"The groom, Peter Jones."

"Surely you cannot still think he is responsible?" Jane said, earning herself a withering look from Colonel Rushton. "Half of your theory was based on the fact he must be guilty because he had fled. Now we know instead that he risked life and limb to ride for Lord Hinchbrooke."

"It doesn't make him any less guilty." Colonel Rushton turned to Jane, towering over her. "It is time to stop playing at this, Miss Austen. *Three* people are dead."

"You imply this is somehow my fault," Jane said quietly, feeling her irritation with the man simmer and start to boil over. "Mr Paulson was killed mere minutes after my arrival. Mr Upton died after he had come to *you*, and you brushed him away. Mrs Paulson…" She trailed off, not willing to confide that neither she nor the magistrate believed Mrs Paulson's death was a suicide.

"You seem agitated, Colonel Rushton," Lord Hinchbrooke said in that calming voice of his. "I can understand it has been a tense few days, and for that I can excuse your tone, but please do not think of speaking to Miss Austen in this way again."

Colonel Rushton opened his mouth to protest but came to his senses in time.

"It does not change the fact that the murderer is out there in that cottage, probably planning his escape."

"The young man that came to fetch me?"

"Indeed. Peter Jones."

"Let us go downstairs and you can tell me your concerns, and then I suggest we get him in to answer the allegations," Lord Hinchbrooke said.

"Finally, a sensible response," Colonel Rushton murmured as he led the way down the wide staircase. Jane saw how much Lord Hinchbrooke struggled with the stairs, moving in closer and offering him her arm. He shook his head, wincing with the effort at trying to maintain a decent speed. The long ride across Hampshire had taken its toll on the magistrate, and no doubt he would struggle with the stiffness in his muscles until he returned to his comfortable home. He did not grumble, though, and he made it downstairs without tripping. He then followed the colonel into the drawing room.

Mr and Mrs Williams were in there, looking nervous, and Jane knew they would be wondering how much she had told the magistrate about them. Mrs Paulson's death freed them from the obligation of having to tell the older woman they had lied about their true identities, but it did not clear them of suspicion over Mr Paulson's murder.

"I wonder if we might have the room?" Lord Hinchbrooke said, turning to Mr Williams, his tone polite but firm.

"Of course, my lord. My wife and I were hoping to speak to you, perhaps…"

"Certainly, after I clear this matter," Lord Hinchbrooke said, guiding the young couple from the room and then closing the door. "Colonel Rushton, tell me your concerns."

"I served in the army for over twenty years, and I know what it takes for a man to kill, my lord. Many people struggle to, even when faced with their own imminent death, and then there are those who have a coldness about them."

"You feel Peter Jones is one of the latter?"

"Yes. He is strong enough to overpower Mr Upton, brutal enough to kill two men without feeling a shred of remorse, and he has a motive as strong as any we could uncover."

"This is his relationship with the maid who was dismissed, Kitty?"

"Yes. Even his own brother spoke of his infatuation with the girl."

"You think he had the opportunity to commit the murders?"

"The house was busy. He could have slipped into the study at an opportune moment, and Mr Upton's murderer was outside — no one would question why he was traipsing about in the snow."

"If he is the murderer," Lord Hinchbrooke said slowly, allowing the colonel to see he was taking the allegations seriously, "do you have an answer as to why you think he would come back to Melmont Hall?"

Jane watched as Colonel Rushton hesitated. Not for the first time, she got the impression he was trying to hurry the case along, to bring it to a quick conclusion. Whether that was out of misplaced confidence in his own theories or for another, more nefarious reason, she did not know.

"Perhaps he thought he was safe from suspicion," Colonel Rushton said.

"I think it is time we question the man. Colonel, will you be so kind as to go and get him? Please do not make him suspect we think he has done anything wrong."

The colonel stood and Jane had the impression he had to stop himself from saluting, then he spun on his heel and marched out of the door.

When they were alone, Lord Hinchbrooke turned to Jane.

"He is very forceful."

"I was wondering…" Jane said, wondering if she was letting her own dislike of the man cloud her judgement.

"Go on."

"Colonel Rushton seems very keen to find the culprit, to accuse someone and have this matter over and done with."

"You think there is something more than a sense of civic duty?"

"I don't know, but why fixate on Peter Jones? He has a motive, yes, but so do many of the other people in this house. The colonel took an instant dislike to him and hasn't wavered since."

"You suspect the colonel?" Lord Hinchbrooke said, tilting his head, genuinely interested in her answer.

Jane considered the question properly. "No," she said eventually. "I find it difficult to like the man. He is abrupt, superior and sometimes disrespectful, but I cannot find it in myself to accuse him."

"Let us see what unfolds when he brings Mr Jones in."

They only had to wait a couple more minutes before the door opened again and Peter Jones stepped into the room, looking round with an air of hostility. He was followed closely by his brother, and bringing up the rear was Colonel Rushton.

"Please come in, have a seat," Lord Hinchbrooke said. Jane noticed how his hands shook as he gestured to the empty chairs and felt a pang of sympathy for him. He would hate for others to see him this way. "I am Lord Hinchbrooke, the magistrate for this area. Miss Austen has apprised me of the events of the last few days, but there are some things I need to ask for myself. Thank you for making yourselves available." He smiled, directing his words at Gabriel, and then turned to Peter. "I wanted to thank you again for taking the risk to ride and alert me to everything that had happened here earlier today. It was a selfless decision."

Peter took the chair indicated, across from Lord Hinchbrooke, whilst Gabriel remained standing.

"Is my brother being accused of something?" Gabriel said, his voice quiet but filled with cold determination.

For a long moment Lord Hinchbrooke didn't answer, and Jane felt the anticipation as she shifted in her seat.

"Not by me, he is not," Lord Hinchbrooke said finally. Jane glanced at Colonel Rushton, who blanched at the comment.

"Nor me," Jane said quietly.

"Then it is you who think I killed my master?" Peter said, looking at the colonel.

Lord Hinchbrooke held up his hands. "My job is to ferret out the facts, to unpick the knotted strands of people's lives and see what is left once they are gone. From what I understand, you had reason to dislike Mr Paulson. I would like to understand those reasons."

"Many people disliked the old man," Gabriel said quickly, "not just Peter."

"That has been made clear," Jane said, trying to give Peter a smile of encouragement to urge him to talk so he could clear his name.

"He was a lecherous old pig," Peter said in a burst of hatred. He looked up, meeting the magistrate's eye and holding it for a long moment before looking away with a sigh of disgust. "I wouldn't expect you to understand, but Kitty was different before he laid hands on her."

"How was she different?"

"She was softer, more innocent." He held up a hand to stop his brother from interrupting. "I'm not saying she *was* an innocent. I knew she had enjoyed the company of others, but she was more carefree; her spirit was lighter."

"What happened with Mr Paulson?"

Peter shrugged, and for a moment it looked as though he wasn't going to say anything.

"I had decided I would ask her to marry me," he said eventually, directing his gaze into the fire so he didn't have to make eye contact with anyone. "I don't think she knew, no one did, but I had decided I would save up for a place of our own and then I would ask her to marry me." In his honesty he was making himself look more guilty, but Jane had faith he would still be able to rebut this accusation. "She told me a few times that Mr Paulson had made some suggestive remarks, but she brushed them off, saying she wasn't foolish enough to get caught in *that* trap."

"What changed?"

Peter shrugged. "I don't know exactly. One day she was murmuring how disgusting he was and the next she started defending him if I said a bad word about him. I do not know what he promised her, but Kitty was no fool."

Gabriel shifted behind his brother and Jane caught a hint of agitation in his face. It was clear he did not care for Kitty, and she wondered if he had been relieved when she had started her relationship with Mr Paulson, taking her away from Peter.

"She stopped coming to see me altogether and I couldn't understand it, so one day I approached her in the kitchen when Mrs Brown was occupied elsewhere. She shrugged me off, told me to leave her alone. Her tone was angry, but there was sadness in her eyes."

"You think she regretted giving in to Mr Paulson's advances."

"Of course. I admit I was devastated. I tried to see her again a few times, but she was careful never to come outside alone or be in the kitchen when I visited. If I did ever try to approach her, she gave me a look that would have warned even the firmest admirer away."

"What happened when things came to an end?" Jane asked, leaning forward. From the beginning she had felt as though Mr Paulson's unsavoury habit of conducting affairs with the maids he employed was likely to be one of the reasons he had come to an untimely end. By the sounds of it, there had been plenty of young women's lives ruined over the years, but the affair with Kitty was the most raw. It seemed too big a leap to think there was another equally devastating motive for his murder.

"Peter knew nothing about it," Gabriel said quickly. "Kitty was gone, marched off the estate, before anyone knew what was happening."

"That's right," Peter confirmed.

"Did you go to see her in the village?"

"Yes, a day after she was dismissed. I couldn't get away from my work before that. At first she wouldn't let me in; she only opened the door a crack and kept telling me to go away."

"Did you go away?"

"I didn't force my way in," Peter said sharply. "I'm not that sort of man." He paused for a moment, looking down at his hands. "I sat on the wall outside her house. I waited for nearly an hour before she came out and sat beside me."

Everyone in the room was silent, engrossed by his story, and Jane felt for the first time she had a true picture of how Kitty must have felt, of the despair she would have been trying to overcome.

"She told me to forget about her and tried to make me promise I would try. I couldn't do it. Then she said things weren't over between her and Mr Paulson, that he had promised he would look after her. I called her naïve and she just went silent. I think she knew that his promises were false, that he had ruined her life and discarded her like a chewed chicken bone."

"What did you do then?" Jane said softly, trying not to break the flow of his narrative but wanting to hear the end of the story.

"I told her I loved her and I would marry her, but she laughed sadly and got up to go back into the house. When I ran after her, she said that if I rescued her now I would spend my life regretting it, regretting her."

"He came back home then," Gabriel said, "and he hasn't seen her since."

Peter buried his head in his hands and kept it there for a few moments, overcome by emotion at re-living the moment he had truly lost the woman he loved.

"So you see, I have a motive. I *did* hate Mr Paulson. He destroyed my Kitty and did not care a jot. We all knew he would move on, unscathed, and wait until the next innocent young girl was brought into the house — then he would be at it again."

"It is a compelling motive," Jane murmured.

Jane felt Colonel Rushton shift and saw him straighten out of the corner of her eye. Peter must have too, for he turned to the colonel.

"I am sorry to disappoint you, but I did not kill Mr Paulson. I hated him, but my mind never turned to murder. I'm not a fool. I know what happens to a man like me if there is any wrongdoing, any challenge. I would be for the noose, no questions. Why would I do that when I still have a chance to build a life with the woman I love?"

"Kitty turned you down," Colonel Rushton said. "You told us that yourself."

"She was upset, emotional. She thinks I do not know she is with child. I decided to give her some time to see that I will still be standing there, steady, when all of this has settled down. I think once she has seen that, she will realise it is better to have a life with a man who cares for her than the terrible one she is condemning herself to at the moment."

"You expect us to believe you would willingly raise another man's child? *That* is your defence?"

Peter Jones looked at Colonel Rushton contemptuously. "I expect you to believe I would choose happiness and the woman I love over revenge."

"Thank you for being so honest with us, Peter," Jane said, and she saw Lord Hinchbrooke nod in agreement.

"To be clear, you are denying your involvement in the murder of Mr Paulson and Mr Upton."

"I had nothing to do with either of the deaths."

"Thank you, Mr Jones. I do not think we need anything more from you for now," Lord Hinchbrooke said. "I wish you the best."

The brothers looked at each other in surprise, neither of them moving.

"I'm free to go?" Peter asked.

"Yes."

"You're not going to arrest me?"

"No. There is no evidence you are involved in these crimes."

Gabriel pulled his brother up from the chair, tugging on his arm as if he half expected the magistrate to change his mind and clap him in irons.

"Thank you, my lord," Peter said, still shaking his head in disbelief.

"You cannot believe his story," Colonel Rushton said, although Jane could see some of the zeal had died in his eyes. He may have been too proud to admit he had got it wrong, but he couldn't hide that he was now doubting himself a little.

"I do, Colonel," Lord Hinchbrooke said. "He is a genuine and honest man, and I believe every word he says. What is more, I have absolutely no evidence he has committed any crime at all."

Colonel Rushton looked like he was going to protest but must have seen that it would not sway the magistrate. Instead he stiffened, gave a curt nod and marched out of the room.

"Interesting man," Lord Hinchbrooke said as he peered after the colonel. "What a mess this house was in, even before the murders. It feels like there must have been so many simmering resentments just waiting to boil over. Someone snapped, but it is going to be difficult to work out who."

"Did you want to speak to the Williamses next? They seemed quite keen to talk to you."

"This is the couple who were to inherit everything but concealed their true identities?"

"Yes, apparently they have a lot of debt."

"A different sort of motive to that of revenge," Lord Hinchbrooke said quietly. "Let them stew for a while. It'll make them more nervous, and nerves make people divulge things they were not meaning to."

"Who would you like to speak to?"

"I think I should see the bodies and talk to the doctor. It is good luck he was here to help with the examinations."

"Indeed. Shall I go and get him?"

Lord Hinchbrooke held up a hand and halted Jane's movement from the chair.

"It has been a few days, Miss Austen, and although I am sure the storerooms are cold, I doubt these bodies are in the best condition. I will not deny the sight and smell of an old corpse has been enough to turn my stomach at times. The last thing I wish to do is to add to the fodder for your nightmares."

Jane considered his words for a moment. Lord Hinchbrooke did not treat her as a weak and feeble woman. In many ways, despite the differences in their social status, wealth and sex, he treated her as an equal, certainly more equal than any other man in her life. He did not give her this warning to protect perceived gentle female sensibilities; he did so because it was a terrible thing for anyone to see, and he did not want to subject her to it.

"I will accompany you downstairs and remain on the peripheries," Jane said.

"Very well. Would you be kind enough to find the doctor? I admit I am struggling with the stiffness in my limbs today."

"Of course. I shall bring him here."

Jane found Dr Histon in his room looking tired and drawn, but he agreed readily to accompany her to meet Lord Hinchbrooke.

"How are you coping, Miss Austen?"

Jane shrugged, a gesture her mother hated, but there were no watchful eyes to pick up these little habits ready to lecture her on deportment later.

"It has been a strain, I will not lie. I find I yearn for the comfort of my family, for my bedroom at home, all the familiar things, yet I am loath to leave before this matter is settled. How about you, Doctor? This is hardly the amiable trip to visit your friend you had planned."

"It is not. Do you know, I don't think I have ever been away anywhere and not been called on to give an opinion, to tend to someone, or to *just take a little look at something*." He shook his head and gave a self-deprecating laugh. "Although I must say, this has been the most demanding and bizarre."

"You have been a great help to me, and I sincerely thank you for everything you have done."

Dr Histon gave a dismissive wave as if embarrassed to have her thanks.

"Despite my grumbling, I do not mind. I knew what I was getting into when I went to study medicine. I had seen how my father rarely got a complete night's sleep, how my mother had to become a font of knowledge, often acting as nurse or assistant when needed. It becomes part of your persona, something that is very hard to separate from the rest of you."

"You went into the army, though. That must have been a very different sort of medicine."

"Yes, that was a swift change of direction."

"It wasn't the plan initially?"

"No. I had planned to set up a practice in Kent, somewhere close to home, then gradually take over my father's patients as he got older."

"What made you change your mind?"

Dr Histon shrugged. "Life changes. I do not regret my decision, not for one minute."

They arrived at the drawing room door and Dr Histon paused, allowing Jane to step inside first. Lord Hinchbrooke was already on his feet and turned as he heard them enter.

"Dr Histon, thank you for coming to see me."

"It is a pleasure to meet you, Lord Hinchbrooke."

"Miss Austen tells me what a help you have been these last few days. I thank you for your service."

"I am glad I could be of service."

"I wonder if I can call on you again? I need to see the bodies of Mr Paulson and Mr Upton, and I hoped you would talk me through your findings."

"Of course, my lord," Dr Histon said, hesitating, "although I must warn you, there may be some deconditioning of the bodies."

"I am aware, Dr Histon, yet I think it is important for us to do."

"Very well."

Lord Hinchbrooke followed Dr Histon from the drawing room with Jane behind, wondering already if she had made the wrong decision in accompanying them.

They descended the stairs to the kitchen, the three of them forming a solemn procession. Mrs Brown was at the table in the middle of the kitchen and watched as they passed, her eyes fixed on the magistrate.

The bodies were being kept in a storeroom furthest from the main hubbub of the kitchen. It was much cooler in this part of the house, but Jane knew these were not ideal conditions in which to keep them. They paused outside the door and Dr Histon seemed to brace himself before going in.

The smell was faint but pervasive, the same smell as when Jane had found a dead chicken in their coop after a fox attack in the summer.

"This is Mr Paulson," Dr Histon said, going to the first of the bodies laid on the stone slabs in the storeroom. He and Lord Hinchbrooke crouched down, while Jane stayed standing in the doorway. She had seen the bodies, already gone through this exercise, but she was interested to see if Lord Hinchbrooke picked up on anything she had missed.

"There is a stab wound to his abdomen, in the right upper quadrant. From external examination, I believe the knife must have cut the superior mesenteric artery."

"A quick death, then."

"Yes, depending on the size of the nick."

"The weapon was a letter opener?"

"Yes."

"It suggests no pre-planning. Something picked up from the desk to be used in a fit of rage."

Dr Histon didn't comment, and Lord Hinchbrooke finished his examination of the body before they moved over to Mr Upton.

"Struck by a blunt object over the back of the head. He wouldn't have seen his assailant coming. The snow muffles the sound, so it isn't surprising."

Lord Hinchbrooke examined the wound and then the rest of the body.

"Have we found what he was hit with?"

"No," Jane said. "There was nothing obvious nearby, and the snow was still too thick to search for long."

"If there is enough light left, we shall have a look today; otherwise, perhaps it will need to wait until first thing tomorrow morning."

"Is there anything else of note, Lord Hinchbrooke?" Jane asked as he straightened.

"No, not that I can see. May they both rest in peace."

They left the storeroom in silence, not speaking again until they reached the stairs up to the hall.

"I cannot imagine you have many cases like this, my lord," Dr Histon said as they left the warm kitchens behind.

"No, I do not. I am sure you have seen some things in the army, though. That must have been an interesting career."

"I was constantly reminded of humankind's capacity for violence and destruction," Dr Histon said with a sad smile, "but it was never dull."

Lord Hinchbrooke motioned for Dr Histon to join them in the drawing room, waiting for the doctor to be settled before speaking again.

"Tell me, Dr Histon, was there anything that struck you about the scene of death for either Mr Paulson or Mr Upton?"

The doctor considered for a moment. "Mr Upton's death was messy, as if someone had struck out in anger or panic. We have not found the weapon, but I would wager it was something nearby, picked up on the way to meet the butler." He leaned forward in his seat, clasping his hands. "Mr Paulson's death... I am not sure what I can tell you. You saw the body. I had a sense of foreboding when I knocked down the door, like I knew what I was going to find in the study, but I do not know why. The door was locked from the inside — I am sure Miss Austen told you this — and all the windows were secured from the inside too."

"Yes, it is a curious matter. Miss Austen tells me you are from Deal, and you are here visiting Colonel Rushton."

"Yes. We were friends in the army, and when I stepped back into civilian life he made me promise I would come and visit once he retired."

"Do you have any prior connections to Hampshire or the Paulsons?"

Dr Histon shook his head. "My early life was spent in Kent. I studied in London and then joined the army. I have travelled with the regiments, of course, but we never lingered in Hampshire."

"What did you make of Mrs Paulson's death?"

Dr Histon sighed and looked genuinely sad for a moment. "Such a shame. I feel partially responsible for that. I gave her laudanum the night before. She was in shock, unable to settle. I did not have my bag with me, but the butler confirmed they had a small stock of medicines in the house. I measured out a small dose of laudanum to help her sleep." He paused, running his hand over his brow. "I enquired last night if she required anything more and her lady's maid said she was fine, but perhaps I should have realised what mental torment she was in."

"Did she seem tormented?"

"Not on the surface, but I have seen similar before. Often those driven to take their own lives are in anguish for weeks before, but when they finally make up their minds a sort of peace settles over them. It is as if all their uncertainty floats away and they are left with the knowledge that their earthly form at least will suffer no more."

"You didn't see Mrs Paulson last night, after the game of cards?" Jane asked.

"No. She retired to her room. I assume the only person to go in after was the maid."

"When you saw her body, were you convinced she had died by an overdose?"

"Yes. Many of the signs of an overdose of laudanum disappear once life has departed, but her repose was peaceful, her lips discoloured. There is a certain look about the eyes as well. It all fits with the empty bottle beside her bed."

"Thank you, Dr Histon, you have been helpful."

"I am not sure what your plans are, Lord Hinchbrooke, but I would suggest we send for the undertaker as soon as it is possible for him to get his cart here."

"I agree, Dr Histon. I am hopeful that tomorrow the snow will continue to melt and we will be able to organise the removal of the bodies."

The doctor stood and inclined his head before walking from the room.

"He seems quite sure it was a deliberate overdose of laudanum that killed Mrs Paulson," Lord Hinchbrooke said.

"I think we should speak to Mary Wright again, now she has had a chance to calm down. She was close to her mistress and will have some insight."

"Where is she?"

"I assume she is upstairs in her room in the attic."

"Let us stretch our legs and see her up there. It may feel less intimidating for the woman."

CHAPTER EIGHTEEN

It took Lord Hinchbrooke a while to get moving, but his muscles seemed to have loosened up by the time they were climbing the second staircase to the top floor. Jane led the way, knowing it would be less intimidating for her to be the one knocking on Mary Wright's door.

It took a few seconds for the door to Mary's room to open, but when it did it revealed her tear-stained face, and they saw that her hair was a mess and her clothes were crumpled.

"I have the magistrate with me," Jane said softly. "We want to try and work out what happened, Mary. May we come in?"

Mary peered at Lord Hinchbrooke over Jane's shoulder and then gave a nod, allowing them into her basic but comfortable room.

"Please make yourselves comfortable."

There was only one chair, for the maid wasn't expected to have company, but Mary perched on the bed and Jane was able to sit on the windowsill, ignoring the cold that permeated through her dress and made her shiver. Lord Hinchbrooke took the chair, lowering himself into it slowly.

"I am sorry for your loss, Miss Wright," he said sombrely. "I understand you had been with Mrs Paulson a long time."

"Ten years," Mary said, giving a sniff and then seeming to compose herself. "She was a wonderful mistress, very kind and considerate."

"Miss Austen has told me you checked on your mistress last night at about ten o'clock, is that right?"

"Yes, sir. She had retired to bed around nine but struggled to sleep and rang the bell for me to attend her just before ten."

"This is when you went to get her some warm milk?"

"Yes, she often would have a hot drink before bed, especially if she couldn't sleep."

"How did she seem to you, Mary?" Jane asked, wondering if after mulling things over for a while the maid would have remembered anything more.

"A little flustered, perhaps. When she had something on her mind, Mrs Paulson would pace around the room, talking to herself. That was what she had been doing earlier in the evening."

"Do you know what she was flustered about?"

"No, she didn't confide in me," Mary said, her voice catching in her throat.

"Was that unusual?" Jane asked, remembering how much the older woman had relied on her lady's maid when Jane had questioned her after Mr Paulson's death.

"Very unusual. Normally she told me everything. One day about three years ago she confided in me about how her husband's affairs hurt her, and after that she told me everything. I think she liked having a confidante."

"But she didn't tell you anything last night?"

"No, Miss. When I went in later at ten, she was clutching the miniature of her son. She normally kept it near her bedside, but last night she was holding it in her hands."

They fell silent for a moment, all considering whether this could mean she had resolved to take her own life at this point and was taking comfort in the memory of her son.

"Do you believe she would take her own life, Miss Wright?" Lord Hinchbrooke asked, giving the maid a few moments to consider her answer.

"I've thought of little else, sir," Mary said, her eyes large and glistening with tears. "I know that is what must have happened, for she was the only one with the key to the medicine box, but I cannot believe it. She was shocked by her husband's death, but there was no great love between them. I cannot believe she would have taken her own life out of grief for him."

"What about if her conscience weighed heavily on her?"

Miss Wright scoffed. "You can't think my kind, gentle mistress would ever hurt anyone. It was not in her nature. She spent her life trying to make the world a better place, little by little."

"What if she thought the world would be a better place without her husband?"

"She wouldn't have been wrong," Mary said softly, "with the number of lives he has ruined. All those young women cast out from their families, without a job, without a position in life. He was a foul creature, but Mrs Paulson knew what she could change and what she couldn't. There was no way to stop her husband from having these affairs, so instead she focussed on what she *could* do." Mary paused and looked at Lord Hinchbrooke and then Jane, her next words forceful. "I will *never* believe she harmed anyone else or took her own life. She felt guilty over things she had no influence over, and she carried the weight of her husband's sins on her shoulders, but she had been doing that for the duration of their marriage."

"Nothing had changed now," Jane said quietly.

"Exactly. Kitty was the latest in a long line of young women ruined by her husband, but there wasn't anything unusual about this time. She would ensure Kitty was provided for, add her name to the long list of wronged women and carry on working away in the background."

"She hadn't finished her work to protect these women," Lord Hinchbrooke murmured.

Mary Wright nodded vigorously. "You're right. She had this guilt, this drive, pushing her. There is no way she would have given in and taken her own life. She would have known it would bring an end to the charitable work that had defined her life these last twenty years. Mrs Paulson told me once that she had stood by and let a young woman suffer once, and that had ended in the most terrible way. That was when she had decided to devote her life to trying to make the world a better place."

"Thank you, Miss Wright," Lord Hinchbrooke said, standing up from his chair.

"You believe me — that she didn't kill herself?"

He hesitated and Jane stepped forward. "We cannot come to any conclusions yet, Mary, but I promise you we have heard everything you have said, and we will not clutch at the easy solution when the truth is there to be unearthed."

"Thank you, Miss."

Silently they left Miss Wright's bedroom, closing the door behind them.

"She was devoted to her mistress," Lord Hinchbrooke said quietly as they descended the stairs to the first floor.

"I wonder what will happen to all the staff now."

"That will be for Mr and Mrs Williams to decide, if they do inherit," Lord Hinchbrooke said with a tilt of his head. "If they are not found guilty of murder first."

CHAPTER NINETEEN

"Jane, I need a moment of your time," Cassandra said, coming down the stairs into the kitchens. Lord Hinchbrooke had decided to interview each of the servants in turn, choosing to do it in the kitchens where they would feel more comfortable rather than in the family rooms upstairs. It was monotonous work, checking where everyone was around the times of the three deaths, and it served only to highlight that anyone could have left their post for a few minutes unobserved and stabbed Mr Paulson or hit Mr Upton over the head. The servants in particular hardly ever stayed still, always running to fetch or carry, to answer a summons or prepare something for later in the day. It made it impossible for anyone to provide an alibi for anyone else.

"Is something amiss?"

Cassandra didn't answer, instead waiting for Jane to rise from her seat and follow her upstairs. Only once they were ensconced in an alcove in the library did she speak.

"I have been outside and I spoke to Mr Jones. He has been out to the main road and tells me the snow is melting fast. He thinks if the weather stays mild, the roads might be clear enough for a carriage to pass tomorrow morning."

"You want to go home?"

"Do you not?" Cassandra shook her head and held up a hand. "Do not answer that."

"Cassandra…"

"I am weary, Jane. It has been a trying few days, and I find myself overcome with nerves all the time. I wish to be at home where I feel safe, where I do not need to look over my shoulder all the time."

"I understand."

"I think it best you return home with me."

Jane felt her heart sink. Slowly everything felt like it was slotting into place. They didn't know who had committed the murders yet, or how precisely, but piece by piece the information was fitting together to make a full picture. Another day or two and they may get the information they needed to be able to name a suspect.

"I know it is not what you want," Cassandra said, reaching for Jane's hand, "but this trip was meant to be relaxing, a diverting time with pleasant company. It has been the opposite."

"It is not that I don't yearn for the company of our parents and the safety and comfort of our home, but I just need a few more days."

"I am not sure this is good for you, Jane. Think how you have been after the last gruesome affair you were embroiled in. You have barely slept, you are wasting away, you are hardly even writing. I don't think we can blame all of that on Mr Tom Lefroy. These murders take a toll on you."

At the mention of Mr Lefroy's name, Jane felt her body stiffen and a chill passed over her skin. She couldn't deny the events of the last few days had worked as a distraction from what she was fast coming to admit was a broken heart. For three days she hadn't found herself wondering whether Mr Lefroy might write, whether he might realise what she meant to him and ride to Steventon to declare himself. Until this weekend her thoughts had consisted of little else, and she didn't want to return to the madness of speculation.

"I will not deny the events of the last few months have been taxing," Jane said, choosing her words carefully, "but I *can't* leave like this, not with everything unresolved. It will torment me, and I will find no peace at home."

Cassandra regarded her for a long minute. "I think you are making a mistake," she said eventually. "Everyone will be leaving tomorrow; no one wishes to stay in this house of death. I am not saying you can't ponder on the matter at home, but return with me, surround yourself with the people you love."

"Please do not press me, Cassandra. I wish to assist Lord Hinchbrooke as much as I can. It gives me purpose."

"It is a noble aim, but Lord Hinchbrooke will cope fine without you. You have done your part; you have kept everything preserved until he could get here and imparted the knowledge you have gathered, but please, Jane, I beseech you, leave it to him now."

"I promise to think on it, Cassandra."

"You forget you cannot stay here unchaperoned."

"Mrs Williams will be here."

Cassandra gave her a hard stare. "Someone you suspect of murder is hardly a suitable chaperon, Jane."

Jane tried to suppress a smile but couldn't quite manage it. She was pleased to see Cassandra's expression mirror her own after a few seconds.

"You would think I would have more cause to worry about Frank or Charles than you, with their dangerous naval campaigns and daring deeds."

"I do not mean to vex you, Cassandra. I promise I will think on what you have said."

"I suppose I cannot ask for any more than that."

Jane took a moment to enjoy her sister's embrace, trying to push away the melancholy she felt when she realised that one day soon, Cassandra would go off to become Mrs Thomas Fowle, and never would their relationship be the same again.

The next morning promised mild and sunny conditions, and Jane felt a flash of disappointment as she peeked through the curtains before Cassandra was awake. She had hoped for one more day. So much could be achieved in that time.

Jane was downstairs before eight, listening to the bustle of the servants as they prepared for another day. Mrs Brown had told them the day before that there were enough funds in the household accounts to pay the remaining servants for the month, so for now they would continue with their duties until someone came to tell them otherwise. Mr Paulson's will would have to be read soon, and no doubt there were complex legal processes that would have to be adhered to before Mr Williams could claim his inheritance, if he were the heir. It would be a time of great upheaval and uncertainty for the staff, and no doubt they would fear for their jobs.

Lord Hinchbrooke emerged a few minutes later, looking tousled from the night. In his haste to get to Melmont Hall as quickly as possible he hadn't brought a valet with him, and there was no one used to this role in the Paulson household. Jane wondered for a moment who had been responsible for looking after Mr Paulson, ensuring his clothes were pressed and ready for the day and seeing to his shave and personal care. She could not imagine the young footman in the role, but perhaps he and Benjamin Grout had shared the duties.

"Good morning, Miss Austen. Did you sleep well?"

"Passably, my lord," Jane said, watching carefully as Lord Hinchbrooke struggled into the room. He was certainly finding moving around difficult today, and she knew he would pay the price for his long ride in the snow yesterday morning.

"I didn't sleep a jot," he said with a wry smile, "and I would wager you did not either."

"There is so much to unpick. I kept going round in circles as I lay in bed last night. Was Mr Paulson killed because of his treatment of one of the young maids he took advantage of? If so, who in this house would care enough about Kitty to kill him? If we don't think anyone came from the village and we do not believe Peter Jones is a likely suspect, then who are we left with?"

The magistrate opened his arms in a gesture of defeat and shook his head.

"If not because of Kitty specifically, who apart from Mrs Paulson would care about the string of misery he has left behind? Or have we become too distracted by his dubious morals and pushed aside too easily another motive: money?"

"That is not forgetting the most puzzling question of all. How did someone enter Mr Paulson's study, stab him and leave, ensuring the door was locked from the inside?"

"Perhaps Mr Paulson realised what an awful man he was and stabbed himself in the abdomen."

"Then his ghost rose from the dead and killed Mr Upton and his wife?" Lord Hinchbrooke said with a rueful shake of his head.

"Everyone will be leaving today, unless you can compel them to stay."

"I do not have the grounds to arrest anyone. I can ask in the strongest possible terms that they do not leave, but I cannot stop them if they really want to go."

"I know," Jane said miserably.

"I want to talk to Mr and Mrs Williams this morning, to see if they reveal anything more."

Their conversation was interrupted by the sound of wheels rolling on the drive outside. Jane crossed to the window, looking out, and saw a cart rounding the corner, heading towards the door to the kitchen.

"The undertakers have arrived."

"Good. I asked Mr Jones to head into the village and ask for the undertakers to come and remove the bodies as soon as the cart could get through. If we leave things much longer, Mr Paulson will begin to putrefy. I should go and supervise," Lord Hinchbrooke said, standing with a groan. "Without a head of household, it is unfair to ask the servants to do such a thing alone. The cook may have been here for years, but never would she have agreed to duties including the disposal of the dead."

Jane didn't offer to accompany him. The smell of the bodies was still fresh in her mind from the day before, and she didn't need the image of the indignity the dead would be subjected to imprinted on her brain. Instead she sat in the comfortable chair and tried to ignore the sounds from the storerooms below.

"Good morning, Miss Austen," Colonel Rushton said as he entered the room. He looked a shadow of his former self, with sallow cheeks and his eyes sunken in his face, making him look a decade older than a few days earlier.

"Good morning, Colonel."

"I understand the undertakers are here."

"Yes. Lord Hinchbrooke is downstairs with them now."

"Good. Although I am sure there will be some delay whilst Mr Paulson's affairs are sorted."

"Surely they will bury the dead and conduct a funeral?"

"They will bury them, they will have to, but until the will is read and an heir named, there is no one to sort this out properly. No one to guarantee payment to the undertakers."

Jane hadn't considered this. She suspected you would have to be cruel of heart to deny someone a fitting memorial, but tombs and headstones were expensive, and if the heir did not know the person they were inheriting from then she supposed there would be the temptation to cut the cost.

"I will speak to the undertakers and give them the guarantee that I will pay for any expenses if no one else comes forward to settle the debt," said the colonel.

"That is noble, Colonel Rushton."

"It is the least I can do. I do not pretend there was any great respect between myself and Mr Paulson, but I had known Mrs Paulson a long time and held her in high regard. It is only right I ensure she is laid to rest properly."

"I am sorry for your loss, Colonel," Jane said softly and for a moment she thought he might break down, but he rallied and gave her a curt nod, choosing to turn away rather than let her see the extent of his emotions.

"Has Lord Hinchbrooke come to any conclusions yet?"

"Not yet."

"The guests will be starting to depart today. The roads are not completely clear, but they are passable. I know Dr Histon is keen to leave, as his journey back to Deal is unlikely to be straightforward."

"I am sure you are keen to go as well."

Colonel Rushton hesitated. "Yes, although I am loath to go with the matter being unresolved."

Jane knew the feeling well. The colonel remained silent for a few moments and then turned abruptly, leaving the room without saying any more.

"Miss Austen," Mr Williams said, his manner hesitant, "am I disturbing you?"

"No, Mr Williams, please come in." He must have been waiting outside for Colonel Rushton to depart.

"My wife and I think it best if we go back to the village today," Mr Williams said as he came in and took a seat, perching nervously on the edge of the cushion. "We are close by if anything is needed, and there is nothing we can do until Mr Paulson's will is read."

"I think Lord Hinchbrooke will want to speak to you first."

"Of course, I wouldn't leave without his blessing. The last few days have been such a horrible strain on my wife; I just want to get her back to some semblance of normality. I know it is our fault for engaging in this deception, but I wish to put at least a little distance between us and Melmont Hall."

"What will you do whilst you wait for the will to be read?"

Mr Williams chuckled, but it was without humour. "I live in fear of being dragged off to debtors' prison, so we will live quietly and hope the solicitor appears sooner rather than later."

"And if you are not named as heir in the will?"

Mr Williams opened his hands and shrugged with such sadness that Jane felt sorry for him.

"Then I think it unavoidable. I will perhaps be able to hold off the creditors for another month, or maybe two, hopefully long enough to make some provision for Lilith. She has a cousin who may well take pity on her in our hour of need."

Jane grimaced. As much as she believed the Williamses had done the wrong thing in concealing their true identities and worming their way into the Paulsons' home, she was well aware of the reputation of debtors' prisons. They were no better than the prisons where they held criminals, for the conditions were dire. Cold cells, damp, uncomfortable beds and food only for those who could spare a coin to pay for it. Without any help or support from friends or family outside the prison, a man would struggle to survive a harsh winter in those conditions.

"I hope it does not come to that, Mr Williams," Jane said softly.

"As do I, Miss Austen."

"Lord Hinchbrooke is occupied with the undertakers at present, but I will suggest we arrange an interview with you and your wife after breakfast. That way, if you do wish to return to your accommodation in the village, you will be able to do so before it gets dark."

"Thank you, Miss Austen."

Mr Williams stood and bowed, leaving the room with his shoulders slumped and his head bent.

Jane considered him for a while, wondering if he was a consummate actor or if he was the misguided, desperate man he portrayed so well. It was difficult to tell. His actions could either be those of a man who had simply run out of options, or they could be hiding malicious motivations.

She was so deep in thought that at first she didn't hear Lord Hinchbrooke return, only noticing his presence as he sat down in the chair Mr Williams had just left.

"At least that is done," he said, closing his eyes for a moment.

"Colonel Rushton was in here a moment ago. He said the undertakers may want a guarantee of their fee being paid before they do more."

Lord Hinchbrooke nodded. "I have given them my word the estate will be liable for the cost of the burial and undertaker's fees. They know the Paulsons were not in any financial hardship, so that should be enough."

"Could the heir refuse to pay?"

"It is a tricky area of the law to interpret, but they can argue they didn't request certain expensive items — engraved headstones, that sort of thing. I had a look through Mr Paulson's papers last night when I couldn't sleep. There was no will I could find, but I did manage to ascertain the details of his solicitors. I will send a messenger with a letter to them today, and hopefully they will attend tomorrow with the will."

"I wonder whether Mr Paulson did change the will so it did not favour Mr Williams or if that was an empty threat, designed to get the man to leave him alone whilst Mr Paulson was alive."

"It will be interesting to see, although I doubt the old man changed his will. Who else would he leave all this to? He may not have known Mr Williams or even wanted to help him in life, but he was a blood relative, and somehow in matters of inheritance that seems to matter more than anything else to many people."

"Mr Williams was here a few minutes ago. He wishes to take his wife back to their rented cottage in the village. I said you would want to talk to him first."

"How did he seem?"

"Like a condemned man."

"I wonder if that is because of his debt or because of a guilty conscience?"

"I'm not convinced he is guilty," she said slowly, "even though out of everyone here he has the greatest amount to gain from Mr Paulson's death."

"Did you suggest a time to talk to him?"

"I did. I thought after breakfast would be good."

"Fantastic. I am ravenous."

As they left the library, they almost tripped over a small pile of bags in the hall. Charlotte was carrying another bag down the stairs, huffing under the weight of it.

"Who is leaving, Charlotte?" Jane asked.

"Mrs Leveritt and Miss Leveritt. They are both having breakfast now, but they are keen to get away straight after."

"I am afraid I must depart soon too," Dr Histon said as he came down the stairs behind Charlotte. "The doctor who is covering my practice will be expecting me back soon, and I do not think the journey to Deal will be an easy one. I can leave my address if you have any more queries, Lord Hinchbrooke."

"Thank you," the magistrate murmured.

Jane found she didn't have much of an appetite and picked at a piece of toast and her poached egg. It felt as though she had failed. Three people were dead and they didn't have any answers, yet everyone was leaving, ready to get on with their lives. Lord Hinchbrooke was right, he didn't have the power to compel anyone to stay, but she wished they had just one more day.

There was no conversation around the breakfast table. Everyone was too subdued to make an effort and Jane thought some were wary of saying something they shouldn't with the magistrate sitting there with them. After drinking her tea and deciding she could not stomach any more breakfast, Jane stood. She felt overwhelmed, and as though the walls were pressing down on her.

"Is something amiss, Miss Austen?" Lord Hinchbrooke asked.

"I need some fresh air."

"Let me accompany you."

"Please do not rouse yourself on my account."

"I insist, Miss Austen."

Seeing he was not going to back down, Jane nodded, murmured a farewell to the rest of the table and then strode from the room. It took her a few minutes to find someone to ask for her outer garments, but before too long the young footman emerged with her coat and the pair of heavy boots she had worn when venturing out in the snow.

"Thank you," she said as she slipped off her satin shoes. Never again would she plan to spend a weekend away in the winter without packing suitable footwear for *all* occasions.

Once they were outside, Jane felt some of the weight lift from her as she filled her lungs with fresh, cold air.

"I feel like I have failed," she said as they set off around the front of the house. "Three deaths and I have been here for all of them. I have spoken to everyone in this house, been a witness myself, yet I cannot fathom who has killed these three people or why."

"You have very high expectations of yourself, Miss Austen."

"If you had been here, I expect there would never have been a second murder, let alone a third."

"I doubt that is true. I have as little idea of the identity of the murderer as you, Miss Austen."

"Has this happened before? Are there cases where you have not found the culprit?"

Lord Hinchbrooke grimaced. "A few. Nothing as ghastly as this, but yes, there have been crimes where either there is no evidence to point towards the perpetrator, or I have suspected someone but not been able to prove anything. They are the ones that haunt you, Miss Austen."

"I can imagine. I feel haunted already."

"We will get to the bottom of this. It is a conundrum, that is true, but not an impossible one to solve. With a little more information and some time to think, I am certain a solution will present itself. The correct solution."

Jane wasn't as convinced. She hated the thought of whoever had committed these crimes getting away with it, being allowed to continue on with their normal lives without any repercussions for their evil deeds.

"Come, Miss Austen, we will prevail. Point out to me where the different rooms are and where Mr Upton was killed."

They walked a little to the left of the main entrance to Melmont Hall, and Jane described the gruesome scene they had been presented with only a couple of days before. As they moved closer, she was appalled to see some blood staining on the stonework. The snow had almost cleared here, washing away most of the details of the scene, but a few splatters remained.

"I wonder," Lord Hinchbrooke murmured to himself, testing the square slabs, but none of them came loose.

"You think the murder weapon was something picked up out here?" Jane had discounted the idea, thinking the murderer had likely sneaked up on Mr Upton with their chosen heavy, blunt object already in their hands. The butler was likely to be jumpy and on edge given what had happened to his employer and wouldn't stand around whilst someone prised a paving slab free to knock him over the head with.

"Perhaps. Mr Upton's murder was the riskiest of all three. I think someone realised the butler was onto them and had to act quickly, without much time to plan. The first murder was meticulous, in many ways a work of art. The whole house has been puzzling at it for days, and no one can work out how it was done. In contrast, Mr Upton's murder was rushed. It was committed in panic and that means the murderer may have made a mistake."

Jane began to cast her eyes around, wondering what could have caused that horrific, bloody injury to Mr Upton's skull.

"Mr Upton's murder was messy, so the murder weapon would be as well. It might have been something brought from inside the house, but I doubt whoever killed the butler would risk taking it back inside, covered in blood and hair."

"You're right. The house was busy. It meant people could come and go without it being suspicious, but it also meant there was a higher chance someone would spot you if you walked in carrying a bloody spade or something similar."

"A spade isn't a bad idea," Lord Hinchbrooke said thoughtfully. "Perhaps we should check the outbuildings for any equipment missing, or anything that has blood on it that shouldn't." Jane nodded as Lord Hinchbrooke straightened. "But for now, shall we continue round the house? I wish to see the study from the outside, to confirm no one could have left that way. I don't want to be focussing on the inhabitants if there is a way to re-fasten the window from outside."

They continued round the outside of the house, Jane with her arm through Lord Hinchbrooke's, gently supporting him. She hoped the deterioration she had seen in him was temporary, brought on by the long ride in the cold weather. He'd confided a little about his condition — a shaking palsy, he called it — and the doctors had told him the tremors would get worse, as would the stiffness. It varied from case to case, but some people with this condition were left barely able to move, trapped inside their bodies, their minds working but with no way of expressing themselves.

Jane knew that was what Lord Hinchbrooke feared. He hadn't told her in so many words, but the look of desolation on his face as he'd described what his future would likely hold was enough to inform her. The only thing he dreaded more was the possibility of slowly losing his wits, reverting back to the infant stage as some old men and women seemed to.

"Over there you have the stables, assorted outbuildings, and the cottage Gabriel and Peter Jones live in." Jane pointed out the different buildings as they rounded the side of the house, and then they were on the wide path that separated the house from the formal gardens. There was a well-kept border filled with hardy shrubs directly adjacent to the house and then the gravel path was set a little above the rest of the grounds, with a few steps down to the neat geometric design of the flower beds.

"Here," Jane said, as they paused outside the study windows.

Most of the snow here had melted with the sun shining directly on this side of the house. Only a little remained on the leaves of an evergreen shrub, caught in the folds and protected from the sunlight.

Lord Hinchbrooke leaned over, stepping into the mud to get closer to the windows. He pulled and pushed, gripping them with his fingertips and testing to ensure they truly were secure.

"There were no footprints either?"

Jane shook her head, holding out her hand to steady him as he stepped out of the flower bed. As she began to turn to continue on the walk around the house, something in the soil caught her eye. The light glinted off it and at first she thought it might be a shard of ice, but as she leaned closer she saw it was a little glass vial.

Crouching down, she reached out her gloved hand and picked it up, regarding it with a frown. It was about three inches long with a stopper in the top. There was a crust of brown around the top and a few dried flakes in the bottom.

"Is that blood?" Jane asked, straightening.

She handed the bottle over to Lord Hinchbrooke but didn't wait for his response, her gaze drawn to the window in front of her. It was one of the study windows, and just beyond the glass was the chair where Mr Paulson had been found murdered.

With a cold dread, all the jumbled pieces of the puzzle slotted together and Jane saw the only way this could have been done, and the only person who could have done it.

"It is blood," Lord Hinchbrooke said, his expression grim.

"I know who the murderer is," Jane whispered.

"You do? From this little glass vial?"

She nodded, not quite believing it herself, turning the theory over and over in her mind, testing it anew.

"I need to ask Mrs Brown one question to confirm everything, but yes, I can see how it was done."

"How? Who?"

Jane opened her mouth to reply, but the clatter of wheels around the front of the house made her hesitate.

"We need to stop everyone from leaving," she said, her heart hammering in her chest.

"I will do that. I'll gather everyone in the drawing room. You speak to Mrs Brown."

"Thank you."

They hurried off in separate directions, Jane heading towards the servants' entrance and Lord Hinchbrooke to the front of the house to stall the departing guests.

Ten minutes later, everyone was squeezed into the drawing room. The carriage had been for the Leveritts, and it had taken all of Lord Hinchbrooke's authority to press them to stay. Thankfully no one else had departed yet and most people were too intrigued to grumble too much about being brought together in this way. Colonel Rushton and Dr Histon stood side by side next to the fireplace. Mr and Mrs Williams were on one sofa whilst Miss Leveritt and her mother were on another. Cassandra sat in one of the armchairs, and Jane was perching on the arm whilst she waited for the room to settle. Lord Hinchbrooke was in the other armchair, looking about him with interest as if trying to see if he could work out what she had concluded before she revealed it. The servants were huddled at one end, Mrs Brown at the front of the group, the rest looking nervous behind her. Even Gabriel and Peter Jones were there, with the younger brother leaning against the doorframe.

"Thank you all for gathering here this morning," Lord Hinchbrooke said, not rising from his chair. "Miss Austen will now address you. I ask that you give her your full attention and answer any questions she has for you honestly and openly."

"Do you know who the murderer is?" Mrs Leveritt asked, her gaze darting from the magistrate to Jane and back again.

"I believe so," Jane said, getting to her feet and taking a few steps so she could survey all of the occupants of the room at the same time. It was unsettling, seeing all the faces there looking back at her, but she knew this had to be done. She *knew* who had committed the murders, or at least she thought she did, but there was no easy way of proving it. It was the only solution that fitted, the only solution that was possible, but she needed the evidence of some of the people in the room today to push her suspect into confessing.

"You know?" Colonel Rushton said, stepping forward.

"Yes, Colonel. I will explain everything." Jane took a deep, steadying breath before she began, knowing her choice of words was important. "Over the course of the last four days, there have been three tragic deaths here at Melmont Hall. Three murders."

Colonel Rushton stirred again and took another step forward.

"Surely you mean two murders."

Jane shook her head. "Three, Colonel. Mrs Paulson was the third victim, and she was murdered just as Mr Paulson and Mr Upton were. However, we have three very different crimes. Lord Hinchbrooke pointed it out this morning — the first murder, Mr Paulson's murder, was meticulously planned. It seemed impossible; how was our host stabbed sitting at his desk behind a locked door? The other two murders were rushed, acts that had not been part of the original plan, something done to cover up the mistakes made."

Jane glanced at Lord Hinchbrooke for reassurance and felt her confidence growing as he nodded at her encouragingly.

"It is with Mr Paulson's death that we will find the motive. The other two were for self-preservation, but the first murder was the one that the murderer was fully invested in."

"What was the motive? Tell us who has done this," Colonel Rushton demanded.

"Colonel, some patience, please," Lord Hinchbrooke said in his authoritative tone. "Allow Miss Austen to speak."

"There were lots of possible motives. It is a badly kept secret that Mr Paulson had numerous affairs with maids and other women in inferior positions, women he could control and manipulate. He would promise them the world, have his fun and then, when they inevitably became pregnant, turn them out without another thought."

"My mistress saw to it they were looked after," Mary Wright said, her voice ringing out clearly through the room.

"That she did, Mary. At first, it made me wonder if Mrs Paulson had a motive to kill her husband. He was committing adultery again and again, right here under her nose. It was humiliating, and I think most would have some sympathy for her situation."

"Mrs Paulson would never harm anyone," Mary said firmly.

"I agree. It wasn't in her nature. She had accepted her lot. She was a woman married to a powerful man. She couldn't stop him having his affairs, so instead she worked around the edges, ensuring the young women had somewhere to go once they had been turned out. Of course, she disliked her husband, but he had been carrying on this way for years. I couldn't see what would be different this time." Jane paused, glad that her audience was enraptured. "I did wonder if perhaps Mr Paulson had fallen for his latest conquest, but there was no evidence of it. He'd had Kitty dismissed, and there was no sign he was planning on breaking his pattern."

"I am glad you ruled Mrs Paulson out," Cassandra said, her voice soft but her eyes filled with tension.

"I am too. She was a kind woman, a good woman."

"If not Mrs Paulson, then who?" Colonel Rushton said, his arm sweeping around the room.

"As I said, there were plenty with a motive. The dismissed maid Kitty, or the footman who was obsessed with her and sent away on the same day after an argument with Mr Paulson. Mr Jones here, with his fondness for Kitty and his strong sense of right and wrong. Or perhaps the business with Mr Paulson's unsavoury affairs with the maids was a distraction. Mr and Mrs Williams, or Mr and Mrs Potter as most of you know them, have a financial claim on the estate. The murder could have been merely a means to speed up their inheritance."

All eyes focussed on the young married couple and Mr Williams stood, his face flushing.

"Sit down, Mr Williams," Lord Hinchbrooke said, and the man complied quickly. "Miss Austen does not believe you are the murderer; she is merely illustrating the point that many have a motive."

"So you see, it could have been almost anyone. The only person I could safely dismiss as a suspect was my dear sister, as she had been with me the entire time in question."

Cassandra looked at her and gave Jane an encouraging smile. Jane was struck by how exhausted her sister looked and felt relieved that this matter was nearly concluded. A few more minutes and hopefully Lord Hinchbrooke would have the confession he needed.

"From the very beginning, I told myself that the way to identify the murderer was to work out how the crime had been committed, how the doors and windows to Mr Paulson's study were secured from the inside. It was only this morning, when I saw *this* glinting in the sunlight under the study window, that everything fell into place." She brandished the little glass vial. "I expect the murderer has been searching for it frantically, but it remained hidden in the snow until it melted this morning."

"Is it a bottle, Miss Austen?" Miss Leveritt asked. She had colour in her cheeks and looked more lively than Jane had seen her for days. Perhaps the prospect of this nightmare nearly being over was making her feel more like her normal self.

"A vial. There are a few streaks in the bottom, rust-red."

"Blood?" Colonel Rushton said, frowning.

"I believe so. Shall we go back to that first night? Everyone was gathering in the drawing room, but it was hectic with guests arriving at different times, servants rushing here and there. People came and went, and as such no one has an alibi for the time Mr Paulson was murdered. Anyone could have slipped out of the drawing room, or up from the kitchen, and into the study."

"I concur," Colonel Rushton said, nodding his head.

"At seven, we all go in for dinner and Mr Paulson does not appear. Mrs Paulson asks the butler to fetch him, but Mr Upton cannot rouse him." She holds up a finger. "This next part is important. Mr Upton comes back into the room and Mrs Paulson leaves. I follow, and so does Colonel Rushton. The colonel bangs on the door, but there is no response, so he goes to knock it down. But before he can put his shoulder to it, Dr Histon steps out into the hall and stops him, reminding him of an old injury."

Colonel Rushton was nodding along as Jane spoke, confirming her version of events.

"It takes him a few attempts, but Dr Histon is able to knock down the door and enter the room. He can tell immediately that Mr Paulson is dead, and we can see it from the doorway, so he instructs us to wait there whilst he checks the body. He declares Mr Paulson has been stabbed, and Colonel Rushton and I enter the room."

Jane turned to the colonel, his face now ashen. She felt a flicker of sympathy and held up the bottle with the remnants of blood in it.

"You know, don't you?"

She watched him hesitate, and then slowly he nodded. "It is the only way."

"And that is what Mr Upton realised, long before us. Although he did have an advantage of a slightly different viewpoint from the door of the study."

"Miss Austen, the suspense is killing me," Mrs Leveritt said, her eyes shining with excitement.

"This plan was very clever and very risky. Carried out by someone who knows how people react in stressful situations, how they do not focus on details, how their perception can be changed, the train of their thoughts guided away from the truth. Isn't that right, Dr Histon?"

Jane could feel the energy ripple through the room as everyone turned to look at the doctor.

"Are you asking for my medical opinion?"

"No. Do you want to explain how you did it, or shall I?"

"I am afraid you've lost me, Miss Austen," Dr Histon said, his voice laced with concern.

"I got myself so caught up with looking for alibis and who could have left the drawing room during the time Mr Paulson was killed, when in truth the finding of the body was all staged. Mr Paulson had died earlier. At some point just after six, Dr Histon slips away and knocks on Mr Paulson's door. He has a quick conversation with Mr Paulson and hands him something he claims is an important document, asking Mr Paulson to look it over in complete privacy as soon as possible. Charlotte has already delivered Mr Paulson's evening drink, and Dr Histon engineers an opportunity to slip something into the whiskey. The strong flavour would hide the taste of many lethal poisons. Dr Histon leaves and Mr Paulson, taking the doctor's advice, locks the door behind him then sits down at his desk to drink his whiskey and look at the letter he has been given."

"The blank sheets of paper on the desk," Colonel Rushton murmured.

"The poison gets to work quickly and Mr Paulson dies in his chair, with the door to the study securely locked, by him. An hour later, we come to dinner time. Dr Histon makes sure he is the one to enter the study first; this is vital for his plans. He has the authority of a doctor, and once everyone has seen Mr Paulson is dead he can ask for a few seconds before other people rush into the room. Hidden by the desk, as he ostensibly checks over the body, he thrusts the letter opener he took earlier from Mr Paulson's desk into the old man's abdomen."

"But dead bodies don't bleed," Colonel Rushton said, his face now deathly white.

"Dead bodies don't bleed," Jane agreed, "which is what this vial was for. I assume it was filled to the brim with blood, and Dr Histon pulled out the stopper and poured it onto Mr Paulson's shirt around the wound. It didn't form a great pool, but it was enough to convince anyone who looked that Mr Paulson had bled when he was stabbed, and therefore his heart was still beating."

Colonel Rushton turned to his friend, despair and rapidly dying hope in his eyes. "You opened one of the windows, when we were there with the body."

"I think he threw this vial out. I suspect he planned to retrieve it later, but it was the one thing that could condemn him if found on him. Later, the snow was too thick and had obscured the bottle, and he was wary of disturbing the area too much in his search."

"What about the other two murders, Miss Austen?" Lord Hinchbrooke said, his tone grave.

"Mr Upton was to the very left of the doorway when Dr Histon entered the room. I think he realised that when he first saw the body, before Dr Histon approached it, there hadn't been a knife protruding from the abdomen. He worked out what had occurred and was going to reveal everything to Colonel Rushton, but when Dr Histon became aware of the butler's request to meet his friend, he convinced Mr Upton it would be worth his while to meet him instead. I still do not know what the murder weapon was, but it was a swift crime — a blow to the back of the head with a blunt object. Then you left him in the snow to breathe his last breath."

Jane glanced at Dr Histon and saw his expression hadn't changed. He looked sorrowful, but more in a way you might if someone was clearly exhibiting signs of madness in front of you, rather than because you had been found out as a murderer.

"Mrs Paulson — I think she was probably the hardest one for you," Jane said quietly, wondering if she saw a flicker of emotion in his eyes. "At first I couldn't work out why, but then I realised you let something slip that afternoon when we were playing cards. Mrs Paulson became flustered and left soon after, retiring to her room. You must have realised what she knew about you and decided you could not take the risk of her revealing it all."

"You think I killed her as well?"

"That evening, you waited until Mary had brought Mrs Paulson her warm milk, and then you lured her from the room by emitting a small cry — rightly deducing that she would think it was Mrs Leveritt, took the key from the bedside table where you knew it would be, and opened up the chest of medicines. You selected a bottle of laudanum and put a few drops in the cup of milk, ensuring it was only a few so she wouldn't notice the flavour in the sweetened milk. Not enough to kill her, but enough to make sure she slept soundly, and then you retreated and waited. I don't know what time you returned, but you coaxed the sleepy Mrs Paulson to drink the rest of the bottle of laudanum, adding another few drops to the milk so it would seem she had mixed it with her drink and consumed it in one go."

"And the paper?" Colonel Rushton said, barely able to get his words out now.

"The scrap of paper. It was an interesting decision, one I expect you regret, Dr Histon. I imagine it was torn from a letter Mrs Paulson wrote to you or your family many, many years ago, apologising for something that she felt a weight of responsibility for."

"It is a clever story, Miss Austen," Dr Histon said, "but fanciful. There is no reason for me to do any of these things. I do not know these people. Before this weekend, I had never once met Mr Paulson, Mrs Paulson or Mr Upton before."

"You are right, you hadn't. When I realised the only person who *could* have killed Mr Paulson was you, everything else began slotting into place. I realised I had settled on the right motive, but the wrong time period." She turned to Mary Wright. "You told me about the governess who took an overdose, the reason Mrs Paulson was so fastidious about keeping the medicines of the house under lock and key."

"Yes, Miss. It was a long time ago."

Mrs Brown shifted. "I remember. I had just taken up my position here as kitchen maid."

"Thank you, Mrs Brown. Can you remember the name of this governess?"

"Rebecca," Mrs Brown said. "Miss Rebecca Histon."

Silence fell across the room, and Jane could see Dr Histon desperately trying to maintain his composure.

"Your sister, I presume," Jane said. "She was the one to take her own life."

Still Dr Histon did not speak and Jane momentarily closed her eyes, steeling herself for what she was about to do next. She would try to provoke him, but her conscience would find the act troubling.

"Of course, I do not know, but I assume something prompted her to risk eternal damnation."

"My sister is not burning in hell, Miss Austen," Dr Histon said, his tone clipped. "Only a vengeful, cruel God would make her suffer after death when she went through so much during life."

"She fell victim to Mr Paulson?"

For a long moment she thought Dr Histon would continue to deny it, and then he let out a troubled exhalation. "I admit nothing, except the fact my sister did use to work here. Mr Paulson, with his lecherous ways, took advantage of her in the most cruel way and left her broken in mind and soul. Seeing no way out, she took her own life. I do not deny that, Miss Austen, but it does not mean I killed the Paulsons and their butler. Why would I wait for twenty years to do so?"

"I do believe you came to Hampshire with no thought of murder in your mind, Dr Histon. You came, as you say, to visit your friend Colonel Rushton. It is only when you arrived that you realised you had been thrown into the very place you would never voluntarily choose to go. Here was the place your dear sister killed herself, and you were invited to dinner with the people that drove her to her death." Jane paused. "I suspect you even thought about turning down the invitation at first, making up some excuse and riding as fast as you could back to Kent, for no doubt these past twenty years you have tried to put the terrible tragedy from your mind."

"For someone you accuse of murder, you make many allowances," Dr Histon murmured.

"It was that Kitty girl," Colonel Rushton said, turning to his friend. "That was what made you stay, wasn't it?" The colonel turned to Lord Hinchbrooke to explain. "The local doctor was caught up somewhere, and a girl came to beg Dr Histon to attend her sister. She said her sister was bleeding and losing her baby. It was Kitty you went to see, wasn't it? You worked out that all these years later, Mr Paulson was still doing the same thing he did to your sister."

"He had to be stopped," Dr Histon said quietly. "All those years, all those lives ruined, and he was sitting here free from any consequence."

Mary Wright lunged forward and slapped the doctor on the cheek.

"How could you do that to my mistress? She was a good woman, a kind soul."

Colonel Rushton stepped in and pried the maid off his friend, passing the sobbing young woman back to Mrs Brown.

"I do regret that," Dr Histon said quietly. "She remembered the surname. I could tell. I mentioned my sister and I could see it made a connection in her mind. It was only a matter of time before she was sure."

"You killed her for that?" Colonel Rushton said, and Jane felt the emotion pulsing from him in waves. To learn his friend had been the one to kill the woman he had once loved must have been heart-breaking.

"We have a lot to talk about, Dr Histon," Lord Hinchbrooke said, standing from his chair and taking control of the room. "Thank you, Miss Austen, for your thorough explanation. Now, I have arrangements to make and I suggest you all go home."

Lord Hinchbrooke waited, but no one moved or said a word.

Finally Cassandra stood, moving gracefully from her seat to the front of the room. She paused by the door and turned back to the assembled company, meeting everyone's eye in turn and then giving a shallow curtsey. As she left the room, the rest of the guests sprung into action, as if released from some sort of spell. They hurried from the room, no one looking back, and Jane wondered if they were worried about getting caught up in any more of the drama.

Finally it was only her, Lord Hinchbrooke and Dr Histon. She turned to the magistrate, who bowed to her formally.

"My sincere thanks, Miss Austen."

"I hope you do not mind, my lord, but I am going to take my leave. Cassandra is eager to get home, and I have to admit that if I never see Melmont Hall again it will be too soon. I am weary and find I have no stomach for what comes next here."

"Rest, Miss Austen. Recuperate. You have done more than enough here. Perhaps you will permit me to call on you in a few days. I can inform you of our progress then."

"Thank you, my lord."

Jane turned to face Dr Histon, unsure what she felt about the man in front of her. Murder should never be the answer, but she could understand his driving need to stop the man who had pushed his sister into such a despair years earlier. If he had stopped there, perhaps she might feel some sympathy for him, but Mr Upton and Mrs Paulson had been a step too far. Not entirely innocent, but certainly there was no way anyone could justify their deaths.

"It has been a pleasure knowing you, Miss Austen," Dr Histon said, inclining his head.

CHAPTER TWENTY

The carriage rattled away from the house along the drive, and soon they were through the heavy metal gates and onto the road into the village. The horses were moving slowly, the driver cautious, but the road seemed passable, and it wasn't long before the village was in sight.

"Mother and Father will never let you leave the house again after this affair," Cassandra murmured.

Jane smiled, leaning her head back against the plush seat. The carriage was borrowed from a friend, and it was comfortable despite the rocking back and forth.

"It was hardly the relaxing weekend you hoped for," Jane said, reaching out and tracing a pattern in the drops of water on the inside of the window.

"I wanted that for you. I hate the strain these last few months have put you under."

For a long moment Jane didn't answer, looking out the window at the snow still piled at the side of the road. The majority had melted now, but where it had been particularly thick some still lingered.

"It was horrible," Jane said slowly, "for three people to be killed whilst we were there, people we knew." She shuddered. "But looking into the crime was distracting. Do you know, I've barely thought of Mr Lefroy these last few days."

"I hardly think that can be your way to cope, getting yourself embroiled in a crime every few days to keep your mind busy."

"No, but this has shown me what complex lives everyone has, and the secrets they keep, hidden there in the darkness. Take Mrs Paulson: on the surface she was this jolly, generous woman of our mother's age, but underneath it all she was battling the damage her husband inflicted, trying to make a positive change in the world. I cannot expect to sail through life unharmed by everything. People are tested; they mourn, they grieve."

Cassandra nodded and reached out across the gap between them, taking Jane's hand.

"So what you're telling me is you are going to be just fine."

"More than that, my darling sister. I am going to thrive. Somehow we will put this horrible affair behind us and together we will focus on the new and the beautiful. I wager next year Mr Fowle will return home and you will marry, and in no time at all I will have half a dozen nieces and nephews to dote on as their favourite aunt."

"You will find love too, Jane."

Jane didn't answer at first but smiled softly at her sister. She didn't mean to be melancholy, but right now she could not imagine ever holding someone in the regard she had held Mr Lefroy, even if it had been only for a few short weeks.

"Perhaps. If not, I have you, I have my writing, I have Mother and Father and I have Lord Hinchbrooke."

"You care for Lord Hinchbrooke?" Cassandra sounded surprised. "I know you spend time with him…"

"I am not in love with Lord Hinchbrooke, Cassandra. Not everything has to be about love. He is my friend, a friend who is opening up a different world to me. *That* is even more valuable than love."

A NOTE TO THE READER

Dear Reader,

Thank you for taking the time to read *Last Impressions*. If you enjoyed the book, I have a small favour to ask — please pop across to **Amazon** and **Goodreads** and post a review. I also love to connect with readers through my **Facebook** page, on **Twitter**, **Instagram** and through my **website**. I would love to hear from you.

Laura Martin

Sapere Books is an exciting new publisher of brilliant fiction and popular history.

To find out more about our latest releases and our monthly bargain books visit our website:
saperebooks.com

Printed in Great Britain
by Amazon

43578787R00155